SHAPECHANGER

The change began with long seconds of terror as she fell, with a small part of her always afraid that this time it wouldn't work. . . . Then fire seemed to run through her body, and the wind rushing along her skin fluffed the downy feathers sprouting from her chest. Her arms stretched to full length and widened, pin feathers extending from her fingertips as her hands fused into her wings. She scooped air with her wings to stop her fall, then banked sharply to catch the updraft at the south side of the castle.

ELISABETH WATERS
CHANGING FATE

DAW BOOKS, INC.
DONALD A. WOLLHEIM, FOUNDER
375 Hudson Street, New York, NY 10014

ELIZABETH R. WOLLHEIM
SHEILA E. GILBERT
PUBLISHERS

First Printing, April 1994

1 2 3 4 5 6 7 8 9

DAW TRADEMARK REGISTERED
U.S. PAT. OFF. AND FOREIGN COUNTRIES
MARCA REGISTRADA
HECHO EN U.S.A.

PRINTED IN THE U.S.A.

for Madeleine and Hugh

CHAPTER 1

Acila finished stirring the mixture in the cauldron and set it on the windowsill to cool overnight. She was very anxious to see if the potion would actually do what it was supposed to. According to the scroll she had found the formula in, it should have some very interesting, and maybe even useful, properties.

It was quiet in the tower, and the late afternoon sunlight flowed across the four-foot-wide stone windowsill. Acila perched on the sill beside the cauldron, enjoying the feel of the sun's warmth on her sore shoulders. It felt as though she had been stirring that potion for hours.

Since the room's only window faced away from the rest of the castle, noises from the courtyard or the other buildings were only faint echoes. Acila savored the quiet, knowing that it couldn't last.

She had no need to look out the window; there was nothing there to be seen, nothing but empty space. She and her twin brother Briam shared the top floor of a simple stone tower which had been old when the rest of the castle was built. From her window the tower dropped to the edge of a cliff which dropped in turn several hundred feet straight down—the legacy of a long-ago earthquake. Fortunately Acila was not troubled by heights.

She sighed, getting up reluctantly from the windowsill. Enough self-indulgence—time to get back to work.

The twins' father had, as usual, gone off early in the spring, taking with him most of the castle guard as well as an entire troop of mercenaries, in his constant quest to add yet another estate to his already too vast domain—much too vast to suit Acila, who was forced to take on the responsibility for its administration. Just because their mother, no doubt hallucinating from the drugs they had given her to ease the birth of the twins, had murmured something about the child ruling over a kingdom, her husband had set to work building the kingdom for his son. It was really too bad, Acila thought, that Mother hadn't lived long enough to realize that she was badly mistaken.

By now it was obvious to anyone willing to admit it that Briam had neither the intellect nor the inclination to do more than ride, hunt, dance, and play any musical instrument he could get his hands on. Even their father, although unwilling to admit that his son was not the perfect young lord and heir, had turned a blind eye as Galin the Steward trained Acila to run the estates that would one day be her brother's. Now, at the age of eighteen, she was very good at it. The domain their father was amassing would remain intact—assuming, of course, that Briam had a child capable enough to hold on to it after Acila was dead. Their father occasionally spoke of finding a suitable bride for Briam, but he had not yet actually done anything about it.

Music had always been Briam's main passion and interest; even when he started to notice girls he spent more time singing ballads of courtly love to whomever he fancied himself in undying love with that month than he did doing anything else.

So though Briam was nominally in charge of the estate during his father's absence, everyone, including Briam, went to Acila with any problems. By now, Acila could run the place better than her father, who wasn't there very often anyway.

Picking up the scroll she had been using for her potion, she headed toward the stairs, closing her bedroom door behind her.

Eagle's Rest, named after her father's device, an eagle flying toward the sun, had started out as a temple, consisting of a single unfortified square stone tower. The sanctuary on the ground floor was still used as the chapel although her father was religious only when it suited him. He preferred to leave religion to the women of the family, which was one of the reasons why Acila was the priestess of the Lady of Fire. Her father had turned her over to the Goddess when she was two—or at least not objected when Marfa suggested it. (The other reason was that the Maiden had chosen Acila, but her father didn't know that and would neither have understood nor believed it if he had.) Marfa, the housekeeper, served the Earth Mother, and Galin served the Lord of Water. The old man who had been priest of the Sky Father had died during the winter, so He was without a priest at present. Marfa, the eldest of the remaining three, told Acila that the Sky Father would call a new priest to himself in his own time.

The tower's second floor, which had originally been the quarters for the priests of the Earth Mother and the Sky Father, was used now only for storage. Both Galin and Marfa, due to their mundane duties, found it easier to live in the main keep. The twins had the third floor (properly the quarters of the priests of the Lady of Fire and Lord of Water, which meant that Acila belonged there and Briam didn't). This gave each twin a bedroom in addition to the common sitting room. Acila had the room to which she was entitled as priestess of the Lady of Fire, and Briam the room which should have been Galin's. The sitting room faced south and was the most comfortable room in the castle, although extremely shabby in its furnishings. Acila noticed as she passed through it that its softwood floor was getting quite a track worn in it between the stairs and the bedrooms. She resolved to see if she could find an old

rug in one of the storerooms. Her father would object
if anything valuable made its way into the tower, but
he wouldn't care if she found some old castoff from
one of the guest rooms.

The guest rooms hadn't been used since she could
remember; her father was not a hospitable man. Her
mother's family had considered hospitality a virtue,
enabling her father to visit, spy out the layout and defenses, and come back with an army to take the place.
He had married his wife, the only known survivor of
her family, to strengthen his claim to the property.
Then he built up the castle's defenses and used it as a
base from which to conquer everything else in range.

The tower had another floor, cut into the rock be-
neath and entered through a hidden entrance built into
the altar. It was a secret known only to the priesthood:
Acila, Galin, and Marfa. Acila had not told even Briam
about it. (She had tried, but she found that when he
was in the room the entrance refused to open for her.)
The secret room contained the temple's only remaining
treasure, its library. Briam wasn't particularly bookish,
and their father, Acila knew, would have seen the library only as a source of revenue. He had already sold
off all of the temple's other treasures or melted them
down to pay the mercenaries he hired each year to help
him amass more land and more treasure to hire more
soldiers.

Acila descended the stone stairs to the sanctuary,
and closed and bolted its door behind her. She made
her way through the familiar, peaceful chamber to the
south side of the altar. The altar was an octagon made
of stone, standing as high as Acila's heart. The south
face of it showed the Lady of Fire in human form at
the left, holding a lightning bolt that stretched from
sky to earth. The next carving, at the center, showed
Her in the form of a salamander, basking in fire, and
the carving at the right showed her as a bird, taking
wing out of the fire with flames trailing from the tips
of her wings as she flew toward the Sky Father's sec-

tion of the altar. The top of the altar held the few implements used in the daily ritual, and each section was carved with appropriate symbols. The Maiden's section was covered with dozens of stylized flames. Acila set down the scroll and reached out to press her hands against two of the flames, chanting softly. The triangle between the fire and air sections of the altar slid out of the way, revealing the ladder to the library below. Acila grabbed the scroll and went quickly down, knowing that the opening would close automatically in only a few seconds. She never had been able to figure out how the entrance worked, or why it would work only for one of the priesthood and not for anyone else. Presumably it was some sort of magic, but Acila had never fully understood its rules.

The altar closed above her, and a soft light began to glow in the darkness. The light had no apparent source, but it always seemed to be brightest where it was needed. It was never bright enough, however to illuminate the entire library at once. As a child Acila had asked why this was so, and Galin had told her that bright light was bad for books; it cracked bindings and faded print.

The light was so dim that Acila had never been sure just how deep the library went down into the bedrock below the tower. The library had the same width and breadth as the structure above it, but its depth was unknown. The ladders from the four corners of the altar led to a wooden catwalk that enabled one to reach the walls. The walls were made up of shelves full of books and scrolls alternating with ladders descending at the corners where the walls joined together. At six-foot intervals a platform stretched between these ladders, allowing just enough room for one person to stand or kneel and examine the contents of the shelves. The ladders and the platforms were made of wooden strips smaller than Acila's wrist, and often creaked alarmingly as one traveled along them. Between the feeling that one was about to fall into an apparently bottomless abyss and having to contend with the dim lighting, only the most dedicated of book lovers would have dared to explore its ancient depths. Acila knew that there *was* a bottom because she had been down there, but no matter how many times she tried, she could never seem to count the levels between it and the entrance. Though Acila loved this mysterious, magical cavern and its fascinating contents, even she was glad that the more frequently needed books seemed somehow to be nearer the top.

Acila had spent as much of her free time as she could exploring the library and had discovered that when she was just browsing, the light would follow her around, but if she were looking for something specific, the light would lead her to it. She had discovered the scroll she now held while browsing on the very bottom shelf.

As the light led her down a ladder, Acila tried, as always, to count levels but soon lost track. By the time she reached the bottom, it seemed as though time had stopped. This was not uncommon; the library often seemed to be a place out of time. Acila would sometimes think she had spent all day there, but when she emerged she would often discover that only an hour or less had passed.

The light illuminated the space from which Acila had taken the scroll. Whatever its source, the light always knew where the item one was replacing belonged, and any attempt to put it elsewhere would extinguish the light instantly until the item was picked up again. Marfa and Galin suspected that this was the work of some long-ago librarians who knew only too well the rule that a book mishelved was a book lost and wanted none of that in their library. And they certainly succeeded, Acila thought ruefully, rubbing her sore arms. If I had a choice, I'd leave this scroll up in the top level, not bring it all the way back down here.

The light started fading slowly as soon as she replaced the scroll and grew steadily dimmer as she climbed. By the time she reached the point where the ladder to her section of the altar joined the catwalk the room was dark again, but as soon as she put a foot on the bottom rung the entrance opened, giving her light from above by which to climb back to the chapel.

Acila looked at the angle of the sun through the small high windows of the sanctuary and went to open the door. Galin and Marfa would be here at any moment for the evening ritual.

In fact, Acila wasn't surprised to see Galin waiting just outside the door when she opened it. Galin was in his early forties, but his short stocky frame and round face made him look younger, even though his brown hair was starting to turn white. He smiled at her, obviously knowing why the door had been closed and where she had been, but he said only, "Good evening, Acila. Did you have a pleasant afternoon?"

Acila grinned at him. She was a good deal fonder of Galin than she had ever been of her father. "Yes, very, and if you had anything to do with my being undisturbed for a change, I thank you."

Galin patted her lightly on the shoulder. "You work too hard, child."

Acila nodded ruefully. "We all do. You, Marfa and I must do at least six or seven people's work among us."

"At least," Galin agreed.

"It's a shame Briam isn't more interested in real life," Acila said wistfully. "I had hoped that the Sky Father would choose him as His new priest."

"Lord Briam is not the stuff of which priests are made," came the tart remark from the doorway as Marfa entered. Marfa had definite opinions on the subject of the twins' characters; she had been housekeeper and priestess as long as Acila could remember, and she had raised Acila and Briam. Unlike Galin, Marfa looked every day of her age and then more; she seemed at once ancient and ageless. "But the new priest will come soon. I feel it in my bones." She moved to her place at the north side of the altar. "Shall we begin?" Galin and Acila moved to their places at west and south, as Marfa picked up the basin at the center of the altar and moved it to the Earth Mother's side.

"In the beginning was Earth, Mother of all life." Marfa scooped a bit of a mixture of rich brown earth, green leaves, and dry twigs from a small bowl on the Earth section of the altar and placed it into one of the shallow divisions of the basin, which was divided into four parts. "From Her body all are born and to Her all return at the proper season. Honor the Mother, thank Her for Her blessings, and remember that our roots are in Her body."

Marfa passed the basin to the Sky Father's portion of the altar, and the three of them stood in silence during the time the priest would have done his part in the ritual. Then Acila reached out and took the basin.

"Fire is the daughter of Earth and Sky, Lightning, the first born of the children which link them." She took a twig from the earth division of the basin and lit it from the small lamp that always burned on the Fire section of the altar. Placing the twig into the fire division of the basin to burn, she continued, "All life is changed by contact with Her, yet Her essence never changes. In all the changes of our lives, remember that, though the form may change, the reality is eternal." As the form of the twig converted itself to a line of ash, Acila passed the basin to Galin.

"Water is the son of Earth and Sky, Rain, the secondborn of the children which link them." Galin picked up a vial of water and slowly poured some of it into the water division of the basin. "Water flows through all that lives, yet Water never changes, however far He may travel. The reality is eternal." Galin placed the basin carefully back in the bare center of the altar, between the carved portions allotted to each of the Elements. He reached out to clasp Acila's and Marfa's hands, and they stood there silently until the last rays of the sun passed below the sanctuary windows. Then they dropped hands and silently left the room. The basin would sit on the altar overnight, and in the morning Acila, as part of her duties as the youngest of the priesthood, would clean it in preparation for the next night's ritual.

Acila had hoped to find Briam in the courtyard outside the temple, or at least in the Great Hall—after all, it was dinnertime and he was supposed to preside at the high table. But when she arrived in the Hall with Galin and Marfa, there was no sign of Briam, although everyone else in the castle was there, the tables were set up, and the food was ready. Marfa muttered something under her breath. Galin's "irresponsible daydreamer" was slightly more audible.

"We may as well all sit down," Acila sighed. "I'm sure he'll be here momentarily." She led the way to the high table and took her seat. Galin sat to her right, Briam's empty chair was to her left, and Marfa sat to Briam's left. Acila put her hands in her lap, fingers interlaced, looked into her cupped palms, and reached out with her mind. As she had expected, she heard a faint thread of melody, apparently played on a lute.

Briam! she sent out a mental call, accompanied by the sensation of her empty and complaining stomach and the feeling of embarrassed annoyance that she always got when she was in a room full of people waiting for Briam.

The lute music stopped with a startled jolt, and she could feel Briam come back to a sudden awareness of the world around him. "He's on his way," she whispered to Galin.

"Good," Galin replied. "It would be helpful to have *him* make the announcement that we start harvesting tomorrow."

Acila nodded. "It would certainly look better that way, since he *is* supposed to be in charge here."

"It would look even better if he were to show up on time for dinner," said Marfa.

Briam entered the room at a brisk trot just in time to hear the last remark. "I do apologize," he said, slipping quickly into his seat and nodding for the servers to begin. "I am composing a new piece, and I'm afraid that I lost track of the time."

Since all three of his table companions had been able to guess that for themselves, they did not bother to comment. The boy who was serving them barely repressed a snicker. Marfa glared at him, and dinner continued without incident. Acila and Galin discussed the work schedule and crew assignments for the next morning. Briam ignored them and ate in silence, his mind presumably still on his music.

When he stood up to leave at the end of the meal, however, Acila prevented his departure with a quick hand around his wrist. *You have an announcement to make, brother dear.* It really did help sometimes that he was her twin; not only could she call him from a distance, but they could speak mind to mind with words when they were in physical contact. This ability was very useful when most of Briam's thoughts were elsewhere, as they were tonight. She prompted him through the announcement of the harvest schedule virtually word by word. When he was done speaking and had escaped back to his lute, Acila wondered if he had any idea of what he had said, or indeed, if he even grasped that the harvest would begin the next day.

Judging from a conversation she overheard a bit later, she was not alone in her doubts.

"Quite an unusual heir our lord has." The voice was male, but not one Acila could put a face to. "Of course, it's not like he has much choice, having only the one son."

"Lord Briam's not so bad." That voice Acila did recognize; it belonged to the armsmaster, now old enough to be semi-retired. "He's a good fighter when he puts his mind to it."

"And what do you have to do to put his mind on

fighting?" the first man challenged. "Threaten to smash his lute?"

The armsmaster chuckled indulgently. "It's not quite that bad. Good dancers are frequently good fighters, and he's quite good at both. No, Lord Briam will do well enough as long as Lady Acila stands by him. She's got the common sense of the pair."

"Of the family, belike. At least she stays here and pays attention to what's going on, instead of being off campaigning half the year. How much land can one man hold, anyway? And our lord sees more of his horse than he does of his children. Small wonder that his son is a dreamer and his daughter takes more after Galin than her own father."

"We can use more than one of Galin—or Lady Acila. We couldn't support more than one of our lord."

"True enough. But I'd pity those children, if it weren't for the fact that if they mess things up, *we* will be the ones to be pitied."

"Don't you worry. They'll do all right, as long as they have each other."

They moved out of earshot then, leaving Acila puzzled. Why should anyone pity her and Briam? And why should they think that the twins would want to see more of their father? Life went much more smoothly when he was away than when he was home finding fault with things and filling the castle with extra soldiers, some of whom were greatly lacking in manners.

Acila had just finished putting the chapel in order the next morning when she heard a commotion in the courtyard. Hastily she went out the door, which was adjacent to the west wall at the very back of the keep, hoping that whatever the fuss was, it would be something minor. Halfway down the courtyard a group of maidservants were gathered, all crowded together around something. Several of them were crying, but Acila recognized the one closest to her as one of the laundry maids, who cried over the most inconsequential matters. She pushed her way unceremoniously toward the center of the disturbance, looking for someone who could give a coherent answer to a simple question.

Her heart sank, when, at the center of the group she found Galin, kneeling beside Marfa, who lay on the ground with her leg at a very odd angle. Marfa's eyes were closed and her face was screwed up with pain, but she wasn't making a sound. Typical, Acila thought. Marfa never had much patience with anyone who made a display of her emotions.

Galin looked up and saw her. "Acila, Marfa has fallen and I believe her leg is broken."

"Oh, no!" Acila said, trying to sound sympathetic rather than the way she really felt, which was frightened and overwhelmed. If Marfa couldn't do her work, Acila would be overburdened indeed. And if she couldn't take her part in the daily ritual . . . it was bad enough being short one member of the priesthood, but with two missing the ritual would be impossible. And bad things happened when the rituals weren't completed. "What happened?"

"Nothing." One of the maids answered, sounding terrified. "She just fell down in the middle of the courtyard. My lady, do you think it be witchcraft?"

Acila looked at her in disgust. "No, Berna, I do not think it anything of the sort!"

"Indeed not," Galin agreed calmly. "Marfa is no longer young, and not as steady on her feet as she once was."

One of the kitchen maids said quickly, "That's true. The same thing happened to my grandmother last year."

"Your grandmother died," Berna pointed out.

"Enough!" Acila snapped. "Galin, get some men and a stretcher and have her carried to her room. Berna, go get the midwife. The rest of you, please calm down and go back to work."

Acila took Galin's place by Marfa's side as everyone

else scattered. She took Marfa's hand, and the bony fingers closed convulsively around hers. "Don't worry, Marfa," Acila said soothingly. "Everything will be all right."

Marfa's eyes opened and looked straight into Acila's. "It's starting," she said softly. "Be brave, girl."

"What's starting?" Acila asked. But Marfa closed her eyes again and did not speak further.

Fifteen minutes later, Acila and Galin stood outside Marfa's room, waiting for the midwife. A horrible thought suddenly occurred to her. "Galin? When she said last night that she could feel in her bones that a new priest would come—"

"I'm sure this is just an unfortunate coincidence," Galin said soothingly. "As I've said, Marfa is not a young woman, and it is not at all uncommon for women of her age to suffer broken bones."

Acila frowned. "I do hope you're right," she said, "but I have a very bad feeling about this."

The rest of the day was a nightmare. Quite apart from her sympathy for Marfa's pain, the housekeeper's incapacity put all of her duties on Acila's shoulders—and on the first day of harvest, those duties were considerable. By mid-afternoon Acila had a pounding headache and had retreated to her room, hoping that a few minutes of quiet would relieve the worst of the pain.

"Acila!"

Acila groaned. Briam's shout echoed up the stairwell, bouncing off the stones of the tower and mingling with the sound of his pounding feet on the wooden stairs. She hoped that whatever Briam wanted was something trivial. Knowing Briam, it could be something as simple as his inability to find his riding boots, which Acila had seen him kick under his bed when he took them off last night.

"Acila!" Briam arrived at the doorway of her room gasping from his run up three flights of stairs.

Whatever he wants, Acila thought wryly, *it's probably not that he can't find his boots.*

"There's an army heading this way!"

Acila started at him in surprise, momentarily forgetting the pounding in her head. "Are you telling me that Father is actually coming home in time for harvest this year?" she asked. "He hasn't done that since we were eight! How far away are they?"'

"Down where the trail starts to get steep and narrow," Briam replied. "They won't be here for at least two hours, and probably closer to three. "But," he paused for emphasis, "it's not Father."

CHAPTER 2

"What?" Acila stared at him incredulously. "Briam, nobody else ever comes here. This place didn't even have a wall around it until Father built one!"

This was quite true. Eagle's Rest had been a secluded spot to begin with, and now was reachable only through large areas of their father's land, but even so he had built a wall around it and reinforced its defenses until it could withstand a siege without serious difficulty, assuming, of course, that it was adequately provisioned. But on the first day of harvest, "adequately provisioned" was the last possible description of their status if they had to close up the castle.

If there really was a hostile army coming up the pass, Eagle's Rest was in trouble. "How could an army get so far without anyone's warning us?" Acila wondered aloud. "Briam, are you sure it's not Father? Maybe he's just hired some new mercenaries you don't recognize."

Briam looked uncertain, but he shook his head. "I could see the banner," he said stubbornly, "and I can certainly tell the difference between red and blue."

"Blue?" Acila asked.

Briam nodded. "A blue banner, with a wolf—at least I think it was a wolf." Briam gestured to the window. "Don't you think that you ought to go take a look?"

Acila rotated her shoulders. They were a bit sore from her work on the potion yesterday, but the muscles still worked. "All right," she said, "I'll go." She indicated the cauldron, which occupied half the window-sill. "Get this out of my way, will you?"

Briam looked dubiously at the potion. "What is it?"

"It's an experiment—and if there is a hostile army coming this way, we may need it, so be careful with it." As Briam gingerly lifted the cauldron and set it on the floor in front of the window, Acila closed and bolted the door, then stripped off her clothes and tossed them onto her bed. Naked, she perched on the windowsill, then dove out of the window.

Even though the change to eagle form was the first one Acila had learned and the one she used most often, she still found it to be the most difficult of the shape changes. It began with long seconds of terror as she fell, with a small part of her always afraid that this time the change wouldn't work. Perhaps the terror came from the fact that she had first discovered her unique abilities by falling off a shed roof as a small child. It was much worse if she was close to the ground when she started. And even once the change was complete and she could control her wings, flying took a lot of physical effort. By the time she returned to her room, Acila knew, she would be dangerously exhausted, but she saw no alternative now. She had to find out about this army.

She continued to fall as the change took hold. Then fire seemed to run through her body, and the wind rushing along her skin fluffed the downy feathers sprouting from her chest. Her arms stretched to full length and widened, pin feathers extending from her fingertips as her hands fused into her wings. She scooped air with her wings to stop her fall, then banked sharply to catch the updraft at the south side of the castle. As the eagle flew, it was only a few minutes to the place Briam had described.

As Briam had said, it was an army, and he was correct about the banner; it was blue, with a wolf against a full moon. Acila tried to remember if she had ever heard or read of this device, but nothing came to mind.

Between the men and horses and the baggage wagons bringing up the rear were several siege engines. *Whoever this man is,* Acila thought uneasily, *he looks determined.*

The leader was easy to pick out; he was riding to the front with several of his lieutenants. For a moment Acila had the oddest sensation of recognition, which was ridiculous, because she had never seen anyone who looked like him before. His hair was dark and cut very short, and there was a blue circle painted between his brows, like the moon on his banner. The circle was creased by his frown as he replied to something one of his men had said. This conversation might be well worth hearing.

Acila landed on a tree ahead of them, trying to hide among the branches. Concealment, unfortunately, was impossible; in eagle form Acila was conspicuously large, but she did her best. At least now she could hear them.

"Lord, you worry needlessly. The man is dead, and none of his guard escaped to carry word here; I swear it. There are few men remaining here, and who is there to order defense?"

Acila dug her claws into the branch, feeling faint. *Dead? Does he mean Father?*

"I hear he had children, near grown now," the leader remarked.

I guess he does *mean Father.*

"Do you think that such a wily old fox would not have shared some of his cunning with his pups?" the leader continued.

"Two children only, my lord, and one of them a girl." That voice was familiar. Acila stiffened in anger. She had tried to warn her father about Stefan after the evening when she had been forced, in defense of her virtue, to push him down the stairs. Her father had called her a missish little fool and told her sternly that he didn't want her upsetting his soldiers, and if she couldn't handle situations like that gracefully, she should not leave her tower without Marfa or one of the maids with her. Acila had spent most of the next few weeks in her room, counting the days until the army left.

"As for the boy," Stefan continued in ingratiating tones, "I assure you he's no threat. He prefers music to weapons practice; it will be easy enough to kill him. Then marry the girl, if you wish, and you will be the undisputed owner of a defensible castle, a good quantity of land, and such serfs as survive the fighting."

"And the pillaging thereafter?" The lord, whoever he was, regarded Stefan without favor. "I have told you, Stefan, and I mean what I say: keep your men in order. I do not wish my honor further tarnished by your actions."

Honor? Acila thought furiously. This might be helpful. *What is his notion of honor? Obviously it won't stop him from attacking "children," but there may yet be things his "honor" will not let him do.* He didn't seem upset by the idea of killing Briam however—or of marrying her. *Does he seriously think I'll marry a man who killed my brother? And why would he want to marry me anyway?* Granted, it would give some slight appearance of legitimacy to his seizure of her home, but was that reason enough to want to marry someone you'd never seen, and scarcely heard of?

There was an uneasy silence among the men for several minutes, during which time they came even with Acila's tree. Stefan looked up, saw her, and reached for his crossbow.

The lord twisted catlike in his saddle at Stefan's movement. "What do you think you are doing?"

Stefan gestured. "The eagle, my lord." Acila tensed for flight, not that she expected to be able to fly fast enough to escape a crossbow bolt at this range. "It's the old lord's emblem."

"Hardly reason enough to kill an innocent beast," the lord snapped. "Leave it be. Unless, of course, *you* wish to eat the dead after the fighting." They rode on in silence, but Stefan scowled as he replaced his crossbow.

Somebody had better watch his back, Acila thought. *Stefan is ill news.* She shuddered, feeling queasy. She had never realized that she could feel sick to her stomach in eagle form—if she had thought about the question, considering the predator's normal diet, she would have sworn it was impossible. But it took her several minutes of shivering and fighting for control of her body before she was able to struggle to an upper branch and launch herself back into flight.

As she headed back to the castle, she pondered their options which seemed pitifully limited. She didn't fool herself that there was any way to defeat this army; they had a lot of men and ample provisions. *Besides, with all of us trapped in the castle, they can help themselves to the crops in the fields.* But she had to do something. Briam was her brother, and all the family she had left. She couldn't stand by and let him be killed!

In addition to Briam, there were all the other people: the castle servants, the serfs, the tenants on their farms, the artisans in the small village outside the castle walls. Acila had known these people all her life, and even though she wasn't responsible for their lives by law and custom, she still felt that she had to find some way to keep them from being killed or hurt or having their homes destroyed. At least the lord didn't seem to want random destruction any more than she did.

Does that mean that the problem is how to lose with as little damage, injury, and loss of life as possible? She banked around the south wall, letting the updraft carry her to her windowsill. *But I don't want to lose!*

Briam looked up inquiringly as she changed to human form and began to dress.

"You were right, Briam, it's not Father's army." She hastily laced her gown, covered her hair, and pulled back the bolt on the door. "We had better go talk to Galin."

They found Galin on the east wall, with the few

men-at-arms who had remained at Eagle's Rest, watching the approaching army. Galin nodded to Briam. "Do you have any orders, Lord Briam?"

Briam looked uncertainly at Acila, who sighed silently. *I should have coached him on what to say.*

"We feel," she began, "that it would be best to bring all the people—and whatever they can carry—inside the walls."

"But, Lady," protested one of the men-at-arms, "surely we can't feed all those people for more than a few days."

"We can't feed those of us already inside the walls for more than a few weeks," Acila pointed out. "If we take in everyone, the enemy may believe us to be adequately provisioned for a long siege." *Not likely,* she thought grimly, *but it's worth the chance, and at least everyone will be safe for a few days, which gives me time to come up with another brilliant idea.* "And I am determined—we are determined—to lose no lives in this invasion, not one villager, not one serf, sheep, goat, chicken, or man-at-arms. We trust that you have no quarrel with that resolve?"

"None, Lady," the man assured her. This, of course, was the answer that Acila had expected; all the young idiots who thought that dying in battle was a glorious fate had gone with her father.

Galin looked amused. The old steward had conducted most of Acila's training himself, beginning in her childhood when she had followed him about whenever she could. "You, and you," he selected two of the men-at-arms, "go call the people in at once." The men hurried down the corner stairs.

Acila followed more slowly, discussing with Galin the housing of extra people and animals and the putting up of a semblance of defense ". . . oil spouts and barrels, and it doesn't matter if the barrels are empty, but we need to look prepared to defend ourselves." Briam trailed silently behind them.

Satisfied that this part of the plan would be carried

out, Acila dragged Briam off to her room to be drilled in his part in the defense. No use to tell him he was the one in most danger; he wouldn't understand that anyone could want him dead. Best to make him think he was doing this to defend her; he'd sung enough stories of gallant knights and fair ladies for that to appeal to him.

By the time the army arrived they were as ready as they could be in the short time they had had to prepare. People and livestock were all crowded safely inside, the castle was closed and looking formidable, and Briam, dressed in freshly-shined armor, stood on the battlements with his hand resting on the back of a large eagle perched on the wall in front of him. It was an uncomfortable perch, but even Briam wasn't strong enough to hold her on his fist—she weighed four times what an eagle would. Wolf-shape would have been a deal more comfortable—Acila didn't like being touched in bird shape any more than a real eagle would—but she wanted to have the eagle's eyesight, and this was the package it came in. She consoled herself with the reminder that they looked imposing—and as long as they were touching she could mind-speak to Briam without anyone knowing he was taking orders from his sister.

Stefan rode ahead of the army to parley. *Good,* thought Acila, *they consider him expendable. At least they have reasonable taste.*

"Lord Ranulf of the Mountains comes to inspect his new castle. Open to him at once."

Briam had a good voice for shouting from battlements, a nice full booming bass. "I do not recognize Lord Ranulf's claim to my castle, and I do not speak to scum like you."

"He claims this castle by the death of your father, boy." Stefan pulled their father's head from his saddlebag and held it up by the hair.

One of the archers on the wall loosed an arrow. The

head dropped to the ground. To the accompaniment of guffaws from the men of both sides, Stefan hastily dropped the lock of hair he still held and checked to be sure he still had all his fingers. Acila made a mental note to see that the archer was rewarded later.

Lord Ranulf rode forward and gestured Stefan back to the ranks. The blue circle on his forehead was furrowed to an oval by his frown.

"Lord Ranulf," Briam called out. "Your choice of men does not commend you to us—nor do your intentions toward my lady sister."

Acila was glad now that she had chosen eagle form; she could see Ranulf's eyebrows rise in shock. If they were very, very lucky he might think Briam was a sorcerer and would go away. But instead, Ranulf was looking thoughtfully at her.

No one alive knew that she was a shapechanger except Briam. Most people didn't believe that such things existed, save in old tales told on the Longest Night. But if Lord Ranulf had a good imagination, and a good eye for feather patterns, and if he had taken a good look at her in the tree . . . no, that was really stretching coincidence too far. All he would have seen, then or now, was an unusually large eagle. He couldn't know, and even the suspicion would be lunatic. But he did not appear ready to leave.

"Lord Briam," he called out courteously, "you cannot hope to withstand me for long. I have plenty of men and supplies; even if I cannot breach your walls, I can certainly starve you out, and I am prepared to do so. Yield, and save us all trouble and grief."

"I will not sell my folk and my sister into slavery," Briam returned. "If my father is dead, this castle is mine, not yours, whatever a fool like Stefan may think." He cast a disdainful glance at Stefan, then looked back at Lord Ranulf. "Leave now, and save *yourself* trouble and grief."

Acila suddenly realized that Lord Ranulf only appeared to be looking at Briam, for when she looked at Ranulf, his eyes met hers.

"I'll stay," Lord Ranulf said calmly, still looking into Acila's eyes. "I'll be here when you change your mind." He reached down in a graceful sweep of his upper body and scooped up their father's head from the ground, then straightened, cradling it in his elbow. "By the way, don't try to send out any messages. My men have orders to shoot any creature trying to leave the vicinity." He rode back to his army and started them setting up in siege formation.

Briam ordered the men-at-arms to keep watch on the army, then strode majestically to Acila's room and bolted the door, while she flew around the building and landed on the window ledge so she could change back. The last rays of the setting sun still warmed the ledge, but the air was getting cold, and Acila was glad to scramble back into the clothes she had left in front of the fire.

Briam started to take his armor off, and Acila automatically moved to help him. "What do we do now?" he asked in the confident tone he always used when asking her that question.

But this time, Acila had no answer.

Lord Ranulf returned their father's body to them the next morning, under a flag of truce. The body had been washed, dressed in the best clothes their father had taken with him, and placed in a coffin, which the village carpenter confirmed had come from his shop. "There's always a few men make it back here and then die each year," he said, "so I always make a coffin or two this time of year to have one ready."

On top of the coffin was a letter and a small pouch. Briam picked up the letter, glanced through it, then handed the letter to Acila and the pouch to the carpenter. "Payment for the coffin," he explained.

Acila looked at him in surprise, then bent her head over the letter. True enough, the first few lines dealt with the matter of the coffin and the payment for it. She turned it over to check the signature. "And Lord Ranulf commends your craftsmanship and the orderly way in which you keep your shop," she told the man.

He hefted the pouch in his hand, looking puzzled. "Strangest invasion I've ever seen—or heard of," he said. "He hasn't fired the village, has he?"

"I doubt it," said Galin calmly. "For one thing, we'd see the smoke if he did, and for another it makes no sense from a tactical standpoint. If he could win, it would be his village and he wouldn't want his own property damaged."

Acila noted Galin's use of the conditional tense with appreciation. She was sure that he knew as well as she did that "it will be his village" was more accurate than "it would be his village." By her reckoning, they had food for three more days.

She forced herself to smile at the carpenter, hoping that her face didn't look as stiff as it felt. "If he had burned your shop, he certainly wouldn't bother to pay you for the coffin," she pointed. "And I am glad that you had it ready made since we do have need of it." She blinked quickly to force back the tears that suddenly blurred her vision. *I can't break down in front of people,* she thought. *I've got to get away for a bit.*

She looked quickly at Briam. He seemed to be holding up just fine. Probably shock, but maybe it could work to their benefit. "Briam, why don't you get some men and take the body to the chapel, while I go see about getting the proper herbs." Briam nodded and he and Galin chose several men from the group standing around them to help carry the body.

Acila headed for her room as fast as was consistent with the dignity she had to maintain under the circumstances. She would rather have run, screaming, but that wasn't an option.

When she got to her room, she bolted the door and collapsed on the bed, shaking violently. Then she blacked out.

CHAPTER 3

Acila awoke to find the sun streaming in her window. It took her several minutes to figure out what she was doing lying fully clothed on her bed in the middle of the day. She felt cold all over, and sick, and too shaky to stand. She twisted to reach the clothing chest at the foot of her bed. When she reached to open the chest, she found that she still held Lord Ranulf's letter clutched in her hand. She dropped it on the bed beside her and opened the chest, reaching inside it for the dried fruit bars she kept there for times when she had been shapechanging and needed extra food in a hurry. She unwrapped one with shaking hands and crammed it into her mouth. Even chewing it took enormous effort, but after she had eaten three of them, she felt at least half human again.

She picked up the letter and looked at the salutation. It was addressed to her.

Well, that explains why Briam gave it to me. But why would Lord Ranulf write to me? Did Stefan tell him that I made the decisions around here—no, Stefan wouldn't know that because Father was here when he was, and besides, I heard what Stefan was telling Lord Ranulf. . . .

She turned her attention back to the letter. After the part about the coffin which she had read earlier, it continued ". . . It may relieve your heart to know that I neither killed your father nor ordered his death. The mercenary Stefan brought his body to me in hope of a reward, which I have not given him."

But Stefan is still with you, Acila thought, *so you must have promised him something, or else he still hopes for something.*

". . . I bear no ill will toward you, nor toward any of your people, and you may assure your brother that my intentions toward you are quite honorable. I ask that you do me the favor of becoming my wife. I feel sure that you have sufficient sense to see the advantages to this plan. You will be able to live comfortably in your own home and remain mistress of your estate. In time, the property will pass to our children. . . ."

Acila dropped the letter, feeling profoundly shocked. It was silly, of course, that the idea of having children should shock her, but children of her own were not something she had considered. Her father had made it quite clear, without ever saying anything explicit on the subject, that she was never to marry or have children. The inheritance was Briam's, not Acila's. Now Lord Ranulf seemed to be looking at it from the opposite point of view. Acila picked up the letter and read it carefully from start to finish. Except for the one reference she had already seen, there was no mention of Briam. *So what does Lord Ranulf plan for him?* Acila wondered.

She continued to wonder during the next several days, during which they buried their father next to their mother in the family graveyard behind the main hall, cut the food first to half-rations, then quarter-rations, and watched Lord Ranulf's army.

Most of the army patrolled outside the walls, but Acila and Galin noted that every morning a large group of men would march off toward the village and fields and would not be seen again until after dark, when they returned to camp. She wished she dared change to eagle shape and find out what they were doing, but she did not think that Lord Ranulf had been bluffing about shooting any creature trying to leave the castle. Even if the shot merely intended to disable—an arrow through the wing, for example (Acila shuddered, visualizing an arrow tearing through feathers, tendons and muscles, and told herself firmly that she had too vivid an imagination), Acila was unsure of her ability to land safely using only one wing and even less sure of her ability to hold eagle shape if she were injured. And the idea of being naked and helpless in the middle of a strange army was terrifying.

They were all down to one meal a day now, a gruel made from the few remaining barrels of last year's grain in the storerooms. There was no meat, no fruit or vegetables. Water was no problem, the castle had a good well inside the walls. But the harvest, the fruit trees, and the wild game that was their usual diet at this time of the year were all outside the walls. They weren't dying yet, although some of the younger children were starting to sicken, but Acila knew that time was against them. They could hold out for a while longer, but they couldn't last forever. And their father had no allies who could be expected to come to break the siege. Acila mentally damned her father; if he hadn't spent his entire lifetime making enemies instead of allies, and then getting himself killed, they wouldn't be in this mess. Lord Ranulf was going to win; there was just no other possible conclusion.

She paced the walls with Galin and Briam, watching a group of Lord Ranulf's troops leave as they did each morning. Suddenly one of the men on the walls shouted and pointed up.

"Look! The great eagle!"

Briam and Acila looked at each other in astonishment before looking up. Sure enough, there was an eagle circling over the castle, bigger than any eagle in nature. "It's a bit bigger than you are," Briam whispered in her ear, "but other than that, it looks identical."

"That's impossible," Acila whispered back.

The eagle folded its wings and dove straight toward

them. Briam and Galin moved in, crowding Acila in an irrational effort to protect her, but the eagle unfolded its wings a short distance above them, scooped air to break its fall, and landed neatly on the wall directly in front of them. It looked sharply at Briam, then Galin, before fixing its eyes on Acila's. Acila met its stare, reminded of the afternoon the army had arrived, when she had been an eagle and had watched Lord Ranulf from the walls. There seemed to be intelligence behind the eyes that stared into hers. Had she looked like that? She forced herself to stand perfectly still and keep her face calm. Animals generally couldn't outstare a human, and as long as its claws were on the wall the eagle wouldn't hurt her. Unlike owls, eagles didn't bite. After several long minutes, the eagle turned, dove off the wall, and flew away beyond the trees.

Acila felt so shaken that it took her several seconds to realize that Galin was talking to her. "The men seem to think it's a good omen," he said, looking around at the few men they had stationed on the wall.

"I wish I thought so," Acila said.

Galin looked sharply at her. "You are tired," he said firmly. "Go and lie down for a bit; there's nothing you need to do right now."

He was right, Acila realized as she went wearily back to her room. There was nothing constructive for her to do, nothing that needed her attention, nothing she could do to save her people, her brother, her home, or even herself. She lay down and promptly fell asleep.

It was early evening when she woke, and when she went to find Briam, she was horrified to find him on the walls, parlaying with Lord Ranulf.

"Lord Briam," Lord Ranulf was saying courteously, "you cannot hope to withstand me for much longer. I may not know to the measure how much food you have left, but you know, and I can guess. I can certainly starve you out, but that is both unpleasant and bad for your people, who need not otherwise be harmed. Yield now, and save them."

"I will not sell my folk and my sister into slavery so tamely," Briam retorted. "I challenge you to single combat."

Acila checked her first impulse, which was to grab Briam, drag him down from the wall, and lock him in his room until he came to his senses. *This must be the most incredibly foolish thing he has ever done in his life!* she thought. *I'll never be able to get him out of this one.*

"If I lose," Briam continued, "the castle is yours; and if I win, you give that turncoat mercenary over to us for justice and depart in peace."

"A somewhat uneven bargain, Lord Briam," Lord Ranulf replied. "Why should I risk the castle in single combat when I can win it simply by waiting a little while longer?" He thought for a moment. "If you want to fight someone, fight Stefan, since you seek his life, and if you win, you go free."

"And my sister goes with me," Briam countered.

"What life would the lady have wandering about with you?" Lord Ranulf asked reasonably. "I pledge to marry her in all honor; she will have her home and position."

Acila came up to Briam's side and grabbed his arm. *Agree, Briam,* she thought at him.

You want to marry him? The thought was hurt and incredulous. *I can't go away without you!*

Of course not, but I'll get out of it. Just agree to these terms.

Briam spoke at her prompting, "I will agree to the following terms: tomorrow morning I will fight in single combat with the mercenary Stefan. If I win, I go free with my armor and weapons, my horse, and my eagle. If I fail to kill Stefan, you will dismiss him from your service and banish him forever from this estate. In either case, the castle will be surrendered to you. In turn you will agree to show mercy to the serfs and castle folk and treat them well."

"I agree to your terms with the following exceptions: you may have horse, weapons, armor, and such baggage as you can carry, but not the eagle."

But he can't *know!* Acila thought. *Can he?*

"And I will marry your sister."

"If she will have you!" Briam retorted.

"Very well, if I can gain her agreement." Lord Ranulf sounded much too confident for Acila's taste. "Then we are agreed upon the terms?"

"Yes," Briam said slowly. "We are agreed."

"Until tomorrow morning, then." Lord Ranulf bowed in the saddle, then turned and rode back to his army.

Briam and Acila retreated to Acila's room to talk in private.

"Acila," Briam said, worried, "can you change into a horse?"

"A colt, maybe, but nothing big enough to carry you."

"I could lead you, and walk."

Tears came to Acila's eyes, and suddenly she couldn't stop crying. Briam picked her up and sat on the ledge holding her in his lap. "Don't cry, Acila, please don't cry!"

"I'm just tired, Briam," she sobbed. She sat up and resolutely began to scrub her face with the hem of her gown. "Why did you challenge Lord Ranulf?"

"In single combat the right side always wins," Briam replied simply.

"Oh, Briam, that's only in a minstrel's tales." Acila sighed. "Have you seen Stefan fight?"

"Yes, I watched the men-at-arms practicing before they set out with Father. Stefan's not bad, but I've seen better. And I have the right on my side."

"Well, I suppose that's some help." Acila tried to remember what it was the guardsman had said about

Briam's fighting ability. "But remember, Stefan will be fighting for his life tomorrow, so he'll fight harder."

"If I lose, I'll be dead," Briam said slowly. Obviously he was just now realizing this. "Do you think it hurts to be dead?"

Acila reminded herself sternly that this was no time to turn squeamish over the predicament her brother had gotten himself into—if he didn't do this, probably they'd just kill him out of hand. Oh, if only she could turn him into something, some form insignificant enough to sneak out safely. But her changing ability was limited to herself, and she could only change herself into an animal. Unless the potion she had labored so hard over worked—it was designed to give her the ability to turn herself into anything. And it had better work.

"Acila?"

What had he asked her? "No, being dead doesn't hurt; dying probably does, but the pain stops once you're dead. But you're not going to die tomorrow, not if I can help it."

"And you'll change into a horse and come with me?"

"No, that won't work." Acila frowned. "I don't know how, but I'd swear Lord Ranulf knows I'm a changer. Remember what he said about not letting any creature leave the castle."

"So what are you going to do? I'm not going away without you."

Acila took a deep breath. "I'm going to turn myself into a sword." It was the first time she'd dared to say the words out loud, and she hoped she didn't sound as scared as she felt. "And you're going to use me in combat, and then walk out of here with me at your side."

Briam looked at her as if she were crazy. "But you can't turn yourself into a sword. A sword isn't an animal. A sword isn't even alive. How can you turn back if you're not alive? Beside, if I can't hold you on my arm when you're an eagle, how do you expect me to fight with you if you turn into a sword? You'd be much too heavy."

"This isn't one of my normal changes," Acila explained patiently. "It's a spell, and the usual limitations about form and size and weight don't apply. The potion I made will let me turn into a sword." She pointed to the cauldron which had been sitting in her room since the day she made the potion. It seemed a lifetime ago. *If I made the potion right and I do the spell right, it should work,* she thought grimly. "And after you get out of here, you will take me to the ocean and put me in the water, and that will turn me back."

"The ocean's a long way away." Briam sounded overwhelmed.

"I know." *Sweet Lady of Life, what am I doing?*

"All right." Briam had come to terms with the idea. He trusted her. He always trusted her, and sometimes the burden was almost unendurable. "What do I do?"

"I'll have Galin pack your clothes and some food for the journey. You go to bed and sleep well, all night. When you get up in the morning, come here. You should find a sword, the cauldron, and this parchment." She pulled the scrap of parchment on which she had copied the words of the changing spell out of her chest and showed it to him. "Burn the parchment, empty any potion left in the cauldron out the window, and take the sword. Have your horse saddled and loaded, and get one of the men-at-arms to hold him during the fight. Kill Stefan. Get on your horse and go to the river, then go downriver to the ocean. When you get there, put the sword in the ocean." She paused for a few seconds to give the instructions time to sink in. "What will you do?"

"Burn parchment, empty cauldron, take sword, get horse, kill Stefan, put sword in ocean."

She fought back tears and gave him a hug. "Good night, Briam. Sleep well."

"Don't worry, Acila. I'll take good care of you. Good night." He returned her hug and left.

Acila went to find Galin and tell him what she needed him to do. Galin looked troubled.

"I've already packed provisions for Lord Briam, and I can have Gris saddled for him in the morning. But I think you and I had better go talk with Marfa."

Acila nodded wearily, and they went to Marfa's room, dismissed the maid who was sitting with her, and closed the door.

"I told you the Sky Father would call a new priest," was Marfa's first comment.

Acila looked at her in horror. "You mean Lord Ranulf?"

"No. He's only the God's instrument."

Acila wondered if Marfa really knew what was going on. "Marfa, our father is dead, and they're trying to kill Briam! I can't just sit by and let that happen."

"Actually," Marfa said with what Acila considered a revolting lack of feeling, "you can."

"No, I can't!"

"Calm down, Acila," Galin intervened, "and do lower your voice. This door is *not* soundproof. I believe that what Marfa is trying to say is that your first duty is to the Gods. And I rather doubt that Stefan is going to kill Briam. Stefan underestimates him to a degree that will almost certainly prove fatal."

"Acila," Marfa said quietly, "there is something you must realize. I never felt it necessary to tell you this before, but your father killed my nephew when he took this place. I was sworn to the Mother, so I pretended to be the housekeeper and remained to serve Her. The people here have been loyal to the priesthood for centuries, even when the current lord pays no heed to it. And the Gods protect their own. You are perfectly safe. And as Galin says, Briam will, no doubt, defeat Stefan and go free."

"Go free where to do what?" Acila shot back. "You

both know that Briam can't possibly look after himself. I'll have to go with him to take care of him."

Both Galin and Marfa looked at her in horror. "You can't," they said in unison.

"I can, and I will—unless, of course, you think the Lady will strike me dead."

Marfa looked troubled. "I'm not sure what will happen to you if you leave. I suspect that the Lady will simply call you back, but I don't at all like the idea of the temple being short two priests, however temporarily."

Acila thought about that. They had not done the evening ritual in days; it was possible to skip the Sky Father's part of the ritual, or the Fire or Water portions, but without a priestess of the Earth Mother the ritual could not be started at all. And Marfa's broken leg had coincided with the invasion, but surely that was only coincidence. The army had to have been on its way here well before Marfa's injury. "None of us knows what will happen to the temple with me gone," she said aloud, "but everyone knows what Briam is like without me. I *have* to go with him."

Marfa sighed and lay back against her pillow, wincing visibly. "I doubt that the Gods will permit you to leave. Certainly Lord Ranulf doesn't plan to let you go, and he seems quite capable."

"Well, if he manages to stop me, I guess we can consider it the will of the Gods," Acila said lightly. "You need more pain medication, Marfa; I'll have one of the maids bring you some." *And I have work to do.* She bent and kissed Marfa lightly on the cheek, then turned to hug Galin, surprised to find tears starting in her eyes. She blinked furiously in an unsuccessful attempt to control them. "If things go wrong tomorrow . . . if anything happens to me . . . I want you both to know that I love you."

Galin put his arms around her sobbing body. "Acila, you're worn out. Go to bed, child; I'll make sure Marfa gets her medicine."

"Thank you," Acila sniffed, wiping her eyes with her sleeve. "I don't know what's wrong with me; I don't normally cry."

"You've had too many shocks lately," Marfa said gently. "Go to bed, dear; things will look better in the morning."

"And remember, Acila," Galin added as she turned to leave, "we love you, too."

For some reason that made Acila start crying again, and she fled hastily to her room, taking care that no one saw her face as she went. *It would be bad for morale if anyone saw me crying.*

She closed her bedroom door, remembering not to bolt it. Briam would need to get in tomorrow morning. Carefully she spread the parchment on the table and read the spell. The words danced in front of her eyes. She couldn't concentrate; it didn't make any sense. *But it has to make sense; I have to do this spell!*

Why do you have to do this? a voice in her head asked. *I don't want to be a sword!*

Do you want Briam killed? she asked her other self.

Not particularly. But why do I have to be the sword? Why can't he use one from the armory?

Because as a sword I can help him fight. I'll be right in his hand and can link with him. He may be able to fight as well as he dances, but he's not a killer—he doesn't even like to hunt! Besides, didn't you hear him? He won't leave the castle without me. And the way Lord Ranulf's acting, I don't think I can turn into a bird and fly to meet him.

You could put a sword here for him and hide someplace. Did it ever occur to you that he just might be able to defeat Stefan on his own? Briam is pretty good with a sword—he does have some ability. Just because he's your 'baby brother' doesn't mean that he's totally helpless. You're just in the habit of doing everything for him.

You may have a point. But I really don't think this is

the situation in which to test Briam's abilities any more than absolutely necessary. And even if Briam can defeat Stefan on his own, you know as well as I do that he can't go into exile without someone to take care of him. And I don't see anyone else offering to do it.

Who's going to look after Briam if you're a sword? Are you still going to be able to mind-speak with him? You don't know much about this spell; if you're a sword, you may be absolutely helpless. How do you know Briam isn't going to lose you someplace? And what if he loses the fight even with you helping him?

Then I'll be a sword forever—assuming, that is, that I ever manage to turn myself into a sword in the first place, with you arguing with me!

Something moved on the window ledge, cutting off the internal dialogue. Acila froze in horror as a spider a full fathom across began to crawl over the sill. Fortunately her paralysis lasted only a second, then she grabbed a torch out its wall holder and used the flame to stop the creature's advance.

It froze on the windowsill, flickered in the firelight, and re-formed into human shape. Lord Ranulf!

Acila willed herself to stand tall and hold the torch steady, even though she felt as though icy water were running through her veins. While she had suspected that maybe, somewhere in the world, there were other shapechangers, she had never been sure that she wasn't the only one in existence—and she had certainly never expected to meet another one. She was horribly afraid that she was going to faint, and she knew she couldn't afford to do that.

For once, the little voice in her mind came to her rescue. *So that's how he knew you were a changer,* it said. *He's one, too. He must have been the eagle this morning.*

Acila felt her mind start functioning again. *And he probably knows that real eagles don't like being touched.*

"Lady Acila." He bowed courteously, apparently quite untroubled by the fact that he was naked.

"Lord Ranulf." Acila glared at him. "What you are doing in my room?"

His eyes inspected the room, and Acila took another step toward him, blocking his view of the parchment with the spell as she did so. There was no way to hide the potion; if he stepped from the ledge he'd land in it. He did not, however, seem inclined to get any closer to the torch she held. His eyes moved from it to her face, and he chuckled. "I thought we needed to speak privately, my Lady." There was a peculiar caress in his voice. "And may I say that you are even lovelier as a lady than as an eagle?"

"Since I am not an eagle, I fail to see any point in this conversation." Acila concentrated on standing straight, keeping her chin up, and playing the great lady for all she was worth. It probably wouldn't fool him, but she couldn't think of anything else to do at the moment.

"You make a beautiful eagle, and no doubt to most people you look quite convincing. But a changer is heavier than a true eagle and needs more wing and less body in order to fly, which means that anyone who knows what he's looking for can tell the difference."

So that's how he knew, Acila thought. But I still have no intention of admitting it. Aloud she said, "I really must request that you leave immediately. For me to entertain a strange man unchaperoned would be unseemly—even were you properly dressed. Are you not cold?"

He ignored the sarcasm. "And you therefore use fire as a chaperon? How considerate of you. Surely no such formality is necessary between a betrothed couple?" His face still reflected amusement, but he was keeping a wary eye on the flames.

"I would remind you, Lord"—I am *not* going to call this man *my* lord—"that I have not agreed to this betrothal. Furthermore, with the current unsettled state of the castle, I do not feel inclined to entertain. So just turn yourself back into a spider and crawl right back down that cliff!" She took a step toward him, holding the torch before her.

Lord Ranulf slid unselfconsciously into a sitting position on the windowsill, making it clear that he had no immediate plans to leave. "But you will agree to the betrothal," he replied confidently. "After all, who else are you likely to find who will understand you so well? And you're exactly what I want for a wife—just think of the children we'll have."

Acila grimaced. "The very thought gives me morning sickness," she snapped.

Lord Ranulf chuckled, apparently genuinely amused.

Curiosity briefly overcame Acila. "Don't you have any children yet?"

"One son, nine years old. But he's not a true changer."

"Did his mother die when he was born? Did yours?" All her life Acila had believed that her mother had died because Acila was a changer. This might be her one chance to find out if bearing a changer child was inevitably fatal.

Lord Ranulf looked surprised. "No, why should they have? My mother is dead now, but she lived a normal life span. And Rias' mother is alive and well."

"Then you already have a wife—"

"No." Lord Ranulf gave a decisive shake of his head. "Rias' mother and I are not married. I am quite free to marry, and I am sure that you and I will deal splendidly together. You are everything I could possibly want, everything I've dreamed of and searched for all my life." He smiled at her, and Acila fought the sense of sudden kinship she felt with him. "Haven't you ever dreamed of finding someone like yourself— someone who would understand you, someone from whom you would not have to hide most of the things that make you the person you are."

Acila shook her head defiantly. "I'm a twin, remember. I have a brother who knows exactly who and what I am."

"Does he really?" Lord Ranulf asked. "Think about it." He rose to his feet in one smooth movement, his head almost brushing the top of the window. "Until tomorrow, my lady wife." He shimmered again, and the spider crawled over the ledge and down the castle wall.

Acila hastily shoved the torch back into the wall holder and bolted the wooden shutters of the window behind him—at least he seemed to have the same size and weight limitations she did—then leaned against them and shook.

Well, she asked her inner voice, *which would you rather be—a sword or womb to birth were-spiders?*

A sword, and pray he doesn't figure it out.

He shouldn't; there probably aren't five people alive who have even heard of the spell. And the potion isn't easy to make.

This time the spell made sense. She took off her clothes, folded them neatly, and put them away in her chest, checking it carefully to be sure she hadn't left any more parchments in it. When she was sure that her chest contained nothing but clothes, she made her bed neatly and checked the room for anything she didn't want to fall into the wrong hands.

Satisfied that she had done everything she needed to do in human form, she placed the spell on the window ledge next to the cauldron, got into the cauldron—with some difficulty; it was rather a tight fit—bathed every inch of her body in the potion—which was very cold by now—and chanted the spell with concentration but very softly, in case there was a spider outside the window. As she intoned the last syllable, she could feel herself compressing, shrinking, becoming incredibly dense and colder than she had ever imagined possible. But to her horror, she was also becoming blind, deaf, and mind-blind. Her last coherent thought was: *Is this what they call 'cold iron'?*

CHAPTER 4

She was covered in warm sticky liquid and she was looking at Stefan's body as her feet—no, her point—no, her feet—slid out of his chest. *Sweet Lady, it worked! But I'm not supposed to be changing back yet!* She tried to halt the change, but she was too cold and weak. In a moment she was sprawled, naked and bloody, on the field—right where Briam had dropped her.

She twisted around to make certain that Briam was all right. He appeared unharmed, but he was staring at her as if he had never seen her before. "But you said you wouldn't change back yet!"

"You have strange taste in weapons, Lord Briam." Lord Ranulf rose from checking Stefan's body for signs of life, stripped off his surcoat and wrapped it around Acila, as quickly and casually as if he were accustomed to scenes like this. Acila struggled to sit up. She was not going to lie there looking helpless in front of this man! The rest of Ranulf's guards were watching them from one sideline and the people from the castle stood crowded on the other. Judging from the babble of voices, they were all still trying to figure out what had happened. She didn't hear any comments on her state of undress, but she didn't doubt that she'd just provided everyone with plenty of gossip fodder for the winter and most of next spring. *Ignore them,* she told herself firmly. *First concentrate on getting out of here.*

"Is he dead?" she demanded.

"Quite dead." Lord Ranulf raised his eyebrows,

turning the blue circle almost to a triangle. "What chance did he have against so determined a pair of opponents?"

"About the same chance our father had against a troop of treacherous mercenaries," Acila retorted. Unfortunately her teeth started to chatter just then, which did rather diminish the effect she was trying for.

Lord Ranulf dug into his belt pouch and pulled out a bar of what appeared to be nuts and seeds stuck together with honey. "Eat this, there's no sense in your going into shock. As for your father's death, it was not by any order of mine! I would have met him in honorable combat."

Acila chewed diligently and swallowed. "As what?" she asked sweetly, taking another bite.

"As a human," he replied calmly. "I have no hand as skilled as your brother's to wield me were I to become a sword. How did you do it?"

Acila's mouth was full, so Briam answered. "She used a spell. She's really good with strange potions," he added proudly.

"You did well," Lord Ranulf said courteously, as Acila choked on a seed.

"But I must have done something wrong," Briam said, puzzled. "She wasn't supposed to change back until I put her in the ocean."

This time Acila had no need of eagle's eyes to see the astonishment on Lord Ranulf's face. "But that spell was lost long ago! Most people think it only a legend."

"Why did she change back?" Sometimes, Acila reflected bitterly, Briam had an extremely limited mind.

"Salt water and blood have the same elements," Lord Ranulf said absently, looking at Acila. "It seems I chose better than I knew when I decided to marry you."

Acila swallowed the last bit of honey and decided she'd live. "May I point out, Lord Ranulf, that I am not going to marry you. Stefan is dead, and my brother and I have won our freedom."

"I said I'd marry you!"

"*If* I agreed. I *don't* agree."

"Whether you agree or not, you were not included in the list of things your brother is allowed to take! Married to me or not, you'll stay here!"

"Do you think you can hold me against my will?" Acila asked. If anyone could, she knew, he would be the one; he could probably figure out some way. But judging from the thoughtful expression on his face, he was realizing how difficult it would be to imprison a shapechanger.

"And I *was* included in the list," she added. He looked sharply at her, and Acila knew that she had won.

"Your words were 'horse, weapons, armor'—and you yourself just called me his weapon." She rose to her feet and wrapped his surcoat more securely around her. She wanted to throw it in his face, but that was hardly practical.

"You can't go off wearing nothing but my surcoat," he protested. "At least go inside and pack yourself some clothing!"

Acila reached for Briam's hand, irrationally terrified that if she left him for so much as a moment, she would never see him again. "My clothing wasn't on the list," she pointed out. "Of course, if you want your surcoat back. . ."

"No!" Lord Ranulf said hastily. "Keep it, if you're too stubborn to take anything else."

Acila looked down at the garment. Last time she had seen it, it had been cream colored with blue embroidery. Now over half of it was blood red. "I'm afraid this is not quite your color any more," she said grimly. "Red was my father's color." She felt very strange, but after everything she had just been through, that wasn't surprising.

She looked at Briam again. He seemed to be all right; the astonishment had faded from his face and there wasn't a scratch on his body, so he was probably capable of riding. Time to go.

She turned back to Lord Ranulf. "You'll just have to console yourself with the estate, the serfs, and the castle—unless, of course, you were planning to break your pledged word."

"I hold by my honor," Lord Ranulf said grimly. "I'll console myself with your library—at least for a time. But I assure you, my Lady Acila, I won't forget you." He smiled suddenly, and it transformed his whole face. Acila was horrified to discover in herself an impulse to smile back. She repressed it at once.

"Here," he pulled a few more of the honey and nut bars out of his belt pouch and handed them to her. "Take these, I don't want you fainting on the road. And remember, my offer holds if you change your mind; this remains your home and you are welcome to return."

"Come, Briam," Acila hastened toward his horse. "Let's go." Briam swung himself into the saddle in true heroic fashion, pulled Acila up in front of him, and they headed down the path.

"I'm afraid I made one serious miscalculation," Acila said many hours later through her chattering teeth. "I *should* have had you pack some of my clothes. Which reminds me, did you bring another sword?"

Briam shook his head. "You didn't tell me to. I did bring my dagger and my eating knife."

"Well, that will have to do, at least until we can get you another sword. But I can't spend the night in this surcoat." She looked critically at the clearing they were entering. Most of the trees around it were pine trees, and the ground was covered with a mixture of leaves and needles which could be made into a fairly comfortable bed. "This looks like a reasonably good place to spend the night."

Briam stopped the horse and slid off easily, then

reached up to lift Acila down. She clung to the saddle
for a moment, waiting for her cold and very tired muscles to agree to support her unaided, while Briam removed saddlebags and water skin and started gathering
fallen branches for firewood.

As soon as she could support her own weight, Acila
gathered up the saddlebags and started to take inven-
tory. Briam's wool cloak was in the top of the first bag,
and she wrapped it gratefully around herself while she
sorted through the rest of the clothing and provisions.
Briam had brought his lute, of course, which was probably a good thing, since music was now his most us-
able skill. A small purse in one of the bags contained
a bit of coin, doubtless Galin's contribution, and two
sets of spare lute strings, undoubtedly packed by
Briam.

There was a pitifully small amount of food for two
people—even if she counted the honey bars Lord
Ranulf had given her, which could really not be considered proper food. Obviously they would have to
hunt soon. Water, at least, would not be a serious problem; streams were plentiful in this area.

As for clothing, Briam was wearing his arming tunic
and armor, she was wearing a badly blood-stained surcoat which was much too large for either of them, and
the packs contained Briam's boots, two pairs of chaus-
ses, two undertunics, one wool tunic, one linen tunic,
and his best festival gown. Acila stared at the last item
with mixed emotions. On the one hand, it was totally
impractical for their present position—had Galin expected Briam to go to the nearest noble estate and take
up residence? But the gold thread and jewels in the
embroidery were valuable and could be sold one at a
time, and Acila was just as glad not to have the results
of eight months of her evening labor left for Lord
Ranulf. Besides, the colors were designed to highlight
Briam's blond hair and fair skin; they wouldn't look
good on Lord Ranulf anyway.

Briam dropped his helm beside her and said, "I'm

taking Gris down to the stream, he needs a drink. Can you light the fire?"

"Fine," Acila said absently. "Maybe it will thaw me out."

"It should." Briam chuckled and disappeared, but within seconds a soft splash followed by loud slurping sounds made his location readily apparent.

Acila carefully scraped a large space in the middle of the clearing down to bare earth and surrounded it with fist-sized rocks. In the center of the cleared area, she piled a small amount of wood into a V, filled it with tinder, and moved to stand at the open end. Even though she had left the altar of the Lady of the Lightning, the salamander was Her symbol, and this transformation had come easily to Acila ever since she had first learned it by copying the shape off the front panel of the altar. Also, it should help remove the cold that seemed to have taken up residence in her bones. She shrugged off Briam's cloak and the surcoat, placed them carefully outside the circle, out of harm's way, moved into the tinder, and condensed herself into salamander form. The tinder flared around her, and she sat in it and basked while she waited for the branches to catch. Briam came back, unsaddled Gris and hobbled him, and sat down beside the fire to wait for her emergence.

The larger branches were starting to burn now, and she had no real excuse to stay in the fire any longer. It felt so good, better than the warmest bed on the coldest morning ever had. But she had a duty to take care of her brother, so she reluctantly moved out of the fire and resumed her human shape.

Briam wrapped the cloak around her and said, "Are you going to wear my clothes?"

"No, you're going to need your cloak yourself tonight, and the rest of them aren't warm enough. We didn't pack enough for both of us to be sleeping outdoors."

"Armies do it all the time," Briam protested.

"Armies are generally better provisioned—I should know; I've made up enough supply lists. Besides, we're going to have to set a watch, and I think the easiest solution to both problems is for me to take wolf shape. I could sleep out in a midwinter blizzard as a wolf, but I'll sleep light enough that I'll know if anything dangerous comes this way."

"All right," Briam said. "I like your wolf shape."

"I know you do," Acila retorted. "I still have vivid memories of the time you tried to ride me when we were four years old—though I suppose it's just as well that you learned that ears aren't meant to be steered with before you tried it on some poor dumb animal."

"You didn't really have to bite me," Briam protested.

"That *is* the major problem with changing," Acila pointed out. "I tend to take on the character of the animal whose shape I use—and the more time I spend in a shape, the more animal-like I become." *And that's something I'm going to have to be very careful with on this trip,* she thought grimly. "Besides, I didn't bite you very hard. It was just the nip you would have gotten if you'd been a fellow cub in the pack. It wasn't *my* fault you didn't have fur!"

They made a simple supper out of their provisions and carefully doused the fire. Then Acila repacked Briam's extra clothes, made sure he was securely wrapped in his cloak and curled up in the best shelter she could find for him (a sort of nest of piled-up pine needles), and shifted herself into wolf form.

The world changed abruptly. Since it was already quite dark, the loss of color vision wasn't very noticeable, but the ground was much closer, the trees were bigger, and everything smelled. Without trying at all, she could locate Gris (sweaty horse), Briam (musky and metallic, with faint overtones of onion), the saddle and saddlebags (leather), the remains of the fire (scorched wood), the different trees around them (varying flavors), and the floor of the forest (pine needles, dead leaves, and leaf mold, in the process of becoming dirt). Sounds were different, too; everything was louder and sharper, particularly the high-pitched chirping of the insects. It was very noisy, but as she adjusted to it, she realized that this was a quiet, peaceful night in the forest, with nothing to alarm or endanger her. Covered by the fur of her wolf form she was warm enough to sprawl out comfortably—no need to curl up in a ball with her legs tucked up and her tail wrapped protectively around legs and face as wolves did when sleeping in snow. She lay down between Briam and the path by which they had entered the clearing and began the series of brief, restless naps a wolf considers a good night's sleep.

Acila woke sometime after midnight. The moon, still high in the western sky, shone into the clearing, slightly veiled by a thin layer of mist. Drifts of mists floated around the trees, and the air was pleasantly moist and cool in her throat. Repressing an irrational desire to howl a greeting to the moon, she listened and smelled carefully. She could see perfectly well now, but by the time she saw danger, it would probably be too late. Much better to depend on her ears and nose for sufficient warning.

She listened drowsily to the sounds of the forest until a different sound reached her ears and startled her into full alertness. It was a faint metallic ring—a horseshoe hitting a stone, perhaps. It wasn't Gris; she could see him sleeping quietly, all four feet planted in the dirt of the clearing. She rose, slipping silently into the trees at the edge of the clearing, and scouted back, parallel to the path. There were two men, both mounted; she recognized them as Stefan's lieutenants. Either they had been fonder of Stefan than she would ever have imagined possible, or they sought to kill her and Briam in the hopes of a rich reward from Lord Ranulf. Or, and she shuddered, to kill Briam and take her back to Lord Ranulf.

As she fled soundlessly back to the clearing to wake

Briam, Acila wondered why she was so sure that they were not acting on Ranulf's orders. It was silly to feel she could trust the man who had taken her home and left her orphaned—it was more than silly, it was stupid and dangerous! But, she reasoned, if Lord Ranulf knew and approved of this, there would be more of them, and he'd probably be leading them himself—if only to make sure they didn't harm her out of ignorance. *Even a slash across the belly could make me useless to him. My ability to bear him a child is his main concern.*

Fighting back the shuddering nausea that idea woke in her, she loped across the clearing and planted a paw on the center of Briam's forehead. *Wake up! Grab your dagger and hide in the trees on the right side of the clearing. There are two men coming on horses. When I hit the first one, you kill the second one. Move!*

Still groggy, Briam scrambled to his feet, dropping his cloak. Acila was glad that he'd taken off his armor last night; it would have glinted in the moonlight as he moved and given them away. In his dark wool tunic he blended into the trees, and with any luck the cloak, the pile of pine needles, and the saddlebags might fool the men into thinking he still lay there, at least for a crucial few seconds. She had no intention of giving them time for a full examination. She slipped into position on the left side of the clearing, opposite and slightly ahead of Briam, and watched as the men rode in.

She sprang at the first man, knocking him out of his saddle and landing on the ground with him, struggling to get her teeth into his throat. Unfortunately, he was wearing a leather helmet which covered nearly all of his neck, and he had managed to get his dagger free as he fell. She hastily shifted her attention to the hand that held it and managed to bite into one of the tendons that held the thumb. The dagger dropped from his grip, and she knocked it away from them with a paw. He was lying on his sword, so that wasn't a problem—at least until he managed to throw her off him, which

wouldn't take long. She prayed that Briam would finish off the man he was fighting and come to help her
before she got into real trouble. She was heavy for a
wolf, but the man under her was bigger and heavier,
and once he got over the initial surprise of being at-
tacked by a wolf, he would realize it. Unless, by the
grace of the Lady, he was one of the humans who had
an irrational fear of wolves.

He was certainly afraid of something; his eyes were
wide with terror. But they were looking beyond her,
and there was an incredibly loud flapping of wings.
Acila pulled her head back as a set of impossibly large
talons dropped almost between her ears, landed at full
extension on the man's face, and pulled in to gripping
position. Blood from what was no longer a face
splashed her as she rolled clear. She had a quick look
at a "bird" stranger than anything *she* had ever been—
almost all wing, with an incredibly small body and
large talons, obviously designed for maximum speed
and striking power. She had no need to wonder who
flew in that form. *He must have his brain in his wings,*
the thought flashed through her mind; *there's no room
for it in that body.*

But the form was shifting, and the smell of the new
form raised her hackles. It was a cat, a very large cat,
with claws even sharper than the bird's talons—and
now, of course, it had teeth as well. And it was much
bigger than she was. She had no hope of beating this in
wolf form; she wasn't even sure she could outrun it.
And she wasn't going to run, not with her brother still
struggling with the second soldier.

She moved between the cat and the struggle, and
growled through bared teeth. *Come now!* said the ratio-
nal part of her brain, *you can't possibly think this will
frighten Lord Ranulf!* But she couldn't think of anything constructive to do, and this was what her wolf instincts were providing in the way of behavior.

The cat, however, was still dealing with the man on
which he had landed. His claws laid open the soldier's

upper leg—including the major blood vessels, judging by the great spurt of blood and the speed with which the body went limp.

Behind her, Briam killed the other man, rolled free of the body, and launched himself at the cat. He was promptly knocked flying by a great paw, but the claws were carefully retracted.

Acila scrambled to stand guard, snarling menacingly, over Briam, but the cat made no threatening moves. He stretched out spine and paws, fastidiously licked the blood off his front claws, and then turned his back on them and scrambled up the largest of the surrounding trees. The branches near the top thrashed violently, and Acila saw a bird shape take wing—and this shape was nearly all wing, without the large talons of the earlier version. It headed back in the direction of the castle, and Acila heard herself start howling.

It was all too much. She'd lost her home, den, pack, family (except for Briam, who was more a cub to be protected than an equal to be depended upon); she was so alone, and so tired, and so miserable . . . and here she sat in the middle of a bunch of dead animals that weren't even any good to eat!

"Acila!" Briam grabbed her and shook her hard. "Change back! Be human!" He sounded scared, and no doubt he was.

Acila changed to human form, her howls changing to sobbing hysterical tears. It was not an improvement. She was making just as much noise, and she was cold and bloody and there was an awful taste in her mouth where she'd bitten the soldier's hand. She went on crying, sure that she would never stop. Briam wrapped his cloak around her and held her close, but she was still crying when she fell asleep.

CHAPTER 5

Naturally, Acila had nightmares. After a day like that, anyone would have nightmares. The Earth Mother was calling to her to return home to the temple, to take her place at the altar, and the Lady of Fire was shooting lightning bolts all around her. She was slipping from one strange shape to another, becoming strange mixtures of all the animals she had ever seen, as well as a good many she had never seen and never wanted to see. And instead of the usual mental blurring as she shifted from one shape to the next, her mind was staying in focus as her body melted from one shape to another. She shuddered at the sight of her limbs melting from hands to paws to wings to tentacles and thanked the Goddess she couldn't see her own face—she had always had a horror of seeing things melting. It was one thing to change shape voluntarily, but quite another to lose it.

She struggled to control the changes, but still she kept shifting. Her stomach alternately burned, as if she had eaten fire, and felt as if something was tearing out handfuls of her essence through her navel. She knew that if she were awake and properly in her body she'd be throwing up, but this feeling was even worse. She was sure that she was going to die, but she was afraid she wasn't. She wished she could die and get it over with.

When the great black wings passed over her and landed at her side, she didn't even care. Lord Ranulf's bird shapes had been horrible perversions of nature;

this one was a reasonably normal looking bat—except for its size, of course. She wasn't terribly surprised to watch it turn itself into Lord Ranulf. It seemed only natural that he'd be invading her dreams; they were the only area of her life he hadn't invaded already.

He looked down at her, frowning, then moved away and disappeared from her sight. She thought briefly of turning her head to see where he'd gone but decided she didn't care; she felt too tired and wretched to move. She closed her eyes and endured as another wave of nausea passed through her.

When she opened her eyes again, he was back. He was also dressed, and she wondered if he'd flown here with a pack of clothes and dropped them nearby or if he'd just gone to the castle and back. It could have been either one; she didn't know how much time had passed, although normally her time sense was very accurate indeed.

He knelt beside her and pulled her gently into his lap. "Poor child, you are having a rough time of it." He put his left arm securely around her shoulder and held her so that her head rested on his left shoulder. "Here, just relax; I'll help you." He put his other hand over the part of her stomach that felt as if it were being torn out, and the pain gradually eased away. She felt rather numb and very tired. "There, now. Rest," he murmured against her hair, "just rest."

It was all right, she could rest; this was only a dream—he wouldn't act like this in real life. Besides, if he were really here, Briam would be awake and fighting him. She sighed and leaned limply against him. "Why did you come after us, and why did you kill that soldier? Wasn't he working for you?" Even knowing that she was dreaming, she was still curious.

"No, he was not!" Lord Ranulf said emphatically. "I would not have you harmed on any account. Do you know how few changers there are in the world?"

"Not any that I knew of but myself—until two days

ago. But Briam's not a changer, and you didn't seem to object to having him killed."

"Killing him in a fair battle is one thing. Pre-dawn ambushes are quite another. He won his life fairly; I do not claim it forfeit now." He sighed. "I would not have thought that Stefan's men wanted to avenge him, or I would have kept a closer watch on them. If I hadn't been wandering restlessly on the walls in the middle of the night and seen them creep out . . . they could have killed you!"

"Oh, no, I don't think so." Acila shook her head. "I was holding my own, and Briam would have killed that man in a few minutes even if you hadn't come along. And I'm very glad that you didn't hurt Briam."

"Oh, he'll probably have quite a few bruises, but I did pull in my claws." Lord Ranulf dropped a light kiss on her hair. "I doubt you would agree to marry me if I killed your brother. You appear to have an extremely stubborn and determined character."

"I'm not agreeing to marry you anyway." *Even if I am dreaming that you're nice.*

His face was gentle, as was the hand that smoothed back her hair. "No, not yet, but I still hope that you will in time. I do wish you'd at least come back home. It's obvious that no one ever taught you anything about shapechanging, and you'd be a lot safer if you were properly trained. And speaking of training, where is your library? So far the only books I've found in the entire castle are the account books."

Acila chuckled. "If you are meant to find the library, you'll find it. If not, you won't."

Lord Ranulf sighed. "That's exactly what your steward said."

Acila felt a brief stab of alarm. "You didn't hurt him, did you?"

"No, of course I didn't." He actually sounded shocked. "What do you think I am—some kind of monster? All of your people are safe and well."

"Thank you," Acila said politely.

"One thing does puzzle me, though. I haven't seen anyone show grief over your father's death, including you and your brother."

Acila shrugged. "I suppose I'll cry for him in time. Right now so much has happened that I feel rather numb. As for everyone else—well, he was away at least half of every year, and he wasn't exactly the sort of person one loved. Everybody obeyed his orders promptly, but—" she tried to find words to explain, "—he didn't care about *people*, except as things: his steward, his son, his daughter." She suddenly realized something. "You know, I don't remember his ever having touched me, not even to take my hand, or kiss me in greeting when he returned from a campaign."

Lord Ranulf blinked in surprise. "He seems to have been a strange man. Where did you get your talent? Was your mother a changer?"

"I don't know. She died when we were born. Nobody knew I was one until I fell off a shed roof when I was three. I was a bird when I hit the ground. Fortunately, Briam was the only one who saw me, and he thought it was a great game. After that, I taught myself, but I was careful to keep it a secret. And once I grew up I was too busy administering the estates to have much time to practice, so I suppose I'm not very good."

"For a wild talent, you're quite good. Your main faults are that you copy real animals too much, rather than making adjustments that fit the shape to your weight better—you can get a great deal more flying speed and range if you don't insist on trying to look like a real eagle—and you haven't learned to recognize and compensate for your limits. You should establish some simple defensive shape that you can shift to and hold when you're exhausted, and practice it until it's automatic. And you need to strengthen your sense of self. No matter how tired you get, you shouldn't be doing that random shifting you were doing just now.

You don't want to lose yourself—you're much too valuable."

His arms tightened around her. "I wish I'd met you when you were younger, and when my father was still alive. He was a good teacher." He sighed. "Please come home, Acila."

"No." At the moment the idea did have a certain appeal, but Acila resolutely refused the temptation. "I have to take care of Briam, and he wouldn't be safe at home anymore."

"But I've told you I don't seek his life!"

"Maybe you don't. But you obviously have plenty of men who'd kill him to do you a favor." She set her jaw and looked him straight in the eyes. "I really don't think Stefan's men were out to avenge him; I think they thought you'd reward them for killing Briam and returning me, even if you didn't order it."

He considered that for a long moment. "You may very well be correct. Well, I'll set my house in order, and you look after Briam—but be very sure that you look after yourself as well!"

He shifted her slightly so that he could reach his belt pouch, and held something to her lips. It was a honey bar like the one he had given her that morning. "Take a bite of this, there's a good girl."

Acila obediently bit off a small piece and struggled to chew it. It wasn't easy, but she did feel slightly better as it softened and melted in her mouth.

Lord Ranulf took the rest of the bar and wrapped her fingers around it. "Be sure to eat the rest of this before you try to move in the morning. If you don't, I assure you that you really *will* have morning sickness!" He laid her limp body gently down and wrapped Briam's cloak securely around her. "Rest well." He walked out of the clearing, still in human form.

When Acila woke, the sun was high in the sky. She lay still, trying to sort out where she was and what was going on. Slowly her memories of the past few days returned: her father's death, the escape from the castle, a fight with a couple of Stefan's men, and advice from Lord Ranulf—but surely much of it had been a dream? Her mind couldn't tell her; to it everything seemed equally real or unreal.

There were no bodies in the clearing. If the fight had really happened, Briam must have disposed of them somewhere. But Briam was sitting across the clearing cleaning a sword, there were now three hobbled horses browsing in the trees at the edge of the clearing, and there were more saddlebags piled with their supplies. So the fight with the mercenaries hadn't been a dream. There was also a pile of bloody clothing. Apparently Briam had grasped the principle that they needed all the food and clothing they could get. Or maybe after last night he'd decided he wasn't that fond of her wolf form after all.

Her current shape was normal human, caked in spots with dried blood; both she and Briam's cloak were going to need a washing as soon as she could move. There was a fruit bar turning sticky in her left hand. Briam must have tried to feed her while she was crying, not that she could remember it, but she certainly appeared to have fallen asleep with the bar in her hand. She pulled it toward her mouth and froze. It wasn't one of her dried fruit bars—it was one of Lord Ranulf's honey bars.

She opened her mouth to ask Briam about it, then decided against it. There was no point in worrying him. She wasn't sure she wanted to know anyway. She forced herself to bite off a piece of the bar and began to chew on it. Wherever it came from, it was food, and she badly needed food. Her mouth still tasted a bit bloody, but now she was too hungry to care.

The honey bar helped; by the time she finished it, she felt merely moderately ill instead of almost dead. "Briam?" Her voice came out as a croak.

"Acila!" Briam crossed the clearing, still holding the

sword. "I was afraid you weren't going to wake up. Are you all right?"

Looking closely at him, she saw that he was red around the eyes; either he'd been crying or he'd sat up watching after she fell asleep—or maybe both. But if he'd sat up watching, wouldn't he have seen Lord Ranulf? Her head ached, so she decided to worry about that later.

"I feel stiff, sore, and very tired, but I'll live." She forced a smile. "How about you?"

He shrugged. "A few bruises—I've had worse. I buried the bodies, but I saved all the clothes and supplies so you could go through them. Was I right?"

"Exactly right." Acila reached out and patted his hand. "Help me up; I want to go wash the blood off me." She gritted her teeth as Briam pulled her to a sitting position, then helped her to her feet. She had aches in every muscle she had ever been aware of, and she discovered several new muscles on her way to the stream.

She was glad now that she had slept until the sun was high. At this time of day the stream was only cold, not icy, at least in the shallow part near the bank. She wasn't even tempted to change into a water-loving shape; at the moment changing seemed impossible. *I wonder if I can lose the talent if I overuse it? No, I'm probably just overtired. After what I've been through the last three days, anyone would be exhausted. At least Briam is holding up well.*

Her internal voice was still with her. *Of course Briam's holding up well. Why shouldn't he be? He's been fighting in his own shape, not trying to make his mind and various sets of reflexes work together with insufficient practice. He's also gotten more sleep than you have, and done much less worrying—if he's done any!*

That seemed reasonable, so Acila turned to the next problem. "Briam, please hand me your cloak and then bring the clothing from the fight over here. We might as well wash it while it's early enough for it to dry before night."

Briam tossed his cloak to her and headed back to the clearing to get the rest. Acila submerged the cloak and started attacking the nearest bloodstain. "If worst comes to worst," she muttered to herself, "I'll kill a few rabbits and dye the whole thing the color of blood."

"Here." Briam came back with the clothing. Acila's nose wrinkled in disgust. She seemed unusually sensitive to smells today—was this a carryover from being a wolf?

"Put it all in the water," she instructed. "Even the stuff that's not bloodstained needs washing. I wish we had some soap."

Briam shrugged. "I didn't know we'd need it."

"Don't worry about it. Even if you did think we'd need it, you wouldn't have had room to pack it. We'll just have to manage with what we do have."

"Umm." Briam looked thoughtfully at the water. "Are we still going to the ocean? Now that you're not a sword, I mean."

"I don't know . . . I mean, we don't have to."

"Then where are we going?"

Good question, Acila thought despairingly. *I wish I knew. Where are we going and what are we going to do with the rest of our lives? Three weeks ago, I knew. We were going to stay home and Briam was going to rule our estates and I was going to run them. Now Lord Ranulf will do that, and he'll probably do a perfectly good job—he certainly seems highly competent at everything he does. But what are we going to do?* Stalling for time, she asked. "Where do you want to go?"

Briam's prompt answer surprised her. "I think we should go find our kingdom."

"What?!"

"You know, the kingdom that Father said we'd rule. I thought he meant our estates were going to be our kingdom, but I guess they're not, so it must be some-place else."

Acila stared at him in shock. *He's actually been thinking about this—or is he making it the beginning of a ballad?*

Briam was obviously expecting a response, so she said the first thing that came into her head. "Father said that you would rule a kingdom, not that you and I would."

"But if I had a kingdom, it would be yours, too." This was obvious to Briam. "We always share things."

Enough of that subject. "All right, where *is* our kingdom?"

Briam looked confused. "Don't you know? You're the one who knows things."

Acila wrung out the cloak as best she could and handed it to him. "Drape this on that bush, please." She picked up a tunic, obviously from the man Briam had killed; there was a slash in the breast. And they didn't even have a needle with them, let alone thread. Why hadn't she done the packing herself?

Briam draped the cloak, then returned to squat next to her. "Acila?"

What was the question? Oh, yes. "No, I don't know where our kingdom is." *Assuming we have one.* "If the Gods mean for us to have a kingdom, they'll just have to arrange for us to wind up there. And in the meantime . . ." her voice trailed off. She wasn't incompetent; she knew that. She'd run a large estate very capably for several years. But that was a different kind of competence—or at least on different scale. There she had lots of help, and it was a matter of directing the steward, overseeing the cook and household servants, going over the clerk's account books. If she wanted dinner, she asked what supplies were available and then issued the appropriate orders. "Briam, were they carrying extra food?"

"Yes, quite a bit. And money, too." He hesitated.

"There was an extra saddlebag with some of your clothes in it."

"My clothes?" Acila looked at him in astonishment. "Why would a couple of mercenaries be carrying my clothes?"

Briam shrugged. "I don't know. They certainly wouldn't have fit either of them. But at least you can get dressed now. And the money should be useful."

Yes, of course, mercenaries would have money. They probably were paid yesterday. That will help when we come to a town, but it might not be at all wise to do that yet. Acila had never been outside the castle walls without at least one man with her (well, not in human shape). A lady of her class did not go without an escort. Presumably other women had ways of managing without armed guards, but she didn't know how. Even with her own clothes available, it might be better if she didn't wear them.

She looked at the clothes spread around her, then down at her body. She was still small and thin, so maybe if she cut her hair she could pass for Briam's younger brother. And now they had two swords and assorted knives. "Briam," she said suddenly, "will you teach me how to fight?"

"Certainly, if you wish," Briam replied, obviously totally bewildered by this strange request. If there was one area Acila had never shown any interest in, it was fighting. "But don't you want dinner first?"

CHAPTER 6

After eating as much food as she could possibly hold, Acila dressed herself in Briam's extra clothes. She decided to put off cutting her hair until she absolutely had to. After all, the weather was going to get colder before it got warmer again; if they had to stay out all winter, she'd be better off with long hair. Briam's cloak and the clothes the men had owned were spread out drying all over the place, and most of them would be dry by sunset. At the moment their camp was very visible from the air, but the only person who might see it from that angle was Lord Ranulf, and he already knew where they were. She hoped that no more of Stefan's men would come after them.

"Acila?" Briam asked. "Are we going to stay here?"

"In this clearing? I think we'll stay here one more night, but tomorrow I'll look for a better place to camp. We're too close to the road here—and I've no desire to have anyone see me before I've learned to act like a boy."

"Why do you want to learn to act like a boy?"

"Ladies aren't supposed to travel unescorted. Once I can convince people I'm a boy, you can be a traveling minstrel and I can be your apprentice or something, but right now I'd look strange to anyone who saw me."

"You don't look anything like a boy to me," Briam looked thoughtful. "But perhaps that's partly because I know you're not."

"Yes, I'm sure that's true, but to convince people I'm a boy, I'll have to learn to move like one. It will probably take at least a month for me to get used to the clothes alone. Even in a short tunic I move as if I were wearing long skirts, and the way I automatically lift the tunic slightly when I climb on top of or over something would give me away to anyone with the slightest perception. You look at me and see your sister, but to anyone else I'd just look *wrong*, even if they weren't quite sure why."

"Can't you just shapechange into a boy?"

"Well, yes and no. I can change my features. I could change my face to be a perfect match for yours and my body to be the same height and bulk—"

"Then we'd be identical twins!" Briam broke in enthusiastically. He seemed to like the idea.

"Yes, and we'd also be conspicuous and easy for people to remember. And with my body spread out like that I'd be too fragile. I'd have to lengthen my arms and legs, and that would make the bones thinner and weaker. We don't want that if Lord Ranulf comes after us again."

"Again?" Briam asked, puzzled.

"Never mind," Acila said hastily. "Besides, it does take energy to change and hold a different shape, and changing from a girl into something that looks like a boy isn't enough of a change. Look, when I change into a wolf, I move like a wolf, right?"

"Yes, and when you change into a bird, you can fly."

"Right. Both of those shapes are different enough from my normal one that their reflexes take over from my human ones. But if I change to look like a boy, I'm still human, so the reflexes don't change. If I step over a log, I automatically lift up my skirts a little bit, and until I learn not to do that, I'll do it without thinking. So I'll need some time to learn to stop thinking like a girl and acting like a lady. And you'll need to learn to stop treating me like a lady and start treating me like a little brother."

"How does one treat a little brother?"

"I'm not sure. We'll have to figure something out as

we go along. I hope we have enough have time. It's still early autumn. We've got some food, and there will be enough game to feed us for a while. If we find a good location, we can live here quite comfortably for a couple of months, but after that it will be winter."

"A couple of months is a long time to camp out."

"True, but it's not as if we had anyplace else to go." They sat in silence for a long time.

Another meal and a quiet night's sleep left Acila feeling much better. After a quick breakfast, she told Briam to pack their belongings while she scouted for a good place to stay. Then she changed to eagle form and went aloft. She paused at the tree-top level long enough to check for the presence of any large, strange-looking creatures who could be Lord Ranulf, but, seeing nothing but clear sky, she continued on up until she was high enough to view a large area.

Most of what she saw below her was either the drab brown of the forest floor or the green and russet of the leaves in the tree tops. The road they had traveled down from the castle was a thin line paralleling the stream. She flew downstream, having no desire to head back toward the castle or the higher mountains behind it. About five miles down, the stream flowed into the beginnings of a river, and about a mile beyond that, another stream ran into the other side of the river. The second stream came down through a marshy area, but beyond that were hills with a good deal of vegetation mixed with rocky cliffs and caves.

This looked promising, so Acila flew lower. The hills had quite a few caves, several of which looked large enough to hold her, Briam, and three horses. The stream was clear, and several of the plants were edible. There even appeared to be enough forage to hold the horses for quite a while.

She landed in front of a line of caves and changed to wolf form—no matter how promising the place looked, it wouldn't help unless they could get themselves and the horses there. She scrambled over rocks, waded along the stream, climbed down through still more rocks along the side of a cliff, and slogged through the marsh until she reached the river. The water was fast moving, but it didn't look too deep.

Bracing herself to change shape in a hurry, she angled her body upriver and stepped in. The water came up along shoulders, belly, and hips, but as long as she kept her nose up, she was able to breathe and see. But ohhh, was it ever cold! Resolving that her next crossing would be made on horseback, she pushed her way onward. She scrambled out onto the other bank and shook herself thoroughly. Well, at least it was fordable, and it would break their trail if anyone else got ideas about pursuing them. She gave herself one final shake, then started running up the path to rejoin Briam. With any luck, the run would dry her off.

The sun was high when she got to the clearing, changed back to human form, and got dressed. Briam handed her a hunk of bread and cheese. "Did you find a place? Are we going now?"

Acila nodded, swallowing a mouthful of food. "Yes, and," she glanced at the sun, "yes. But we had better start right away, we've got some distance to go, and there's a river to ford, which we want to do while there's still sun to dry us afterward."

"All right." Briam quickly finished the last of his food and began to load the packs onto the horses. "This is really an adventure, isn't it?"

"Considering that I've been dividing my time between being wet and cold and being scared out of my mind, yes, I'd say that this definitely qualifies as an adventure," Acila replied dryly. "Are you planning to turn it into a ballad?"

"Of course." Briam grinned.

'Why did I even bother to ask?" She gulped the last of her food and mounted one of the spare horses.

They made good time to the river and forded it without much difficulty; the horses were a good deal taller than Acila's wolf form. But the horses didn't care for the footing in the marsh, and Acila didn't blame them. She had hopped from rock to rock herself.

Briam had other concerns. "What," he wrinkled his nose distastefully, "is that awful smell?"

Acila had noticed it on the way through before and had hoped that it would not be as annoying when she was in human form. It was still quite noticeable, but compared to the way it had smelled before it didn't bother her at all.

"Don't worry, you'll get used to it. I believe it's called skunk cabbage."

"I can well believe it, but I don't think I am ever going to be used to it enough to eat it!"

Acila laughed for the first time since before she had heard about Lord Ranulf's army. "Relax, I don't think it's supposed to be edible."

"Good!" Briam's response was heartfelt and emphatic.

It was twilight when they reached the end of the marsh. Briam looked at the overhanging cliff and asked, "Where do we go now?"

"Over there," Acila gestured to their left. 'There's a sort of stairway."

Briam looked at it in disbelief. Coming down the cliff side on a fairly steep slope was a mess of large rocks. " 'Sort of' is right. It looks as though a giant's child had a temper tantrum and threw his building stones around. How are we ever going to get the horses up there?"

"Force of personality, I guess; and quickly—we don't want to be caught there in the dark. Don't worry, I tested the stones on the way down, they're stable and won't tilt under us." Acila moved her horse to the edge of the bottom rock and dismounted. "Tether the third horse; we'll have to take them one at a time. It's not impossible, but it's not going to be easy."

It wasn't easy, and it was full dark by the time they had persuaded the third horse up to the top of the cliff and gotten all of them to the caves. The moon hadn't risen yet, but the night was clear and the stars were bright. Acila could see pretty well, although she wasn't sure whether this was natural or whether she was shifting her eyes into something else without knowing it.

Briam looked around uneasily. "Is this it? It looks scary, all dark gray with black holes in the rocks. And the ground is awfully hard and rocky." He fumbled along the horse's flank to the saddlebags. "At least we don't have to worry too much about having our campfire spread out of control. Is there anything here to build a fire with?"

"No!" Acila said quickly. "We took longer to get here than I expected, and even if we did find the makings of a fire, I don't want to advertise our presence here."

"But there can't be anybody within miles of here!"

"If we light a fire out here on this hillside, it will show for miles and miles." *And I'm not even going to discuss the possibility that Lord Ranulf may decide to stretch his wings a bit before turning in for the night.* "Tomorrow we'll gather wood and find a good place inside one of the caves for a fire pit. Tonight we eat a cold supper and wrap up warmly."

"What about water?"

"Is there something wrong with your ears?" Acila wavered between annoyance and concern. "There's a stream right over there."

"Oh." He listened for a minute. "I still don't hear it."

Acila frowned. True, the stream wasn't that loud, but she could hear it perfectly well. Maybe he was getting a cold. "You dig out some supper and hobble the horses—not that I think they're stupid enough to try to go anywhere. I'll get water and find a sheltered corner for us to sleep in tonight. Tomorrow we can set up a proper camp in the caves."

"All right." Briam began removing saddlebags and tack from the horses. "I certainly don't want to try exploring the caves in the dark. There could be bears in them, or even wolves!"

Acila laughed. "Just don't snore loud enough to wake anything up!"

Briam slept like a log and didn't snore a bit. Acila, dozing restlessly beside him, felt thoroughly resentful. *It must be wonderful to be placid and not worry about things and trust the rest of the world to take care of you. If I hadn't been so clever about getting us both out of the castle, I could still be home in my own bed, not freezing out here in the hills wondering what to do next.*

Yes, her internal voice shot back, *I'm sure that Lord Ranulf would be happy to help keep your bed warm! And I'm sure he'd make sympathetic noises about Briam's unfortunate death.*

Tears flowed down Acila's cheeks, but she forced her body to remain still; she didn't want Briam to wake up and ask why she was crying. *It's not that I want Briam dead or Lord Ranulf as a husband, but this isn't fair! It's all too much. I don't know where to go or what to do, and now I'm responsible for Briam and three horses, and I don't have anybody to help me. Am I going to have to spend the rest of my life looking after my brother?*

Not necessarily. He could die long before you do—or he could get married. And isn't lumping him in with the horses just a little bit extreme? After all, he is smarter than they are.

Yes, but the way my luck's been running lately, he'll marry some pretty little idiot and I'll have yet another person to look after.

Well, he can't marry anyone while you're hiding out

in the woods—unless you expect some princess in distress to come wandering through here.

Of course not! What do you think this is—a fairy tale?

Try to relax and go to sleep. It's nearly dawn, and you have to set up a proper camp today. You'll have plenty of time to be angry at the world and brood over your fate after that's done—if you really want to follow such an unproductive course of action.

Some help you are! Acila mopped her face with the end of her sleeve, closed her eyes, and concentrated on slowing her breathing until she fell asleep.

"Wake up! Are you planning to spend the whole day sleeping?" Briam sounded obnoxiously cheerful.

Acila cautiously opened one eye, then closed it again. The sun was high, the clearing was warm and Briam had obviously been up for some time. She felt as if she never wanted to get up again. Her restless night had left her feeling drugged and heavy-eyed, and all she wanted to do was sleep for the rest of her life, even if she did keep hearing the Goddess calling her every time she fell asleep.

"I don't know why you were worried about my snoring," Briam teased. "You sound just like a frog."

"Thanks," Acila snarled, pulling herself unwillingly to a sitting position.

"I checked the caves," he went on. "No bears, and the middle one has a couple of side rooms toward the back. One of them is big enough for the horses. The cave nearest the stream isn't really big enough to hold both of us, let alone the horses, and the rest are just large holes, not really proper caves."

"All right," Acila said, dragging herself to her feet. "Let me splash some water on my face and pry my eyes open. Then I'll see about setting up our stuff and making a fire—I assume you want breakfast."

"Of course. I'm starved!"

They spent the rest of the day settling in to their new home. Fortunately there was a spot toward the back of the cave where they could light a fire. The smoke from it drifted up and out a fissure in the ceiling. Acila had insisted on checking to find out where it went before lighting the fire; she didn't want either a forest fire or a highly visible plume of smoke to give their location away. The task was not easy. The hole was too small for her eagle shape to fit through, and any smaller bird shape wouldn't be able to fly. She could always go outside and try to find the hole from above, but there seemed to be some sort of vegetation around it and she didn't think it would be readily visible.

Finally, she sent Briam back to the front of the cave with orders to move the saddlebags in. Then she concentrated, remembering Lord Ranulf as he had left her room, and shifted to spider shape. It was a strange feeling, as if she were pulling all of herself into the center and stretching out in rays all at once. It was horribly disorienting, but when the flowing stopped, she was a large spider with very sticky feet.

She moved carefully over to the wall, testing to see how this body performed, then slowly started to climb. That part wasn't too bad; she'd done a little rock climbing even in human form. But crossing the ceiling was another matter. She hated being upside down, and only the sternest of self-scoldings kept her moving across the ceiling.

I'm going to fall straight down and land splat! on my back.

No, you're not. Come now—have you ever seen a spider fall on its back? Now, move your, uh, right center front foot, that's right. Now the left center front foot . . .

She made it across the ceiling and maneuvered through the hole, one leg at a time. She turned back to human shape very thankfully, not even caring that she was standing naked near the top of a windy hill. The trees and bushes around her broke the force of the wind, so she wasn't as cold as she might otherwise have been. They would also serve to break up and hide the smoke from the fire, and the ceiling of the cave was high enough that the heat from the fire wouldn't harm them. It was also too far for the sparks to jump, unless she was stupid enough to build too large a fire. It would do nicely.

Reluctantly, she changed back into a spider. The transformation was easier this time, and she didn't seem to have quite as many legs to maneuver through the hole this time. *Just goes to show you can get used to anything.* She was heading across the ceiling when Briam screamed.

She lost her grip and started to fall, but was pulled up short by some sort of sticky rope exuded from her stomach. It stretched to lower her to the floor, where she changed back as she hit.

Briam stood there, sword in hand, staring at her in horror. "Acila! You scared me half to death!"

"Likewise!" she snapped. "You idiot, you could have gotten me killed! You ought to know better than to make sudden loud noises when I'm learning a new shape!"

"I didn't know it was you."

"You thought four-foot spiders were native to these parts?"

She was shaking from the adrenaline pouring through her body, and she hoped she wasn't going to throw up. "Put away the sword, for pity's sake!"

Briam looked at it as if he'd never seen it before, then sheathed it. "How did you learn to turn into a spider?"

If you're lucky, brother dear, you'll never know. "I needed something that could climb up and crawl through that hole—it's too small for me to fly through." *Change the subject.* "We're in luck; there are bushes above that will break up and hide smoke, so we can put a fire here."

"Great!" Briam seemed to be recovered from the shock. "I'll go get some wood." He looked around the cave approvingly. "This should be a good place to live." He turned and went out.

Acila dressed with trembling hands, dug a fruit bar out of the saddlebag Briam had dropped, and ate it, shaking all the while.

CHAPTER 7

They had been living at the caves about six weeks when the wolves arrived. There were three of them: two males and a pregnant female, and they came loping up alongside the stream at mid-morning, while Acila and Briam sat in front of their cave, cleaning their swords.

Briam leaped to his feet at once, raising his sword. The larger of the male wolves stopped and stood his ground, teeth bared in a growl. The other male and the female, also growling, stood just behind him. For a long moment none of them moved, and Acila had the odd idea that one could do a painting of the scene and title it "Confrontation."

"Acila," Briam spoke through clenched teeth, "what are you just sitting there for? Why do you think I've been teaching you to use a sword?"

Acila rose to her feet, transferred her sword to her right hand, and used it to sweep the point of Briam's sword down. "Not, I trust, so that I could kill innocent wolves returning to their den."

"What?"

"The cave nearest the stream—didn't you notice the shed fur in it?"

"Is that what that was?" Briam turned to look at her, and the pack leader advanced another two steps toward him. "Hey!"

Acila tossed him her sword. "Take these, and go into the cave."

He looked doubtful. "Are you sure you can handle this?"

"Briam," Acila said patiently. "I weigh half again what a full-grown wolf does, and I certainly hope I'm more intelligent. And after everything else I've survived lately, I should certainly be able to handle a wolf."

"Three wolves."

"No, just one. If I can overcome the pack leader, I become the new leader, and they all obey me."

"Sounds thrilling." Briam retreated to the mouth of the cave to watch. Acila was thankful that the horses were in their stall in the back of the cave; she certainly didn't need them getting in the way.

She pulled the heavy leather gauntlets out of her belt and put them on, then advanced toward the wolf, never taking her eyes from his.

"Aren't you going to change to wolf shape?"

"Briam," she said, keeping her eyes on the wolf's, "be quiet, and stay quiet."

The wolf retreated as she advanced, but he continued to meet her eyes and growl at her. The rest of his pack fell back with him until they reached the stream. Then the female whined anxiously. Acila kept her eyes on him as he tensed and sprang at her.

She twisted as he hit her, and they landed on the ground tangled together, side by side. Quickly she rolled so that he was under her and grabbed his front legs. She was glad she was wearing a short tunic; it would have been very difficult to kneel straddled over a wolf if she had been wearing skirts. She squeezed her knees against both sides of his rib cage to keep him from rolling and shoving her over, and gripped both his forelegs firmly. His shoulders didn't rotate enough to pin them to the ground, the way one would do with a human's arms; they stayed close to his body, with the paws flopping limply over her hands.

He certainly wasn't quiet though; he was thrashing as much as he could in the position he was in and was doing his very best to claw her with his hind legs, which fortunately didn't quite reach her back, and to bite her hands. Luckily, he couldn't get his teeth through the thick gauntlets. She managed to knock his jaw aside without losing her grip on the legs, and after several attempts he finally gave up trying to bite her and just lay there and stared at her. She stared back.

"Acila?"

"I told you to be quiet." She listened carefully for the other wolves, keeping her gaze locked with the one she held. They were shifting restlessly nearby, but she didn't think they were going to attack her.

"Are you going to hold him like that all day?"

"If I have to. It depends on him." The wolf broke eye contact and turned his head aside briefly but then looked back at her. She kept staring straight at him. Behind her she could hear Briam start to approach her. "Stay where you were, Briam," she ordered. The noise behind her stopped. The wolf looked away and quickly back again.

It seemed that she spent hours kneeling over the wolf. She lost track of the number of times he'd look aside for a few seconds, then look back. Finally he turned his head to the side and left it there. She counted out a minute under her breath, then cautiously released his left paw. He stayed still. She gently rubbed his stomach and under his jaw. "Good boy," she crooned in a low voice. He stretched a little and tilted his head back so she could scratch his jaw better. "That's right, good boy." She swung her knee aside and released him, and he scrabbled urgently to his feet and went to join the other two wolves.

She waited a few seconds and then walked over to them. They crowded around her and sniffed her as she stood and scratched behind three sets of ears. When none of them made any hostile moves, she risked removing her left gauntlet and petting them with her bare hand. They sniffed and licked it, but made no move to bite her. She moved with them over to their cave and sat beside the opening while they settled back down.

She twisted her head to the right. Briam still stood at the mouth of their cave, staring at her. "I thought you were going to turn into a wolf."

"Shapechanging is not the answer to every problem, Briam. Put your sword down and your gauntlets on and come let them smell you."

He obeyed slowly, looking dubious. The wolves looked pretty dubious also, but they did no more than growl at him. Acila scolded and coaxed until they let him pet them. It wasn't full acceptance, but it would do for the minute. They'd have plenty of time to integrate the packs later.

The autumn rains started the next day. Autumn had always been Acila's least favorite time of the year; the castle was cold and damp; everyone was cooped up together and tempers flared, so that she spent half her time settling quarrels between servants, and there was never enough light to do the needlework she used for relaxation. But the rainy season in the castle was idyllic compared to her current situation.

After several weeks of near-constant rain, the stream swelled to what was surely a new high. After all, if it flooded out the wolves' den every year, they would have chosen another den. As it was, they simply moved in with her—and Briam and the three very nervous horses. The wolves were nervous, too. They were beginning to accept Briam, but the horses were new to them. Acila made a wall of the saddlebags in the side of the cave where the ceiling was lowest, and the wolves took over the cubbyhole this made for their den.

As the weeks went on the female went out less and less, but the males continued to take turns going out in the rain to hunt and dragging their kill back to the den. As the hunting got worse, both of them started going out at once. One day, when they hadn't returned by dark, Acila lit a small torch and crawled back to check on the female. She was getting too big now to move easily, but she lifted her head at Acila's arrival. Acila scratched her under the jaw and looked at her carefully. Except for her bloated abdomen, she was looking suspiciously thin, and Acila worried that she wasn't getting enough to eat. She crawled back to the other side of the pile of saddle bags and rummaged in the one that held what was left of their food. She could afford to go a bit short of food; she wasn't pregnant. She pulled out some dried meat and took it back to the wolf, who accepted it eagerly. Acila sat beside her while she ate and prayed that the pups would be born early and easily.

The males returned an hour later with what looked like the scanty remains of a squirrel, not that Acila looked at it terribly closely. The female inhaled her share in one gulp, and Acila resigned herself to the idea of short rations until the hunting improved.

The next few weeks were miserable. The rain continued, but Acila, Briam, and the male wolves had to spend most of their time hunting anyway. Acila and Briam also had to take the horses out for exercise and forage. They could eat what they and the wolves killed, but the grain for the horses was running out and the horses did not consider rabbit stew an acceptable substitute. And after a couple of days of leading the horses over terrain they didn't like, Acila was wishing she could turn one of the wolves into a human—or herself and Briam into triplets—anything to get a third human to take care of the third horse. And every day of hunting in the area of the caves meant that they had to go farther to find food.

"Acila?" It was still raining, and Acila was struggling to convince the third horse that it wanted to leave the cave. Ahead of her Briam stood in the rain holding the bridles of the other two. He got on with the horses much better than she did; she had never been much of a horsewoman.

"What?" Acila gave the bridle an impatient tug, and the horse threw back its head in protest.

"Why don't you let me take the horses, and you take the wolves hunting? If we both spend all morning with the horses, we won't have time to go far enough to find enough food." He looked back at the wolves, who were waiting at the back of the main cave until the horses were out of the way. "Will they still obey you if you turn into a wolf? You can run much faster in wolf form—I should think it would make hunting easier."

"I can try," Acila said thoughtfully. "I'm not as big in wolf form, but I'm still pretty heavy. I think I could hold my own in a fight, and I'm hungry enough to be willing to try it."

"I should think so! Do you have any idea how much weight you've lost? You look awful."

Acila looked at Briam. His face was noticeably thinner, and his clothes were looser than they had been when they left home. And she knew she probably did look worse than he did, since she'd started sharing her food with the female wolf even before they'd really begun to run low. "All right, I'll try it—if you can get this wretched beast out of the cave."

Briam made a clicking sound with his tongue, and the horse stepped daintily past Acila and went to join the others. Acila sighed, shook her head, and started peeling off the several layers of clothing she was wearing.

She was very cold as she undressed—did this mean that the snow would start soon? How long had they been here anyway? Maybe she only felt the cold more because she'd become so thin. She looked down at herself and was horrified to see that her lower ribs were all plainly visible. Oh, well, in wolf form the fur would cover them. In fact, she'd be a lot better off as a wolf. She changed quickly.

It was odd to see the cave from a different eye level;

she'd gotten used to seeing it from a human's point of view. The wolves cringed back against the wall, looking upset. She didn't blame them; this was bound to be outside their experience. She approached them slowly and cautiously, but when she got within a couple of yards, they suddenly sniffed the air, came over and sniffed her, then started bouncing happily about her, just as they usually did when she came in.

"What on earth?" Briam said. Since she could no longer answer him verbally, Acila walked over to lean against his legs so that he could hear her. *I guess I still smell the same.*

"Probably," he agreed. "Everything in the whole cave smells like wet wolf these days." The horses shifted restlessly, and he stepped back with them. "I'm taking the horses downstream—why don't you all go the other way?" he suggested. He turned and headed off, and Acila gathered her pack and went hunting.

They ran pretty far, but the hunting was good, and they returned with full bellies and an extra rabbit apiece. Acila changed back, got dressed, and cooked up Briam's share of supper, while the wolves curled up in their den and ate their share.

"This was great," Briam said with satisfaction, licking the grease off his fingers. "We'll all sleep well tonight."

Acila certainly had no trouble falling asleep after the day's exertions, but she awoke during the night in horrible pain. She felt as though someone was sticking knives into half a dozen places in her abdomen, and even though she was sweating, she felt horribly cold and shivery. She tried to figure out what was wrong, but racking her memory only assured her she'd never felt like this before. Had she caught some sort of ague running around in the rain? All the wolves seemed fine; she could hear their soft, even breathing in the darkness. She closed her eyes, clenched her teeth and set herself to endure the pain. There didn't seem to be anything else she could do about it.

It seemed like hours later when someone shook her. "Acila?" Briam shook her harder. "Wake up; you're having a nightmare."

Acila opened one eye, then closed it again. Even the dim light seeping into the cave hurt. "No, I'm not, I'm dying. And I am awake."

"You can't die!" Briam protested. "I need you. What's the matter anyway? I thought it was one of the wolves whining in its sleep at first."

Now that he mentioned it, Acila had noticed the sound; she just hadn't realized that she was the one making it. "I don't know what's wrong—it feels as though someone is sticking knives in my stomach."

"I felt like that once, after I ate a bunch of green apples. What did you eat yesterday? You didn't have much stew with me."

"No, we ate while we were hunting." She tried to think back. "I think I had a bunch of mice and a part of a rabbit."

"Fur, bones, and all?" Briam sounded slightly ill himself.

"What did you expect me to do—turn human in the middle of the woods when I didn't even have any clothes so I could skin and clean it? We all just gobbled down what we could get—and I didn't notice you turning up your nose at supper last night!"

"Yes, but I don't think humans are supposed to eat exactly the same thing as wolves—aren't our stomachs different?"

"I never thought about it before, but I guess it makes sense. And if this is what a baby with colic feels like, I can understand why they scream!" Acila rolled herself into an even tighter ball. It didn't help. "Holy Mother, this hurts! How long did it last when you ate the apples?"

"About half a day," Briam replied hesitantly.

Acila whimpered, then set her teeth. "Oh, well, at least I'll probably live—though at the moment I'm not enthusiastic about the idea."

"The wolves ate the same things you did, didn't they?" Briam looked over at the pile of fur, snoring softly behind the saddlebags. "Maybe if you turned back into a wolf, it would stop hurting."

"It's worth a try," Acila agreed. "I can't feel much worse." She dragged herself out of her clothes, changed, and curled up on her blankets.

Briam sat beside her and stroked her head. "Do you feel any better?" he asked several minutes later.

I think I'm beginning to, Acila thought back at him. *But do you realize what this means? It means that I'll have to stay in wolf form for a long time.*

"Can't you just not eat while you're hunting?"

No! Even the idea seemed perverted to her wolf self. *The whole point of hunting is to eat.* She looked up at him, then sighed and rested her jaw on his knee. *I'm afraid you're stuck with a wolf for a sister until the food supply gets better.*

"But that could take all winter! What happens if you stay in wolf form for several months?"

You get your clothes back, Acila quipped. *Seriously, I don't know, but I'm afraid we're going to find out.*

CHAPTER 8

Once she settled into it, Acila found she rather liked being a full-time wolf. It was much easier to hunt, and she didn't have to take care of the horses—in fact, Briam sternly told her not even to go near them. She didn't have to worry about clothes or take time to dress and braid her hair in the morning. Her fur kept her not only warm but even surprisingly dry; unless it was absolutely pouring rain, the water caught in the outer layers of her coat and could be shaken out easily. Her paws hardened quickly with all the time she spent on the cliffs and stopped getting sore. Her hands would probably be horribly callused when she changed back, but the thought didn't bother her. The fact that it didn't bother her, however, did bother her. Would she want to change back when then time came? Would she even be able to?

As the days passed, Acila dimly realized that she was happier than she had ever been in her life—or, if not precisely happy, content. Compared to her responsibilities at home, being a wolf was simple. Yes, hunting was hard work, and she got tired, but it was physical weariness, not the sort of exhaustion she used to get from having people depend on her, demand she solve all their problems, criticize her, and gossip about her. And if, as she slept at Briam's side at night, she dreamed of Fire and heard the Maiden calling to her as she slept, the memories faded as soon as she ran out with the pack each morning.

Even when the winter snows came, she remained

content. Her body was designed to cope with snow, and she grew more comfortable in her body with each passing day. She and the smaller of the two male wolves became an efficient hunting team, and she became so accustomed to communicating with him that she sometimes wondered if she would still "speak" with whines, growls, head movements and eye contact when she turned human again.

Briam grumbled a bit about the cold and the difficulty of finding forage for the horses, but he never suggested leaving and trying to find other humans. He, too, seemed content to simply exist, with his activities confined to finding food, keeping the fire going, and playing his lute next to it in the evenings, although he did once comment that he would be glad when spring came and his fingers warmed up a bit more.

They had a mild winter, and soon the snow became rain again. Acila scarcely noticed. Her life was reduced to bare essentials, and calculating the progress of the seasons wasn't part of it anymore. She no longer remembered that at home she would have been working out the schedule for spring planting. She was a wolf, and she was content to be one.

It was pitch dark, and the rain was dripping down at the front of the cave. Acila raised her head and listened again for the sound that had wakened her. There it was, a faint whine. Leaving her position at Briam's side, she crept back to the wolves' den. It was too dark to see anything, but Acila thought the female was giving birth. This was enough of a departure from the daily routine of hunt, eat, and sleep to make the human, analytical part of Acila's brain start working again.

The female sounded unhappy, but not agonized, and the males were restless, but not howling, so presumably it was all going well enough. Acila didn't have any idea of what to do if something went wrong anyway. She lay there, with the two males crowded in on either side of her and waited for dawn.

When the birth process was over, and there was enough light to count by, Acila discovered that the litter consisted of eight pups—the absolute maximum the mother could feed. At least by the time they were old enough to get underfoot, the rainy season would be over. If she had to live cooped up in this cave with Briam, three horses, and eleven wolves running around, she really would lose her mind—what little was left of it.

"Acila?" Briam had wakened and missed her. "Where are you?" He crawled to the edge of the den and looked over her shoulder. "Mother of Life! How many of them are there? Eight?" Briam contemplated the puppies. "They're kind of cute, but can she feed all of them?"

Acila laid her head against his leg. *Only if she gets enough to eat. We're going to have to do a* lot *of hunting.*

"I'll help hunt," Briam said. "It's getting much easier to find food for the horses now, so I have more free time."

As far as Acila was concerned, the puppies were absolutely perfect and adorable. She loved to curl up by the other female and help look after them, even though she couldn't nurse them. Sometimes she wistfully wished she could—and then she sternly reminded herself that she only felt that way because she had the strong maternal instincts of a wolf. When she changed back, they'd be merely cute.

Time passed, and the puppies grew. All too soon they were crawling around the cave, and then beginning to venture outside. Fortunately, as Acila had anticipated, this coincided with the end of the rainy season. The sunshine made everyone feel better. Game became more plentiful as more animals came out of their burrows, and hunting no longer took all available time. Acila and the other wolves began looking after the puppies in shifts; one adult to chase after and round up the babies and three to lie in the sun on the warm rocks and watch.

Forage for the horses was much easier to find as well, but Briam still ranged far with them, usually in the downstream direction. He told Acila that he wanted to explore as much of the area as possible. She and the rest of the pack went with him sometimes, now that the horses and wolves were getting used to each other.

It was late afternoon and they were all far downstream. The puppies were running about, sniffing at everything—they'd never been in this area before. They'd had a good day's hunting, and several extra rabbits hung from Briam's saddle. Acila took a good drink from the river, then flopped limply on the bank, next to the smaller male wolf.

"Acila!" Briam called. "It's late and we should be heading home. Round up the rest of the pack, will you?"

Acila turned her head and looked at him, then stretched into a more comfortable position. She felt no desire to move; the sun was warm, the air was fresh, and she was perfectly happy where she was.

Briam dismounted and came over to touch her so he could carry on the argument. *Come on; we won't get back before dark if we don't hurry.*

So take the horses and go ahead. There's plenty of moon these nights for the rest of us—and besides, it's warm enough to sleep out.

Acila? Briam suddenly seemed to find her behavior strange. *What are you thinking of? We can't sleep out here.*

Why not? There's nothing dangerous around here.

Suddenly, as if to prove her wrong, they could hear screams coming from the direction where the puppies and the larger male wolf had disappeared. From the sound of it, the screamer was human and female, although neither Acila nor Briam stopped to analyze the sound. Acila raced toward it at her top speed, flanked by the other two wolves. Behind her she could hear the thudding hooves of Briam's horse. She hoped he wouldn't be thrown riding breakneck over uneven ground, but there wasn't much she could do to stop him.

A girl, about their own age, was standing with her back flattened against a tree, while the puppies sniffed at this strange new creature and the male growled. Her screams were subsiding to terrified whimpers until she caught sight of three more wolves, at which point they went back to full volume.

Acila stood and contemplated her dispassionately. She'd probably be quite pretty if she'd stop screaming and close her mouth. Of course, she'd need to be cleaned up a bit. Her long pale hair had come half undone from its braids and was liberally festooned with leaves and twigs, and her eyes were swollen from the tears that were making tracks in the grime on her face. The hem of her dress was in tatters, and the sleeves were almost as ragged. They had fallen back to her elbows when she clasped her hands at her breast, revealing an assortment of scratches and insect bites on both forearms.

A crashing noise behind her announced the arrival of Briam's horse—hopefully still accompanied by Briam. "Get back!" Briam dismounted and pushed between her and the larger male wolf. "Get those puppies away from her!" He reached to grab the nearest one, and the mother sprang on him, knocking him over. The girl screamed even louder, though Acila would have sworn that was impossible. In defense of her own ears, she sprang forward and shoved the female off Briam, who scrambled hastily to his feet and moved to defend the girl. Acila started chasing the puppies back. The puppies thought this was a great game. The other wolves moved to help, and soon the wolves were gathered together several yards from the girl, who was now sobbing hysterically in Briam's arms.

Acila stalked over and leaned against Briam's leg. *Quiet her down, will you,* she thought impatiently.

What do you expect? Briam thought back indignantly. *She's terrified!*

And I'm getting a splitting headache! Shut her up, or I'll really give her something to scream about!

Don't be such a bitch! I really think you've been a wolf too long! Briam stepped away from her, drawing the girl with him.

Acila stared at him in disbelief. *What does he mean 'bitch'? I'm his sister—and all my life I've taken care of him! And he's always loved me and listened to me. What is the matter with him? Granted, she's pretty enough, but anybody stupid enough to scream like that at the sight of a few wolves—there'd be some sense in it if the screaming were likely to scare us away. As it is, her behavior is idiotic! What does he see in her?*

"Hush, now," Briam murmured soothingly to the girl. "It's all right; they won't hurt you. Most of them are just babies."

"But they're so big! And one of them knocked you down!"

"That's the mother," Briam explained. "She didn't want me to hurt them. It's all right, really. They're just pets."

Pets! Acila thought in outrage. *He'd have starved without us! And he dares call us "pets!"* Briam couldn't hear her, of course, since he was several feet away, but her internal voice replied.

And "pet" is hardly a proper thing to call one's sister. It had the gall to sound amused.

I can think of a few things I'd like to call him!

Oh, come now, he's always had a romantic streak, and here's the perfect damsel in distress.

Probably due to her own stupidity. Acila sniffed. *I wonder what he thinks he's going to do with her.*

The girl was making a valiant, if rather obvious, effort to control herself. She did manage to get her sobbing under control, but she still clung to Briam as if he were the only thing that could save her from a Horrible Fate. "I'm sorry, truly I am. I know it's silly of me, but I just can't stand wolves. You see, there was this horrible creature—" She shuddered and leaned against Briam's shoulder. "Have you ever heard of were-wolves?"

Briam shook his head. "Try not to be scared," he said comfortingly. "Truly, they won't hurt you. What is your name, my lady?"

The girl dried her eyes on what remained of her left sleeve and looked up at him, her eyelashes fluttering very slightly. "Druscilla."

"Druscilla." Briam gallantly kissed her grubby hand. "I'm called Briam."

Druscilla blushed and pulled her hand away. "Thank you for saving me from the wolves." She looked nervously at the pack, who were sprawled about looking at her.

Briam followed her gaze. 'Really, it's all right." He turned to Acila, and held out a hand. "Here, come say hello to Druscilla."

Acila stalked over, eyeing them warily. Druscilla shrank back, then gulped, reached out and patted her tentatively on the head. "Nice wolf," she said in a quivering voice.

Acila endured it stiffly for a moment and then leaned on Briam. *Tell her not to try that with the others. Wolf instinct says to flinch and snap when someone reaches for the top of your head like that. She should put her hand out low and palm up and let them smell her.*

Can't you tell them to behave? he thought back.

Not the way you can tell her. Come, brother, there are eleven of them and one of her—and I hope she's more intelligent than they are!

Briam reached out and took Druscilla's hand, turning it as Acila had directed. "Here, my lady, like this."

Acila sniffed the outstretched hand reluctantly. *She stinks!*

If you think perfume smells worse than damp wolf, you've certainly been a wolf too long! Briam shot back.

And if you'd rather be with a ninny who can't even take care of herself than the wolf pack that's been keeping you fed, fine! Go ahead! But you can do your own hunting from now on! Acila turned and fled blindly into the hills. The rest of the pack followed her.

She ran until she was ready to drop, then she burrowed into the underbrush and curled up in a miserable, whimpering ball of fur.

How could he? I've taken care of him all my life, and he just brushes me off as if I were nothing—as if I were just a "pet" wolf. No, that's not true, he takes better care of his horses; at least for them he feels some responsibility. I'm just in the way all of a sudden. "Be nice to her, Acila; make the rest of the pack be nice to her." As if I could control the behavior of eleven wolves without even trying!

If she were in human form, she'd be crying. As it was, she was frightening the wolves; all eleven of them were crowded around her trying to comfort her. *And I can't even talk to them!* She threw back her head and howled in despair. It didn't make her feel any better.

I might just as well go back home and marry Lord Ranulf. He seems to be the only person alive who might still want me, now that Briam thinks I'm a bitch and doesn't love me anymore. She lay there and thought about home, about sleeping in a bed instead of on rocks and dirt, having the people she'd known all her life around her instead of being out in the woods with no one to talk to, having servants to bring food to the table without her having to turn into a wolf and go catch it herself. At the moment the idea was almost unbearably attractive. She contemplated it for a long time before the sense of duty her father had carefully trained into her ("take good care of your brother, Acila") finally triumphed.

No, she told herself firmly, *I swore I'd take care of*

Briam, and I shall—even if he does suddenly think I'm a monster. Besides, Lord Ranulf doesn't really want me; what he wants is the land, and he already has that! She dragged herself to her feet and headed back to the cave, with the rest of the pack trailing behind her.

It was very late when they got there, and the cave was dark. Apparently Briam had remembered to bank the fire for the night—if he had even returned. Acila halted at the cave entrance and sniffed the air. Yes, Briam was there, and so were the horses and—Acila's nose wrinkled at the scent of perfume—so was Druscilla. Maybe things would look better in the morning. She and the wolves crowded into the corner behind the saddlebags and went to sleep. But something had changed now in her soul; she felt restless in wolf form, and the Earth Mother was calling her back to the altar again while the Maiden threw lightning behind her as if to herd her home. It was the old dream, which had stopped after she had been a wolf for a while. *Why is it back now?*

She woke to the sound of Druscilla's screams, followed by Briam's "What's the matter?" as he sat up and reached for his sword. Acila struggled to the front of the pack, which was difficult since they were all pulling back trying to get away from Druscilla, and went over to lean against Briam.

I swear, that girl has a more limited vocabulary than I do right now! Briam, she must *stop this stupid screaming every time she lays eyes on us—after all, we live here, too!*

All right, all right, Briam thought back at her, sounding harassed. *I'll explain it to her.*

Good luck. Acila sprawled in the middle of the floor, prepared to derive some amusement out of the coming discussion.

"Lady Druscilla," Briam said deferentially, "I know you're not used to having a pack of wolves sharing your living quarters, but please do try to be reasonable.

None of them has laid a paw on you, and it's certainly not likely that they're going to. Look at them!" He gestured toward the wolves, who were trying, with limited success, to hide all eleven of themselves behind six saddlebags. "I swear to you, my lady, that they are every bit as frightened of you as you are of them."

"They can't possibly be," Druscilla quavered. "And that one certainly isn't." She pointed to Acila.

"I assure you that she won't hurt you," Briam said grimly. "She wouldn't dare, would you?" The last phrase was addressed to Acila.

It was all so silly; Acila just couldn't resist. Opening her mouth and letting her tongue dangle between her lower fangs, she shook her head carefully from side to side.

Druscilla pressed a trembling hand to her mouth, and Briam took an angry step forward. "Stop that. This isn't funny!"

Acila rose, butted her shoulder affectionately against his leg, and went back to join the pack.

Briam tried again. "Really, my lady, they're very helpful. They've been catching food for me so that I can take care of the horses."

Druscilla cast him a look of total revulsion. "How can you eat anything a wolf killed?"

To Acila's relief, Briam's infatuation had not totally overcome his common sense. "After it's skinned, cleaned, and cooked, what difference does it make how it died?"

Druscilla's lower lip trembled. "This is awful! I wish I'd never run away from home!"

"I'm glad to hear you say that, Druscilla; I feared I might have difficulty persuading you to return."

Both Druscilla and Briam jumped to face the speaker, a woman who stood at the side of the cave entrance, sword in hand. Acila scrambled to her feet. *If Druscilla hadn't insisted on running away with a full supply of perfume,* she thought angrily, *I would have smelled her coming. That girl deserves every insect bite she's got—and I hope she has a lot of them!*

"Who are you?" Briam snatched up his sword and thrust Druscilla protectively behind him. Acila, glancing from the tunic Briam had been sleeping in to the heavy leather overtunic the swordswoman wore, moved to stand beside Briam, growling softly.

The woman did not advance toward them, but stood her ground calmly, seemingly prepared to stand there all day.

"She's Leader of the Queen's Guard," Druscilla said nervously from behind them. "Shield-Bearer," she added, " did my aunt come with you?"

Acila did not wonder at the respect in Druscilla's tone; the woman before them commanded it. She looked somehow more real than the cave around her, she seemed to know exactly and totally who she was and what she was doing. She would be a formidable ally; and trying to face her down was terrifying.

Suddenly she smiled, as if she had weighed them, their actions and thoughts, and understood them. "No, Druscilla, the Queen is still in the city, preparing for the Spring Festival. It will no doubt relieve your mind to know that she has decided you are not yet ready to take part in it." Druscilla shuddered and pressed her lips together, and Acila wondered what the Festival was.

She turned her gaze on Briam. "You can put up your sword, young man; I mean none of you any harm." She sheathed her sword, and held her hand out toward Acila, looking her straight in the eyes.

Acila walked forward, meeting the woman's eyes squarely. She liked this woman, she decided; her eyes were honest and direct. She also knew how to treat a wolf, which was a welcome change from Druscilla. She stood at ease, scratching Acila behind the ears, and said to Druscilla, "I've come to escort you home, Lady Druscilla, so if you'll gather up anything you may have brought with you, we can go."

Druscilla made some inarticulate sound and clung to Briam's arm.

"She doesn't have to go if she doesn't want to," he said gallantly. "I'll look after her."

The Shield-Bearer looked amused. "I very much doubt that she'd be happy here, but if you wish to accompany us to the city, you are welcome."

"Please come with me, Briam," Druscilla whispered softly.

"All right," Briam said. "We'll all go."

Oh, wonderful, Acila thought, *another adventure. What a great time for Briam to start developing a mind of his own.*

CHAPTER 9

Briam gathered up his clothes and went into the side cave to dress. Acila followed him, feeling that they had a few things to discuss. "What are we going to do, Acila?" he whispered.

Shhh! she thought at him, hastily sitting on his foot. *You don't want them to know that I'm not really a wolf, do you—or did you tell Druscilla already?*

No, of course not; I've never told anyone about your shapechanging! At least he had switched to mind-speaking, so she didn't need to worry that they'd be overheard. *But you can't stay a wolf forever; can't you change back now?*

Not unless I'm willing to be overcome by acute indigestion on the road someplace—and that does tend to make travel rather difficult. And how would you explain the sudden appearance of a sister who has been with you for months and has virtually no clothing? Besides, unless the Shield-Bearer brought extra horses, there are three of you and three horses. She was startled to hear what she had said—how long had Briam been "one of you" rather than "one of us" in her mind? Had she been a wolf too long to be human again?

But you'll come with me, won't you, even if you have to be a wolf? Briam's thoughts sounded anxious. Was he wondering the same thing she was?

Yes, little brother, I'll come with you. Once we see what the city is like, we'll figure out what to do about getting me back to human form. Acila wasn't at all sure she wanted to change back; she'd been happy as a wolf, and being a human was so complicated—beginning with explaining how Briam's sister suddenly appeared out of nowhere. Well, she'd just have to think about it on the road; she should have time to come up with some plausible story. Although any story that would fool the Shield-Bearer would have to be quite plausible indeed.

Briam finished dressing and started to saddle Gris. "Acila," he said absentmindedly, "would you get the saddlebags, please?"

Acila rammed her shoulder into the back of his knee hard enough to make it buckle under him. *With what?* she thought in exasperation. *My tongue?*

Briam looked down at her in confusion. "I'm sorry," he whispered. "I forgot. I'm so used to having you help me. . . ."

Briam, please try *to pretend I'm just one of the wolves. I have a feeling that swordswoman doesn't miss much.* Acila broke the contact and went back to join the rest of the wolves. Druscilla shrank away from her as she passed, but at least she didn't scream this time.

Briam came out of the side cave, leading Gris. "Do you have horses, Shield-Bearer?" he asked.

"No," she replied. "Since I was tracking, I came on foot."

"I have two more, and you are welcome to ride them," Briam said politely. Then he turned to Druscilla and added, "Can you ride?"

"Of course." Druscilla sounded surprised at the question. She looked puzzled for a moment and then laughed. "Just because I don't like wolves doesn't mean I'm helpless!" She glanced uneasily at the wolves. "Are they going to come with us?"

"I don't know," Briam said. "Probably some of them will."

"I don't think they'll follow you out of the forest," the Shield-Bearer said, "but we'll find out. Would you like me to help you saddle the other horses?"

"Yes, thank you," Briam said. "I'm not used to doing it all alone."

The swordswoman raised an eyebrow. "Then perhaps you should have brought a groom with you when you left home."

Briam smiled faintly. "I think most of our grooms would quit before they'd live in a cave with a wolf pack. Besides, I wasn't given a choice. When our estate was invaded, my sister and I barely escaped with our lives. Then a couple of soldiers came after us—that's where I got the extra horses, and my sister and I got separated."

"Aren't you worried about her?" The Shield-Bearer seemed a trifle suspicious of his apparent lack of concern.

"Not much," Briam assured her. "She's very good at taking care of herself, and I'd know if anything really bad had happened to her."

"Really?" Druscilla asked. "How?"

Briam shrugged. "I just would. I guess it's because we're twins." He reached down to grab a saddlebag, then stood and looked at Druscilla. "Is this city we're going to a place where many travelers come?"

"Oh, yes," Druscilla said proudly. "A lot of people come to Diadem." She looked at him curiously. "Does being a twin let you know where she is?"

Briam shook his head. "Not exactly. All I can sense is that she is alive and well somewhere. She's better at telling things than I am; she says she can sometimes tell what I'm doing. At home she used to be able to call me in to dinner from anyplace on the estate, but I'm not sure if we could do that anywhere else."

The Shield-Bearer brought the other two horses out of the side cave and she and Briam saddled them. Druscilla leaned against the wall and watched them; obviously she was so accustomed to having servants around that it didn't occur to her to offer to help.

They had to walk the horses down the rocky part at the side of the cliff, but once they got to the swamp they could ride, although very slowly and carefully, and when they reached the river there was a path of sorts along the bank. Even so, they were held to a walk by the rocky ground and the overhanging branches.

Acila and the other wolves trailed along after them. They had a much easier time of the route than the humans did, which left Acila free to worry. *Briam's really acting strange; he never just decides to go off someplace without asking me about it first. And now he suddenly says, without so much as consulting me about whether I want to go or not, that we're all going off to a city we've never seen or heard of, where we don't know anybody except Druscilla. Sweet Lady, what a recommendation! We don't know anything about this place; we don't even know what this Festival that Druscilla doesn't like is! And a festival that could make her run off into the woods to escape it—even as a wolf I don't like this, and I suspect that I'm going to like it a lot less as a human being. What's gotten into Briam? Druscilla's not* that *pretty!*

They rode until it was nearly dark, then found a wide part of the path to camp in. Acila noted with amusement that the Shield-Bearer was careful to sleep between Briam and Druscilla. Acila and the wolves curled up in a pile on Briam's other side.

They reached the edge of the forest late in the afternoon four days later. The river they had been following was much wider now, and ahead of them were a group of small fields under cultivation, surrounding a village of thatched huts.

"We'll spend the night here," the Shield-Bearer said. Druscilla gave a soft groan, and the woman turned on her in considerable annoyance. "Don't choose this time to put on noble airs, Lady; you should have been prepared for rude housing when you decided to run away. Remember that you are a princess of the land and that these are your people, and act accordingly!" She looked Druscilla straight in the eyes, and after a moment Druscilla silently dropped her eyes to her saddle.

The Shield-Bearer then turned to look at Briam. "Do *you* have any complaints to voice?"

"Indeed not, Lady," Briam assured her. "Compared to my recent living conditions, this is sumptuous." He looked uneasily down at Acila, standing at his horse's left side. "How do these people feel about wolves?"

Acila wasn't sure how the villagers would feel about them, but she knew very well how she felt about the open fields. Every part of her seemed to be screaming inside at the thought of having to cross them. *Danger! No cover to hide behind, no bushes to burrow into, no caves to lair in.* From the soft whining behind her, she knew that the other wolves felt the same way.

The swordswoman looked at the wolves. "I don't think they'll leave the forest, Lord Briam. But if they do, we shall find out how the villagers feel about wolves. She dug her heels into her horse's sides. "Come along." She headed along the edge of a field toward the village, and Druscilla sighed and followed her.

Briam started after them, looking back to where Acila and the rest of the wolves stood frozen at the edge of the forest. "Well, come on!" He whistled, as if calling a dog, and to Acila's surprise the smaller male wolf bounded out after him. The other adults and the cubs melted back into the forest, and Acila followed Briam, hurrying to catch up with him before they entered the village. Bad enough to have to go there without going in alone.

The villagers didn't look at all happy with the idea of two wolves in their midst, but none of them dared to argue with the Leader of the Queen's Guard. The headman and his family moved out of their house for the night so that the party could stay there, and Druscilla managed to wait until they were out of earshot before making her remarks about the inevitability of fleas.

The headman returned a short time later and offered to slaughter one of the village's few goats to feed them, but the Shield-Bearer politely declined, saying that they had no wish to cause the village any hardship by their visit. She then invited the headman to join them in their meal, which consisted of the remaining rabbits. Briam carefully fed both wolves a portion of the cooked meat, thinking to Acila, *Eating this won't stop you from turning back, will it?* as he handed it to her.

They went to bed immediately after supper. Druscilla and the swordswoman slept at the back of the hut, with Druscilla next to the wall. In the best heroic tradition, Briam spread his bedroll by the door and kept his sword near to hand. Acila thought the Shield-Bearer looked a bit amused by this; presumably she knew the people of the village, although even she kept her weapons within reach. Acila and the other wolf curled up behind the saddlebags, and Acila wondered where the wolf would sleep in the city, when the saddlebags were unpacked and put away. Under Briam's bed, no doubt. It was odd; she hadn't realized that the wolf was so devoted to Briam.

They left early the next morning. The headman thanked them for the honor of their visit with expressions of great esteem. From the looks he cast the wolves, Acila was sure that he had counted all the poultry before coming to bid them farewell.

The road they were taking veered away from the river, circling around the cultivated fields. "We should reach home around mid-morning," the Shield-Bearer remarked.

"The Festival will be over by now, won't it?" Druscilla asked anxiously. "I've lost count of the days."

"The Festival need not concern you, Druscilla," the Shield-Bearer replied coldly. "The Queen has decided that you are not ready to take part in it." Her tone of voice was sufficiently dampening that Druscilla kept silent for the rest of the ride.

Diadem, Acila decided, must take its name from its setting. It was a semicircular walled city, situated on the highest land for miles around. She wished she could change to eagle form and get a better view of the city and the surrounding land, but as long as she was with the others, she couldn't. The river they had left that morning, which was still visible to the west even now, ran along the far side of the city, and judging by the sound of it, there was a waterfall beside the city. From their current route she couldn't see the water below the falls, but she thought the river must widen below it.

As they approached the city, Acila saw that there was a gate on the north side of the wall, but the gate their party used was the east gate, in the center of the semicircle, where the largest jewel would be in a tiara. There didn't seem to be anyone watching the gate, which struck Acila as odd. The streets were paved with flat stones and had gutters at their sides, between streets and the sidewalks. The streets were immaculately swept and the houses had garlands of flowers hung along the edges of the awnings which shaded the sidewalks. There was a fountain bubbling gently at each intersection, making Acila suspect that there must be an extensive system of pipes carrying water from the river and distributing it throughout the city. The walls of the houses were whitewashed, adding to the general impression of light and cleanliness. Was everything always this clean or was this part of the Festival Druscilla had mentioned? Considering the normal state of her old home, no matter how many people were trying to keep it clean, she suspected the latter. What kind of festival was it anyway?

Being in the city was making Acila very nervous after all the months in the woods. She could attribute some of this feeling to being a wolf—the other wolf was keeping so close to her that their fur was touching—but she suspected that she might well have been uncomfortable even as a human. After all, she had never been beyond the boundaries of her estate in human form before. Fighting her instinctive desire to find a quiet alley in which to hide, she forced herself to look around and examine what she was seeing. The city was undeniably beautiful, but it was the most alien place she had ever seen. Compared to this, the forest was cozy and homelike.

The streets were empty of people, yet Acila was hearing the sounds of singing. None of the humans seemed to hear it, but the other wolf was whining softly. When they came to the center of town, Acila could see why the gate and all the streets had been deserted. Except for a cleared space leading from the street they were on to a platform at the far end of a large plaza, the entire area was packed with people. *Every single inhabitant of the town must be here,* Acila thought. They were singing some sort of hymn, but Acila couldn't quite make out the words. This must be the Festival, but what kind of festival was it?

The Shield-Bearer swung easily down from her horse and moved to lift Druscilla down from hers. Druscilla stood where she had been placed, pale and frozen, looking sick and horrified. Briam dismounted also, and a man dressed in a plain dark tunic came out of the crowd, bowed to Druscilla, and led the horses away. Briam nodded politely to the man and moved to stand beside Druscilla. Acila, with the other wolf still at her side, went to lean against Briam's leg.

Acila, Briam thought, *what's going on? Do you know?*

I have no idea, Acila thought back, *but I suspect it's the Festival Druscilla was talking about.*

The hymn ended and the people fell silent, looking toward the platform and the woman who stood there. Even after she had resumed human form and seen the Queen with normal vision, Acila always remembered the black and white of her first sight of her. She was a tall woman with pale skin and dark hair, which had been whipped around by the wind until it formed a cloud around her face. Her dress was dark, but was liberally ornamented with something that glittered in the sunlight. A matching cord tied just below her breasts barely saved the dress from being indecent. The neck was cut in a deep V, and only the cord kept the point of the V fixed between her breasts and stopped the dress from slipping when she breathed. The gown was sleeveless, and the skirt, fitted with a few almost invisible pleats, fell loosely to cover her feet. She wore a thin bright chain tight about her neck just above her collarbone, which made her dress seem less low-cut than it actually was by making her exposed bosom seem to be part of the gown. She stood there, straight and still as a statue, looking simultaneously regal and oddly vulnerable. Her head was tilted back slightly and she seemed to be waiting for something, or perhaps listening to a voice that only she could hear. Then she looked at Briam and smiled, nodding slightly. She drew a deep breath, which made the sunlight flash off her dress, and began to sing.

The song was like nothing Acila had ever heard before. It seemed as though all of creation was singing, and the music filled her head. It felt as if her brain had turned to air, providing a space for the music to fill and echo back and forth in. The words were in a language she didn't understand, but even in wolf shape she found her lips trying to shape the words as the woman sang them. She couldn't imagine why this was happening; it didn't make sense. She felt drawn to this woman, a pull even stronger than her bond to Briam, but Briam was her twin and she had never seen this woman before in her life. The feeling of power about her reminded Acila of the power of the sanctuary back home, but this woman, though she appeared to be a priestess, did not have the feel of either the Lady of Fire or the Earth Mother about her.

Acila glanced up at Briam and saw that his lips were moving in the words of the song, whatever they were and whatever they meant. The Queen, Briam, and Acila were all breathing in the same rhythm—and so, Acila noticed, was the other wolf. The song was compelling, as if it held them under a spell, unable to think, unable to breathe except when the singer did. It was the breathing which made Acila sure that she wasn't imagining the whole thing, for aside from that things seemed dreamlike and far away.

The song flowed, pulling them forward, drawing them all together. Briam started to move across the plaza, with both Acila and the other wolf still at his side.

Behind them, Acila heard Druscilla protest. *"Briam, no! Don't!"*

"Be still!" the Shield-Bearer said in an urgent undertone. "Don't disrupt the ritual."

"No!" Druscilla's voice was not loud, but it was intense enough to carry. "She can't! She can't have him—" Her protest ended with a sudden choking sound, but at the moment none of this seemed at all important to Acila.

The song was part of her now; her true self had always known it. It was telling her that she was home; she was where she belonged. Or perhaps it was telling this to Briam and she was picking up his feelings. It felt as though she, the other wolf, Briam, and the Queen were all part of one person. It was natural for them to be moving toward the Queen. Soon they would all be together, bathed in the great warmth and light which called them.

They were near the foot of the platform now, and the Queen came down from it to meet them. As Briam walked up to her, she reached out, took him in her arms, and kissed him.

Acila didn't know whether she was feeling her own feelings or Briam's, but everything seemed to spin about them and a strange energy ran through their bodies. It felt a little like shapechanging, but more intense. She became aware that she was sitting on the Queen's feet and leaning against her leg only when the Queen moved and Acila nearly fell over.

The Queen kept an arm about Briam and led him to

a stone shrine at the left side of the plaza. People drew back to make a path for them, but Acila scarcely noticed. She and the wolf trailed Briam and the Queen as if they were all part of the same pack.

The shrine was small and cavelike, and was furnished with nothing but a low bed which took up most of the floor. It was too low for even a wolf to fit under, but there was just enough room at its foot for the two wolves to curl up together. The wolf huddled in the corner there, and Acila slid in next to him. At least it had the feel of a proper den, and it was the only remotely normal feeling thing about this entire situation.

The Queen dropped the curtain over the entrance to the cave, untied the cord at her breast and removed her gown, and assisted a dazed Briam to undress before taking him in her arms again. At that point the whole room started spinning around Acila and she passed out.

CHAPTER 10

Acila came half-awake in darkness and spent several minutes trying to remember where she was and why she felt so strange. After several minutes the events of the previous day returned to her: the journey to the city; the people all crowded into the plaza; the Queen; the song ... *that's right,* she thought. *I'm in that shrine, the man-made cave in the city.* Listening carefully, she could hear the breathing of two sleeping humans, and the scuffling noise made by the wolf beside her.

He was awake now, too, sniffing at her and trying to move closer to her. She felt oddly restless, as if she were searching for something she shouldn't have, but she didn't know what. And something in the shrine smelled different than anything she'd ever smelled before. She flopped over and leaned against the wolf, and suddenly she realized what she was feeling—it was a very strong wave of desire for him. And the way he was sniffing at her, she'd seen that before, in the kennels at home—*Holy Mother! she realized in horror. I'm in heat!*

Almost before she finished the thought she was back in human form, shivering violently. The wolf whined, unhappy at the transformation, and she shushed him hastily. Miraculously, he stopped whining and lay down again.

What am I going to do now? she wondered. *I'd better think of something fast; the Queen won't sleep forever, and I really don't want to explain this to her. I guess I should shift to something else, find out where they put the horses and our baggage, and find some clothes ... except that I have no idea where my clothes are, and I really shouldn't be wearing Briam's. One thing's certain; I can't change back to wolf form now. The puppies are darling, and I do miss them, but that doesn't mean I want some of my own. I wonder what would happen if I got pregnant in animal form? I don't think I want to find out—at least not this way!*

Signaling to the wolf to stay where he was, she crawled very carefully toward the door, listening intently to the breathing of the sleepers. Near the doorway, she felt coarse fabric under her knee; investigation revealed that it was Briam's undertunic. She slipped it on; he was bound to have enough else on his mind in the morning that he wouldn't miss it.

She peeked cautiously around the edge of the curtain covering the entrance. Luck was with her; the plaza was deserted. Keeping to the shadows as much as possible, she ducked into the nearest alley and bumped into a small figure completely covered by a dark hooded cloak. Even in human form, however, Acila recognized that perfume.

"Who are you?" Druscilla demanded in a low voice, "and what are you doing here? Don't you know it's forbidden to disturb the Queen and the Year-King on their wedding night?"

Acila collapsed against the wall, almost sure that this time she really was going to faint. "Year-King?" she whispered in horror. She had read of this custom—of places where the Queen ruled, and where a new king was chosen each year to be her consort until the time for him to be sacrificed. She had always thought that it would be nice to live in a place where a woman ruled, where she wouldn't have to pretend that all of her orders and ideas were Briam's. But she had not given much thought to what having a Year-King would be like—and she had certainly never cast Briam in the role.

"Are you in love with him, too?" Druscilla asked bitterly.

"He's my brother."

Druscilla gasped, then grabbed her roughly, and led her along the alley, around a corner, to a door with a torch burning beside it, and looked hard at her face. "Yes, you do look like him."

"Don't be silly," Acila protested dazedly, "Briam's blond."

"But you have his mouth, and nose, and eyebrows." Druscilla looked down at Acila's tunic and bare legs and feet. "You can't run around like that! Come with me." Dragging Acila behind her by the wrist, she led the way past two blocks of housing, until they reached the wall where the city hung over the river. "Can you climb?" Druscilla asked anxiously in a low voice.

"I think so," Acila murmured softly. "How high and how far?"

"Not very high," Druscilla said reassuringly, "just don't look down at the river, and follow me." She made sure that her cloak was securely fastened at the neck, pushed it back over her shoulders to leave her hands free, and scrambled up the corner where the river wall joined the wall of a building. The wall of the building was considerably higher, but when Acila got on top of the river wall, she found that it dropped down to allow a view of the river from the garden behind the building wall.

Druscilla led the way down, aided by a fairly strong vine on the inside of the garden wall, and Acila followed her carefully, paying close attention to what she was doing with her hands and feet. It felt strange to have hands instead of paws, and her fingers were rather stiff.

Once they were safe at ground level, Druscilla concealed herself in her cloak again, pulling Acila close to her so that she would be hidden behind Druscilla if anyone should happen to look out from the building. Fortunately, this side of the building did not seem to have anyone awake in it, although Acila could see a dim glow, probably from a night candle, coming from a second-floor window at the far side of the garden. Druscilla dragged her across the garden, past the pool in its center and around a group of stone benches, and up to the building, just under the window with the light. They stood next to an ornate column which held up the second-floor window ledge.

"Climb up the column," Druscilla said in a low voice, "and go through the window where the light is—that's my room. I'll be right behind you in case you have trouble climbing, but you shouldn't; the column has lots of places to put your hands and feet."

Acila looked at it dubiously. Quite a bit of the column's ornamentation jutted out, but which parts of it would take her weight?

"Come on," Druscilla whispered, "we can't stand here for long—the Queen's Guard *does* patrol the garden every so often." She placed Acila's hands on two projections, and indicated a stone branch that twined around the column at knee height. "Put your left foot here to start."

Acila took a deep breath and resolutely started up the column. Druscilla followed only inches behind her, shoving her feet into the proper niches when Acila hesitated.

The width of the window ledge at the top was less than the length of Acila's foot. She wedged her right foot on it at a precarious angle and clung to the side of the window frame. Druscilla came up beside her, scrambled over the windowsill with the agility of a squirrel, and reached back to pull Acila in. She was stronger than she looked, and much stronger than Acila would ever have expected her to be.

Well, at least now I have some idea of how she got as far as she did before the Shield-Bearer caught up with her. She only looks fragile and helpless. But if this is a place where women rule, why does she pretend to be less than she is? What is she trying to escape?

Druscilla's bedroom was far more luxurious than anything Acila had ever seen. Soft furs covered most of the marble floor, and the bed had a coverlet and curtains made of a beautiful woven fabric. There were three beautifully carved wooden chests, two chairs with embroidered cushions on either side of a small table, and a tapestry frame set aside beside one of them. Acila crossed the room to look at the embroidery on the frame and was impressed; it was an elaborate design being very well executed. "Your work?" she asked.

Druscilla nodded. "Briam said you like embroidery. Do you do a lot of it?"

Acila looked ruefully down at her grubby hands. As she had feared, they were callused in strange places and her fingernails were worn down. "Not lately," she replied.

"You'll want to wash," Druscilla said getting back to practical matters. She led the way to the far side of the bed, where there was an ewer of water, a bowl, and a towel. "Get as much of the dirt off as you can, and I'll find you some decent clothes. Tomorrow you can have a proper bath, but even I can't justify demanding a bath three hours before dawn!"

She gestured at the night candle, which still showed three time marks on its sides, then turned to burrow into one of her clothing chests.

Acila gratefully slipped off the tunic and began to scrub as much of her body as she could reach. She wished she could wash her hair; she never had gotten around to cutting it, and now it was a tangled, matted, filthy mess. She tried to untangle it with her fingers, without success.

"Leave it," Druscilla advised, dumping an armload of clothes on the chair. "Here," she grabbed a cloth, wrapped Acila's hair up in it, and tied it in place, "this will keep it out of your way until you can wash it and untangle it—and I assure you it will take hours! I spent half the afternoon doing mine." She tossed Acila a fine cream-colored shift, twin to the one she was wearing under the cloak which she now took off, shook out, folded carefully, and put away in a chest.

Acila put on the shift while Druscilla climbed into bed, adjusted the bed-curtain, curled up against the headboard, and patted the bed next to her. "Sit down, and I'll try to explain what's happening. To begin with, you're probably wondering who I am."

Well, no, I wasn't, Acila thought, *but I appreciate the reminder that I'm not supposed to know. What I'm really wondering about, however, is this sudden character change—I thought you were a total idiot.*

Druscilla demonstrated her complete lack of telepathy by continuing, "My name is Druscilla, and the Queen is my aunt. She's getting old—"

"Old?" Acila echoed, startled. The Queen hadn't struck her as old at all.

"Old to be marrying the Year-King—she's almost past child-bearing age. And she hasn't any daughters, so I'm her heiress, and she said it was time for me to take her place in the Ritual this year, and I don't want to marry somebody in the spring and sacrifice him at summer's end—I just couldn't, and I couldn't think of what to do to stop them, so I ran away, into the forest, and that's where I met Briam, but I really didn't think we'd be back in time for the Festival, because it took me weeks to get to where I met him, and I certainly never meant for him to be Year-King, and we've got to figure out some way to save him!" She stopped, out of breath, upset, and obviously feeling guilty.

"How long do we have before the sacrifice?" Acila asked.

"Four months."

"How do they do it?" Acila braced herself for the answer, and relaxed slightly when it came.

"They give him to the river—off the city wall."

"Tied up?"

"No, he's supposed to go willingly."

"Do any of them survive?"

"One did, about ten years ago," Druscilla shuddered violently. "But mostly they don't—the water's very turblent under the waterfall, and there are so many jagged rocks. I get nightmares!"

Acila suspected that she would, too. "The one that survived, did they try to kill him afterward?"

Druscilla shuddered again. "No, the Queen said the Goddess had given up her claim to him, and he went away someplace. He scared me; I wouldn't have minded too much if *he* had died. The Queen had a son by him, too." She changed the subject abruptly. "What's your name?"

"Briam didn't tell you?" Acila frantically tried to remember if Briam had ever called her wolf-self by name in Druscilla's hearing. "It's Acila." To her relief, Druscilla's face didn't change.

"I am happy to meet you, Acila," she said politely. "We'd better try to get some sleep; in the morning we've got to sneak you out of town so you can come in to town looking for your brother."

"All right," Acila agreed, lying down. "It's better than trying to explain how I did get here." *And it is very odd that Druscilla hasn't asked me that. Not that I want her to, but I do wonder why she doesn't.*

Acila was becoming almost accustomed to strange awakenings. This time Druscilla was shaking her violently. "Someone's coming! Quick, under the bed!"

Acila didn't bother to answer; she rolled off the far side of the bed and under it in one smooth motion. She listened to the booted feet approaching and recognized the step. Is the Shield-Bearer the head of the Queen's Guard or Druscilla's governess? she wondered. If Druscilla usually takes up this much of her time and energy, I wonder what the Guard is like.

The door was flung open and the booted feet stopped at the side of the doorway. From her position under the bed Acila could see bare feet slipping from under a long purple gown as someone passed the

Shield-Bearer and came into the room. The Shield-Bearer then entered the room and shut the door.

"Well, Druscilla? What have you to say for yourself?"

It's the Queen! Acila realized with surprise. But her dress was black yesterday—no, that's right, I was a wolf then, so it only appeared black.

Receiving no answer from Druscilla, the Queen said, "Is she unable to talk? Did you damage her voice when you knocked her out yesterday?"

"I assure you she can talk," the swordswoman replied dryly. "You should have heard her yesterday after I carried her here."

"She strangled me!" Druscilla burst out indignantly. "She could have killed me for all you care—but then you wouldn't have an heiress, would you?"

"I'm not sure I do in any case," the Queen replied grimly. "Whatever possessed you to disrupt the ritual?"

"I thought you didn't notice minor incidents like that when you were in ritual trance," Druscilla said sarcastically.

"I'd have to be deep entranced indeed not to notice my heiress trying to stop the Sacred Marriage! Why on earth did you do it?"

"I love Briam, and I don't want him killed!" Druscilla snapped.

"Oh, Sweet Lady!" the Queen sighed. "I really don't need this. Am I correct in assuming that Briam is the new King?"

"You don't even care!" Druscilla's voice was anguished. "How can you do this, year after year, marry a man in the spring and kill him at summer's end, and never even notice he's a person! Well, Briam is a person and there are people who care about him, and you can't have him!"

"Druscilla," the Queen sighed tiredly and collapsed to sit on the edge of the bed. "I *do* have him. Haven't you paid any attention to all we've tried to teach you?

How can you hope to rule this city if you don't understand the Sacrifice. If Briam had been bound to you—or to anyone else—he would not have come to my call. Only those who are not tied elsewhere can hear it."

"But he likes me!" Druscilla protested.

"Darling," the bed shifted as the Queen reached out to Druscilla, "liking isn't enough. He would have to be committed to you, and obviously he's not."

Druscilla burst into tears. Acila drew back slightly to avoid being kicked by the Queen's restlessly swinging foot, which was uncomfortably close to her nose. The booted feet of the Shield-Bearer approached the bed as well, and Acila could well imagine the look the two women were exchanging over Druscilla's sobbing head.

"Why do you have to kill him anyway?" Druscilla wailed. "You're the Queen and can do what you want—why don't you just abolish the Sacrifice?"

"Don't be silly, Druscilla!" the Shield-Bearer said sharply.

"Druscilla," the Queen said quietly, "the Queen can not do just anything she wants to. Think about it. What makes me the Queen?"

"Your mother was Queen," Druscilla replied crossly. "Anybody knows that!"

"And when she died, I became Queen," the Queen agreed. "And if I were dead, my crown would also be passed on to my successor, and it wouldn't be difficult for someone to kill me; I lead prayers on the balcony every day."

"But why would anyone kill you?" Druscilla asked in astonishment.

"Queens have been killed before when they did something their people wouldn't accept. We say that the Queen rules by the will of the Goddess, but it's also true that she rules by the will of her people. The last Queen who tried to abolish the Sacrifice *was* killed."

"I remember that story," Druscilla snapped, "but, first it was over a hundred years ago, and, second, she was killed by some crazy farmer—it's not as if everyone wanted her dead!"

"One man struck the blow, true," the Shield-Bearer said. "But if her people had still supported her, he would have been disarmed before he could have reached her. He killed her, but everyone else stood by and let him—and then they dragged the king to the river and threw him in."

"And considered themselves specially blessed by the Goddess when the crops were good the next year," the Queen added.

"But that's just superstition!" Druscilla burst out. "There's no proof at all that the crops failed because the Year-King didn't die at the appointed time, or that they were good the next year because the people killed him and the Queen. You can't believe that nonsense!"

"It doesn't matter in the slightest whether *I* believe it or not, Druscilla," the Queen said. "What matters in this case is what my people believe. Perhaps one year the Sacrifice will be abolished. But as long as the people want it, it will take place, one way or another. When you are Queen, you will have to do it."

"Never!" Druscilla cried. "And I won't let you kill Briam, either!" She burst into tears again.

"You'll have to send her away," the swordswoman said with a weary sigh.

"Yes," the Queen agreed. "No sense in keeping her here to witness what will come."

Druscilla sobbed harder. "Child," the Queen said gently, "wash your face and go call your maids. You are going to your mother's estate as soon as you are packed. I want you ready to leave by midday."

"No!" Druscilla protested.

"Yes," the Queen said firmly. "I will not have you moping around court making eyes at the Year-King for the next four months. Go call your maids."

* * *

Druscilla ran weeping from the room, slamming the door behind her. The swordswoman dropped to sit on the bed with a groan. "What are we going to do with her?"

"I just don't know, Wesia," the Queen sighed.

So the Shield-Bearer does have a name, Acila thought. *I wonder what the Queen's name is.*

"I had hoped she would outgrow this foolishness," the Queen continued, "but she seems only to get worse. Fancying herself in love with the Year-King!" She sighed. "I can't keep her as my heiress."

"But, you have no choice," Wesia protested, "there is no one else."

"I shall just have to bear a daughter, then, shan't I?"

"The odds of your surviving that . . ." Weisa's voice trailed off in anguish.

"It's more important that my daughter survives," the Queen replied grimly. "You'll have to be regent and guardian for her if I die."

"You know I'd do anything for you, but there are some things I'd rather not have to do!"

"I also, but things will go as the Goddess wills them." The Queen stood up abruptly. "I'd best go robe, collect the King, and introduce him to his Companions. I hope that escorting Druscilla to her mother's estate isn't one of the things you'd rather not do, because I'm afraid that's your lot for today."

"With the amount of time I spend dealing with that wretched girl, we're undeservedly fortunate to have any discipline at all left among your Guard," Wesia retorted.

"Take the dozen most in need of your personal attention as an escort on the road," the Queen suggested, sounding amused. "I don't doubt your ability to handle both Druscilla and the Guard."

The door opened again, and Acila could see the hem of Druscilla's nightgown along with three other sets of feet, presumably the maids.

"Ah, there you are, child," the Queen said. "The Shield-Bearer will escort you on your journey and return to fetch you for Winter Court. Do you wish to take one of the maids with you, or have you enough staff at the estate?"

"I'll manage with the staff there," Druscilla said in a subdued voice. "But I thank you for the offer, Lady," she added hastily.

"Very well," the Queen crossed to the door, held open for her by one of the curtsying maids. "Shield-Bearer, gather a proper escort for the Lady Druscilla."

"As you command, My Queen," the swordswoman said, following her from the room.

What now? Acila wondered. She wasn't entirely happy with her present position. What if one of the maids decided to check under the bed for dropped clothing?

But it was Druscilla who dropped the night-candle under the edge of the bed and snapped at the maid who reached for it, "I'll get it! For the love of the Goddess, pack quickly; the Queen wishes me on the road by midday!"

"Listen, Acila," she whispered urgently. "I'll leave you some clothes. Sneak out after we've gone and follow us. We'll be going downriver. I'll make sure we travel slowly, so you can circle around and come up to us as if you were coming from inland. Say you're traveling to the city in search of your brother and ask if we've seen him."

"All right," Acila agreed. She wasn't sure exactly what Druscilla was planning, but she was beginning to develop considerable respect for the girl's abilities in her own environment.

CHAPTER 11

*F*or once, Acila thought, *something in this wretched adventure is going smoothly.* Druscilla had left her plain clothes, suitable for someone who had allegedly escaped from her home and been wandering in the woods ever since, and Acila had slipped unnoticed out of both the palace and the city. She had then bundled up the clothes, changed to her eagle shape, and flown high over the river until she sighted Druscilla's party. She couldn't see Druscilla, who was traveling in a closed litter, but Wesia and the dozen guards were easy to identify. She flew another few miles downstream and inland, then landed and changed back to human form.

Her body felt extremely strange. She wasn't surprised that her fingers were clumsy on her bodice laces—after all, that wasn't a skill she'd had much practice in lately, but her perspective had shifted; it seemed to be farther to the ground than it used to be, and her balance felt different and wrong. She rolled briefly in the dirt to mess her clothes suitably and grind dirt into all exposed skin, being thankful that they hadn't been able to do anything about her hair yet. It would certainly make her tale of months in the woods believable! She then headed toward the road, pausing to wash her hands and face as best she could in a stream she passed. She wanted to look as though she'd been surviving in the woods, but not as if she'd descended to the level of an animal—even though that *was* what she had done.

She reached the edge of a bluff and looked up the road. The travelers were just coming into view around a bend, so she started to scramble down the debris left from a recent rock slide to reach them. The late afternoon sun, descending toward the river, was in her eyes, but that couldn't be helped.

She quickly discovered that her rock-climbing reflexes were still adapted to four legs instead of two. For perhaps half a minute she managed to keep her footing among treacherously tilting rocks, but she knew she was starting to fall—and in front of the Queen's Guard, she didn't dare shift, though it took all her concentration to remain in human shape as she skidded and tumbled down the hill in a mass of sliding rocks. She heard her voice whimpering in terror, felt something strike her forehead. . . .

"Easy, now, just lie still." The voice was familiar, but she couldn't place it. "You had a nasty fall, but you're all right now."

A thin arm lifted her gently and a cup of cool water was held to her lips. "Here, drink some of this." Acila swallowed the water gratefully; her lips were cracked and her mouth was horribly dry. She tried to speak, but only managed to croak.

"My name is Druscilla," the voice said.

Oh, yes, of course, Acila thought. Slowly her memory began to return. They'd been in the woods, she and Briam, and Druscilla had come, and been afraid of the wolves. "Where's Briam?"

"What?" a voice demanded from across the room. Acila heard booted feet approach the bed. She tried to open her eyes, but the light hurt them and she closed them again. It was daytime, and there were two women near her, but that was all she could tell. "When did she come around?"

"Just now, Shield-Bearer," Druscilla replied.

"Shield-Bearer"—she came to fetch Druscilla and

they took Briam to the city. . . . "What did you do with my brother?"

"Briam is your brother?" the swordswoman asked.

You know he is, Acila thought, but it was too much trouble to say more than "Yes."

"He's in the city," the Shield-Bearer said soothingly. "We'll send a message telling him you're safe; I know he was worrying about you. We were, too; you've been unconscious for a full three days and then some."

"Oh," Acila said, barely understanding the words as she fell asleep again.

When she woke up, it was night, or rather just before dawn. She lay quietly, trying to sort things out in her aching head. The rest of her memory had come back now; she knew that Briam was in the city as Year-King and she had less than four months to come up with a plan to save him—*again,* she thought wearily. Druscilla had been banished to her country estate, which must be where they were now, and Wesia, *no, I'm not supposed to know her name, call her "Shield-Bearer,"* had escorted her and was still here. She cast her mind over what she'd said when she woke up before and decided she hadn't uttered anything too incriminating. *After a knock on the head, "what have you done with my brother?" doesn't necessarily imply anything more than that I'm looking for him.*

But what do I do now? She looked around in the dim light that was starting to come through the windows. She lay on a cot in what was presumably Druscilla's room; the furniture was arranged in the same way as her room in the city. The bed curtains were partly open on the side nearest her, and she could see a thick blonde braid and a little bit of the top of Druscilla's head. The rest of Druscilla was buried under the blanket.

Acila turned her attention back to her own body and started taking stock. She felt battered and she ached all over, especially her head, and she was sure she would discover a fine crop of bruises when she tried to get up. She moved her hands in front of her face and studied them in the dim light. The palms were scratched, but healing, and the calluses had protected them somewhat. Tough, hardened skin didn't tear as easily as the delicate soft skin a lady was supposed to have. Someone had obviously washed her and put her into one of Druscilla's nightgowns; she had never owned one with lace at the wrists. She reached up and felt her hair; it was still the tangled mess it had been when she changed back from being a wolf. No doubt they hadn't wanted to pull it about while she had a head injury.

A noise came from Druscilla's bed, something between a moan and a whimper. "Druscilla?" There was no reply, unless one counted Druscilla's continued whimpering.

Acila cautiously sat up and set her teeth against the pain. Her head felt ready to split open and her ribs felt as though someone had been using them for drums. She managed to swing her feet over the side of the cot and reach the floor, but when she tried to stand up, her legs refused to take her weight. Fortunately the space between her cot and Druscilla's bed was narrow, so when she pitched forward she landed on the bed—and, of course, on Druscilla. Druscilla awakened abruptly with a shriek.

It wasn't a loud shriek, but it produced a guard before Acila could move. "What's amiss, my Lady?"

"Nothing, thank you," Druscilla replied hastily. "I had a bad dream, that's all." Both girls held their breath, afraid that the guard would open the bed curtains, but she merely closed the door and returned to her post.

"How are you feeling, Acila?" Druscilla whispered softly. "I'm sorry your hair is still such a mess; I wanted to wash and comb it, but the Shield-Bearer wouldn't let me."

"That's all right," Acila whispered back. "The way my head feels I don't even want to try to wash it now, to say nothing of trying to get the tangles out. I may have to cut it off."

"Oh, I hope not," Druscilla said. "Briam has such beautiful hair, and you must, too."

"Under all the dirt?" Acila's hair was not her major worry. "What day is it? How long have I been here?"

Druscilla reckoned it on her fingers. "You met us in the late afternoon on the first day of our journey. Do you remember?"

"All I remember is that I saw your party on the road and then fell down with a rock slide."

"Yes. About a third of the rock slide came down with you—it's a mercy it was a small one. You were unconscious when we picked you up, and you stayed that way for the rest of the journey here, that's three more days, and you didn't wake up until the afternoon of the second day we were here. Then you were awake only a few minutes before you fell asleep again, and now it's," she glanced out the window at the graying sky, "very early morning of the third day here, so you missed six nights and four days."

"Oh, no!" Acila whispered. "What's happening to Briam while I'm away?"

"Nothing," answered Druscilla in surprise. "It's a very bad omen if the Year-King dies before the appointed time. Believe me, the whole city will make sure nothing happens to Briam before Summer's End. Even when he goes out hunting, his Companions go with him. It's their special job to make sure no harm comes to him."

"His Companions?"

"Eight youths of good family, who attend the Year-King whenever he's not with the Queen. It's considered a great honor, and unless the Year-King is very unpleasant and difficult to get along with, it's a pretty comfortable job."

"So they keep him safe until summer's end," Acila said, trying to make certain she understood the situation. "And then they kill him."

"The Companions don't kill him; the Queen and Shield-Bearer do—if we don't stop them," Druscilla said through gritted teeth. "But we will stop them. Somehow."

She took a good look at Acila. "We'd better get you back to bed. Can you sit up?"

With a great deal of help from Druscilla, Acila made it back to her cot, where she promptly fell asleep again.

When she woke again, the sun was streaming in through the window across her bed. It was warm, and it felt wonderful. Druscilla was sitting on a cushion on the broad windowsill, still in her nightgown. Acila tried to speak aloud, but her voice came out as a croak.

"Oh, you're awake." Druscilla jumped off the windowsill and went to the table, which held a pitcher and several cups. "Let me get you some water."

There was a noise of booted feet hurrying down the hall away from their door. "Brace yourself," Druscilla warned softly. "We're about to have company." She propped Acila up, using the pillows from both beds, and held the cup of water to her lips. Acila sipped it gratefully.

It was only a minute before they heard footsteps coming toward them. "Act dumb," Druscilla advised hastily just before the door opened.

I suppose that under the circumstances, that's good advice, Acila thought, *but why does she always do it? Does she have enemies, or is it just that she doesn't get on with the Queen?*

"So you're back with us," the Shield-Bearer said pleasantly. "How are you feeling?"

"Battered," Acila replied ruefully.

Wesia laughed. "I can well believe it. You're very lucky not to have broken bones. How is your sight?"

It took Acila a moment to make sense of that, to realize that Wesia was referring to eyesight rather than clairvoyance or the changes in vision that resulted from changing shape. "Fine, thank you."

"Good. Do you think you could eat something?" Acila considered that. She didn't feel hungry exactly, but she wasn't nauseous and she was obviously in need of fluids at least. She nodded and hastily clutched her head. Nodding hurt!

"Better practice saying 'yes.' You're not going to want to move your head much for a bit," Wesia advised. She spoke to the guard at the door, who went off down the hall.

"So you're Briam's sister. You do resemble him."

"Yes, a bit," Acila replied. "We're twins."

"Are you, now?" That seemed to interest Wesia; Acila wasn't sure why. She glanced at Druscilla, who seemed unconcerned, so presumably it didn't have any relation to Briam's upcoming sacrifice.

If twins could be sacrificed in place of each other, would Druscilla try to sacrifice me to save Briam? It was a disquieting thought. "Where did you meet Briam?" she asked.

"In the forest north of the City," the Shield-Bearer replied, "saving Druscilla from her own stupidity."

"I'm not all that stupid," Druscilla retorted indignantly. "I just have a horror of wolves, ever since one of the Year—"

"Enough!" The swordswoman cut her off sharply. Druscilla looked rebellious, but she did not try to finish her sentence.

Ever since one of the Year-Kings—what? Acila wondered. What could a Year-King have done to make Druscilla afraid of wolves?

"It's high time you dressed and went about your day's business," Wesia told Druscilla firmly. "Genia," she added to the guard who was returning with a tray of food. "Go call Lady Druscilla's maid to help her dress, please." She took the tray from the guard, who promptly set off on her new errand.

Wesia set the tray on Acila's lap. It contained a bowl of some sort of porridge, which smelled delicious. "Can you hold a spoon, or shall I help you?"

"I can manage, thank you." Acila was beginning to feel much better. She had always healed more quickly than most people around her, and apparently that hadn't changed. The smell of the food made her realize how hungry she really was, and she had to force herself not to gulp down the porridge like the wolf she had been.

"You're looking much better," Wesia said approvingly. "If we put you in a litter, I think we can start back to the city today."

"But she was so badly hurt!" Druscilla protested. "She should stay here until she recovers."

"She survived three days in a litter immediately after being hurt," Wesia pointed out. "I doubt that she's in worse shape now. And I do have to get back to the city; I've been here three days longer than I should have been already. The Queen will be worried."

"You sent her a messenger bird the night you got here," Druscilla argued.

"There's no guarantee that the bird got to the city," Wesia replied. "And, in any case, I have work to do there. We'll leave as soon as we can be ready. Please have your kitchen pack food for us."

"Very well," Druscilla gave in to the inevitable with good grace. "Please tell the Queen my aunt that Acila can have my room at the palace. Since I won't be there, she might as well use it."

"Thank you, Lady Druscilla," Acila said, carefully remembering to be formal.

Druscilla smiled at her. "You're welcome," she said. "And I'll gather together some clothes for you, since yours got lost. We seem to be much the same size."

Acila murmured her thanks and ate another bite of porridge.

The guard Genia returned, followed by Druscilla's maid. Wesia promptly sent Genia off to set the guards to packing and loading the animals, but she remained where she was, sitting on the foot of Acila's bed. *She doesn't want to leave me alone with Druscilla,* Acila realized. *She's afraid that Druscilla will tell me about Briam's being Year-King. I'd better remember that all I'm supposed to know about him is that he's in the city.*

She ate her porridge quietly and watched Druscilla dress. The prospect of wearing such clothes did not cheer her; they appeared to be designed to make it impossible for the wearer to do much of anything. Over the lace-trimmed shift, loose and suitable for sleeping in, went three petticoats, so trimmed with lace and flounces that they stuck out and made Druscilla look like a handbell. The maid put Druscilla into a corset, which, in addition to lacing in back, so that she couldn't dress unaided, fastened so tightly that Druscilla would be unable to run in it. Probably a fast walk would make her feel faint. Then there was an underskirt, heavily embroidered and coming to within an inch of the floor. Over that went an overdress of some sort of fabric with small designs woven into it. The bodice of this was boned and it laced up also, but at least it did so in the front. The sleeves, however, were long and loose, calculated to get caught in or dragged through everything one reached for. The skirt was split in a wide triangle so that the underskirt could be seen and, presumably, admired. Well, it was a beautiful piece of embroidery, but the whole outfit was very confining. The maid had to kneel on the floor to put on Druscilla's shoes and stockings and tie the garters; there was no way Druscilla could bend over enough to reach her feet.

Some of what Acila felt must have showed in her face, for Wesia chuckled. "Don't worry, child, you don't have to get dressed for the journey. We'll just wrap you in blankets and put you in the litter, and you can sleep through the whole trip. We'll wake you up for meals."

"Thank you," Acila said with heartfelt gratitude.

She did sleep through most of the trip. Since they kept the curtains of the litter closed, there was nothing to see. The party camped out on the road each night, instead of staying with villagers as they had done when bringing Druscilla back from the forest. Acila supposed they were still trying to limit her contact with others. *Just wait until I recover and can change shape again,* she thought, *and then see how ignorant you can keep me!* But she slept and ate and smiled and thanked them for the food and the care they were taking of her, and said nothing to any purpose. Best to play a waiting game until she knew more.

By the time they arrived in the city, four days later, she could walk a bit. She insisted on putting on one of Druscilla's simpler dresses and walking into the palace leaning on Wesia's arm. She didn't want to be carried in and worry Briam.

Unfortunately her efforts to spare Briam any worry were wasted. When she tottered into the atrium, leaning on Wesia, the Queen was seated on the dais. Briam sat on a lower chair beside her, and on his forehead was a blue circle, just like the one Lord Ranulf bore. Acila took one look at him and promptly fainted.

CHAPTER 12

I seem to be spending my life waking up in strange places, Acila thought. *I wonder where I am this time. I wish I were back home—I miss it.* She opened her eyes long enough to recognize Druscilla's room in the palace, then shut them again and concentrated on the shouting match going on in the doorway.

"Lord, will you let the healers deal with this? At least let them come into the room and look at her!" Wesia's voice was exasperated.

"What did you do to her? You said she was all right!" Briam was rapidly becoming hysterical.

I know he's not used to my being sick or hurt, but I do wish he wouldn't shout so.

"I said she was going to be all right, not that she was now," the swordswoman retorted. "She's apparently been living off the land for months, and then she fell down a hill, a third of which fell down with her. She's half-starved and had a head injury, but she didn't break any bones, and she was recovering nicely—before she insisted on trying to walk into the palace so she wouldn't worry you. If this is how you customarily act when you're worried, I can see why she made the effort, and I'm only sorry she didn't succeed! Now will you stop acting like a spoiled two-year-old and let the healers do their job?"

"Truly, my Lord," the Queen said soothingly, "the healers are skilled at their job—and the Shield-Bearer is quite good at judging how badly someone is hurt. Pray calm yourself. If you like, you can draw up a stool by the head of the bed and hold her hand, but do stay quiet and out of the way."

Briam stalked across the room, scraped a stool across the floor, flopped down on it (it creaked ominously), and grabbed Acila's hand.

Briam, she thought at him, *I love you dearly, but if you shout like that around me again while I still have this headache, I'll turn you into a toad.*

You're alive!

Of course I'm alive! I don't die that easily.

Why don't you open your eyes?

Acila shuddered. She didn't want to open her eyes; she wasn't yet ready to see her little brother looking like a younger version of Lord Ranulf. *How did you get that mark on your forehead?*

Briam shifted slightly to let one of the healers examine Acila's head. Acila hoped the healers weren't telepaths. Having someone "overhear" this conversation would necessitate awkward explanations.

Apparently some of her unease about the mark had reached Briam through their link. *The mark? Is it something horrible? I've never seen it; there are no mirrors in our rooms—that is, the Queen's and mine. Acila, you'll never believe it; she's chosen me to be her King. We've found our kingdom.*

Oh, no! Acila's response came before she could stop it. It was much more difficult to stop thoughts than to hold one's tongue.

What's the matter? Don't you think this is what the prophecy meant?

I don't know. Acila thought it over. *Actually, I suppose this could very well be what Mother foresaw. But it doesn't feel right, somehow. Why did she choose you?*

I don't know. Obviously this was not something Briam was prepared to worry himself about. *Maybe she liked the way I look. Druscilla seemed to like me, too. They said you were with her; how is she?*

*Upset, but otherwise all right. She wasn't very happy
to leave court.*

Is her estate nice?

I don't know; I didn't see any of it but her bedroom.

*Oh, well, the city will be good for you; this is a won-
derful place. They have musicians to play at dinner every evening, and I can go hunting any time I want. I
even have Companions to go with me, and if I go down
into the city and admire something in a shop, the shop-
keeper just gives it to me!*

Why?

*Because I'm the King. That's what the mark is for, so
everyone will know who I am.*

Oh. I see. Acila certainly did see. She remembered
Druscilla's words: "it's very unlucky for the King to
die before the proper time." The mark would ensure
that no one would quarrel with him and kill him by
misadventure. And the merchants probably figured that
he wouldn't be here long, so they might as well make
him happy while he was here. After all, between
Spring Festival and Summer's End, how much of a
merchant's stock could one man use? The was no
profit in pointing this out to Briam, however, especially not now, in front of their audience. Let him be
happy as long as he could.

The healer stood up and moved away from the bed.
"There's nothing wrong with her that food and rest
won't cure," she said. "She simply fainted, that's all."

"Then why is she still unconscious?" the Queen
asked.

The healer chuckled. "She's not."

Perforce, Acila opened her eyes. The Queen stood at
the foot of the bed, with Wesia standing just behind her
right shoulder. Acila met their eyes; at least that way
she didn't have to look at Briam. "I'm sorry if I
alarmed you, Lady," she said. "I guess I was simply
more tired than I thought. The Shield-Bearer took such
good care of me on the road that I was feeling fine,

and I failed to realize that my feeling well wouldn't survive my standing up."

The Queen smiled at her, her face lighting up in a way that made the whole room seem brighter. *She has an incredible smile*, thought Acila. *Nobody could see her smile and not smile back.*

"I've been known to make the same mistake," the Queen said. "The Shield-Bearer is a wonderful nurse—and she's very good at making her patients stay in bed."

The Shield-Bearer smiled, too; obviously this was some sort of private joke. "And bed is where you had better stay for a few more days, young lady. When you've had some rest and a few more meals, you'll probably feel a good deal more human."

Does she know about you? Briam thought.

No, Acila thought back. *Nobody does, except you, so don't tell anyone.*

I won't, but everybody on our estate must know by now.

Maybe, but at least they're not here to tell anyone.

The Queen came to detach Briam's grip on Acila's fingers. "Come, my lord, it's time for dinner." She smiled again at Acila, who felt warmed all over by it. "I'll assign a maid to wait on you and bring your meals. When you're feeling up to it, we'll have you measured for new clothes. Rest well." She left, towing an unresisting Briam and followed by the Shield-Bearer.

Acila lay there, feeling puzzled. *She seems so nice*, she thought. *But how can she be a nice person and still want to kill Briam?*

Want to kill Briam? her other self asked. *What makes you think she* wants *to kill him?*

Druscilla said so, and so did the Queen and the Shield-Bearer. They all said she was going to sacrifice him!

"Is going to" is not the same as "wants to."

What difference does it make? He'll be dead either way!

It may make a big difference. If you will think back to what the Queen said while you were hiding under this bed a few days ago, you may remember that she's much more concerned with keeping her people happy than with being sure the Year-King actually dies.

Acila thought about that for several moments. *Then if I can come up with something that makes the people think Briam's been properly sacrificed, the Queen won't make a fuss if she finds out he's not dead.*

Precisely.

That gave Acila quite a lot to think about.

The next few days were boring. At first Acila slept most of the time, but as she began to feel better she became restless. The maid who waited on her never spoke, leaving Acila to wonder whether she was a mute or had simply been told not to gossip and was carrying her instructions to extremes. At least she did provide a bath when Acila finally felt well enough to demand one. She also helped Acila wash and comb out her hair. As Druscilla had predicted, this took an entire afternoon.

Briam did not visit her, and Acila wondered why. *Granted, he seemed happy here when I last saw him, but I'm his sister. In fact, I'm now his only living relative. And he can't be hunting all night, even if he does go out all day—and he wasn't all that fond of hunting before, but maybe it's more fun with his Companions than it was with Father. Still, he could at least stop in and say good night. Doesn't he even worry about how I'm doing?*

Probably not. Why should he? You're doing fine.

I'm dying of boredom. At least at home people would come talk to me, even if I were sick.

Yes, they certainly would. "What should the cook make for dinner?" "Do we start the grain harvest tomorrow or next week?" "One of the maids is in labor

*and not doing well, may we send for the midwife?" You
should be thankful that nobody's bothering you.*

So I'm ungrateful. But I'm not used to doing nothing. I feel so worthless, lying here and eating their
food and not doing anything in return! And I'm worried about Briam; I'm used to knowing where he is and
what he's doing. Who knows what kind of trouble he's
getting into without me to watch him!

*Considering the trouble he got into with you right on
his heels, your presence is obviously no guarantee
he'll stay out of trouble. And he's probably safer now
than he's ever been in his life; there's a whole city
making sure he comes to no harm.*

Yet.

*He's safe enough until summer's end, so turn your
thoughts to how to get him out of the Sacrifice. At least
you know now that it is possible to survive being Year-
King, assuming that Lord Ranulf was one, and it certainly seems likely.*

Yes. I'll find out if it really was Lord Ranulf
and exactly how he survived. Too bad Druscilla's so
far away; I have a feeling that no one else is going to
be willing to talk to me about the Year-King, past or
present. But I'll find out, somehow.

*I'm sure you will. And don't worry about Briam.
You've seen the Queen; do you have to look any further for the reason he's not spending his free time with
you? Remember the way he reacted to Druscilla.*

I remember. He's certainly picked the worst possible
time to develop an interest in women. I liked it better
when his affections were confined to his lute and the
idea of romance, not the reality.

The Queen appeared suddenly in the doorway, almost as if thinking about her had summoned her.
"How are you feeling now, Lady Acila?"

Acila swung out of bed and stood up. After two days
of surreptitious practice she had stopped falling over
every time she stood up. "Much better, Lady," she said
formally. "I thank you for your care of me."

"You are welcome," the Queen replied, seating herself in one of the chairs and gesturing Acila to the other. "You do look much better. Tell me, have you reached the 'losing my mind with boredom' stage yet?" She smiled her enchanting smile, and Acila smiled back. She felt a bit like a traitor, feeling any liking for the women who planned to kill her brother, but it could be valuable to have the Queen's good will and trust.

"I'm afraid so. I hope there's something around here I can do; I'm accustomed to running an estate, and I find doing nothing very unsettling."

The Queen looked thoughtful. "There's no strictly defined role for the King's sister, but perhaps you could take over some of Druscilla's duties while she's away."

"I'd be happy to," Acila said, adding cautiously, "if they are within my abilities. What does Druscilla usually do?"

"The sort of thing you're probably used to—planning menus, assigning work to the spinners and weavers, and so forth. We'll have to get you some more clothes, though; you can't run around the palace in a bedgown. I'm afraid you'll have to either stay in bed or wear Druscilla's clothes for a few days until we can make you some of your own."

"I'll wear Druscilla's clothes," *anything to get out of this bed and this room,* "but do I have to wear all of them?"

The Queen threw back her head and laughed. "So you share my opinion of her taste?"

"Her clothes are truly lovely, Lady," Acila said sincerely, "but they're so elaborate! I don't see how she can move in them!"

"Years and years of practice," the Queen laughed. "I suppose I spoiled her, but it seemed harmless enough at the time. After all, most girls like pretty clothes, and Druscilla has done beautiful fine sewing and embroidery from the age of five."

"And the more she did, the more cloth she needed to display it, and the more elaborate her clothes got." Acila started laughing, too. "Let's hope she develops other interests. If she lived with me I'd give her the Great Hall to furnish. By the time she did a complete set of banners, cushions for all the seats, and hangings for all the walls, she might conceivably get tired of embroidery. And if she wasn't tired of it after one set, you could develop a sudden desire for a set of hangings for each season."

The Queen looked at her approvingly. "That's an idea. I'll have to try it when she returns; it might work. In the meantime, see what you can find in her clothing chests. As I recall, her riding habit isn't too elaborate, and you can probably detach the sleeves from a couple of her other gowns—just be sure to sew them back on when you return them, or she'll be furious with both of us."

"I shall," Acila promised. "Lady Druscilla has been very kind to me, and it would be a poor return to damage the clothes she has been kind enough to lend me."

"I'm glad that you got on well with her; she's been too much alone since her mother died." The Queen stood up, and Acila hastily rose to her feet as well. "Find yourself something to wear and join us for dinner; your maid will show you the way to the hall. After dinner I'll introduce you to the household staff. The Shield-Bearer will be glad of your recovery. She's been keeping an eye on the household as well as the guards, and it's been keeping her very busy."

Acila rang for her maid as soon as the Queen left, and they spent an enjoyable hour sorting through the clothing chests. The gown Acila finally chose for dinner was a beautiful deep green, embroidered with gold thread. She removed the sleeves, as the Queen had suggested, for although she was thinner than Druscilla, her arms were more heavily muscled. *Especially after running on them for months,* she thought ruefully. *Well, the loose sleeves of the undergown will conceal that.*

Moving carefully and reminding herself not to spill anything or wipe her hands on her skirts, Acila made her way to the dining hall. The Queen and the Shield-Bearer stood talking by one side of the fireplace, and Briam sat on a stool at the other side, petting the wolf who had come to the city with them.

With everything that had happened to her since arriving in the city, Acila had quite forgotten about the wolf. The wolf, however, had not forgotten her. He abandoned Briam without a backward glance and tore down the hall at top speed, bouncing and whining excitedly. Acila shrieked, afraid that he'd tear Druscilla's dress and Druscilla would kill her. It was only afterward that she realized that she had inadvertently presented a beautiful portrait of a terrified maiden.

Hastily, Briam ran forward to grab the wolf, who was bouncing around Acila and whuffling in welcome. "Down, boy," the twins said in unison. The wolf sat, with Briam holding him down, and Acila reached out and let him lick her hand. Then she stroked him behind the ears until he calmed down and Briam could release him.

As they walked toward the table, with the wolf dogging their heels, Acila tried to think of an explanation of how the wolf could have met her before. Not coming up with anything, she decided to keep her mouth shut and hope nobody asked.

Fortunately the Queen confined her comments to, "I hope the wolf didn't frighten you too much; he and Lord Briam are virtually inseparable."

"No, Lady," Acila assured her. "I was merely startled, that's all."

Wesia said nothing, but she appeared to be giving the matter a good deal more thought than Acila would have liked.

With my luck, Acila thought, cautiously glancing at the Shield-Bearer, *she's seen enough of wolves to recognize "greeting a pack member's return" behavior. Oh well, even if she has, there is nothing I can do about it now.*

CHAPTER 13

Over the next few days, Acila discovered that living with a wolf in a cave in the woods and living with it in the Queen's house in the city were two very different things. Although nominally the wolf was Briam's pet—and Briam, with an unusual lack of originality, had named him "Wolf"—the beast appeared perfectly willing to regard Acila as the pack leader; once she was up and about, he followed her everywhere. When Wesia made a pointed remark about the animal's sudden liking for Acila, Acila shrugged and replied that she and Briam must smell alike, being twins. If Wesia didn't believe her, she did at least drop the subject.

The wolf still slept in Briam's room—at least Acila assumed it did, since she shut it out of her room every night and bolted the door. She knew that when she had regained a bit more of her strength, she was going to be sneaking out at night in changed form, and she didn't want a wolf having hysterics in her room to alert everyone in howling range to the fact that something odd was going on.

This left Acila free to worry about more urgent problems, like fur. In the woods, even before she had turned into a wolf, she had worn rough clothes, so it hadn't mattered when Wolf leaned affectionately against her and left a layer of hair behind. But she was quite sure that Druscilla would not tolerate this as an addition to the trim on her skirts. The first thing Acila did was to acquire several large aprons and wear one tied over her skirts at all times. Even when Briam went out hunting and took the wolf with him, they were apt to return without warning and seek her out to tell her they were back.

The next problem came to light when they joined her in the carpenter's shop one day. "What are you doing here, Acila?" Briam demanded. "I thought you were in the laundry, finding out where they hid all my shirts."

"I was," Acila retorted, "and I found your shirts; they were mixed in with a pile of old sheets, which were shoved in a corner because the chest that was supposed to hold them broke when someone put a heavy washtub on it. Then they shoved the pieces under the sorting table and forgot about it. I brought the pieces here to be fixed, so the sheets can be put away properly and so they won't lose your shirts anymore. I trust this meets with your Worship's approval?" she concluded sarcastically.

"All right, all right," Briam threw up his hands. "I didn't mean to imply that you weren't working. Anyway, I got a deer, so we can have venison for dinner."

"Tomorrow's dinner," Acila corrected him. "The cook is already cooking today's."

"Fine, tomorrow's." Briam was being agreeable. "Sister, dear sister, could you do me a tremendous favor?"

"What?" Acila wasn't going to commit herself to anything he asked for in that tone of voice without finding out what it was.

"Sleep with the wolf."

"What?" Acila's mind flashed back to the morning she had awakened in the shrine, with the wolf beside her. She stared at Briam in horror.

"Just let him sleep in your room," he pleaded. "He won't get on the bed, but he insists on sleeping under ours, and he gets upset any time we move."

Acila considered the implications of that and bit back a giggle. "Very well, I'll take him." She beckoned to the head carpenter. "I have a small project for you," she told him. "I need a cube, three feet square, solid top, bottom, back and right side, with the left side and front made of latticework and the front hinged on the right so it can swing open."

"Certainly, Lady Acila," the man replied. "How soon do you need it?"

"By this evening, if possible," she replied.

He looked around the shop. "I reckon I can have it done," he said.

"Excellent," Acila smiled at him. "Have it put in my—Lady Druscilla's—bedroom when it's done."

He nodded, but looked at her oddly. "If I may ask . . . what's this for?"

"It's a den for the wolf," Acila replied.

"But, Lady Acila," he protested, looking down at the wolf. "Latice work won't hold that beast if he really wants to get out."

"It doesn't have to hold him like a cage," Acila reassured him, "It's just to give him a den of his own where he'll feel secure."

"Secure?" the man echoed incredulously. "What makes a wolf feel insecure?"

Acila looked down at the wolf, who stood between her and Briam, leaning affectionately against her leg while she absentmindedly rubbed his ear. "Any number of things," she replied. Wolf twitched his ear free of her fingers and tilted his head to look up at the carpenter.

"If you say so." The carpenter did not appear to be convinced of Wolf's alleged timidity, but he went off to cut the wood, shaking his head.

Acila and Briam headed toward the great hall, accompanied by their faithful wolf. "Briam," Acila said softly, after looking around to make sure that no one would overhear her, "are you happy here?"

"Yes, very," Briam said, sounding surprised. "Aren't

you? You have a household to run again, and you were happy doing that before, weren't you?"

"It's a little different running somebody else's household, but I'm happy enough," Acila said. "I'm asking about your feelings, Briam, not mine. Is this what you want to do for the rest of your life—hunt, eat dinner, play music, listen to music, dance a bit . . ." her voice trailed off, but Briam finished the sentence.

"Lie with the Queen at night? Yes, why not? What else should I be doing?" He frowned at her. "You don't want to leave here, do you? I won't hold you if you do; you don't have to stay on my account."

That's what you *think, little brother!* "Do you love the Queen?"

Briam looked at her as if she had taken leave of her senses. "Of course I do; she's my wife!"

Somehow I don't think that's quite the way she sees it. "But what about Druscilla? I thought you loved her."

"Well . . . I like her—she's nice, but she's not even here now—and I'm married to the Queen. What would you have me do?" He sounded totally bewildered.

"Don't you ever think it might be a good thing to leave here?" Acila probed.

"No," Briam said positively. "I couldn't leave the Queen."

"You go out hunting."

"For a little while at a time, but that's different. I don't leave the land."

"The land?"

"The land of which I am King. I can't leave the land, and I won't leave the Queen. And why should I? Don't you like her?" he asked curiously. "I thought you did; everybody likes her."

Oh, no, Acila thought. *He's bewitched. Maybe we all are, because he's right; everybody does like the Queen. Even Druscilla seems to like her as a person, she just doesn't like the Sacrifice—and I like the Queen very much, in spite of knowing that she plans to kill my brother, which doesn't make sense—unless I'm be-witched, too.* "Do you plan to stay here the rest of your life, then?"

"Yes, of course I do!" Briam was thoroughly exasperated. "What on earth is the matter with you these days? We have a home again, a beautiful one, good food, lovely clothes, people who appreciate us. I should think, after the way Father always complained about what you had done every time he came home, that you'd be *happy* to have people like what you do for them! Is this really the time to try to analyze the meaning of life? Can't you ever stop worrying?"

Acila forced herself to smile at him. It didn't feel at all convincing to her, but Briam seemed satisfied. "Maybe not, it seems I've been a worrier all my life."

"Well, try to stop it," Briam advised. "I'll see you at dinner." He patted her shoulder and strode off in the direction of the rooms he shared with the Queen. Acila sighed and headed toward the back garden to think. Predictably enough, Wolf chose to go with her.

Alone in the garden, except for Wolf, who promptly crawled under the bench she was sitting on, she gave herself over to serious thought. Briam was happy enough now, but she didn't think he truly wanted to be sacrificed. He was certainly fond enough of the Queen that her plans for him would come as a dreadful shock, and he wasn't a good enough actor to hide it when he found out—assuming that Acila could ever get him to believe her. He certainly wasn't listening to her now. Before he married the Queen he might have noticed that something was bothering her. Therefore, Acila realized, she couldn't tell him until she was able to get him out of the city—with or without his cooperation.

She would have to take his place at the Sacrifice, that was the only way out of this mess that she could see, but if she would be at the Sacrifice, somebody else would have to take care of Briam. And she'd have to have a good excuse for Acila to be elsewhere if she was going to be Briam; she couldn't be both of them at once. She was going to have to have help.

She considered the degree of help available to her. For rigging the Sacrifice—and perhaps kidnapping the Year-King—it was virtually nil. Obviously, the palace servants would be useless for this, although they were certainly around her all day, ready to do whatever household tasks she assigned, advise her as to how things were traditionally done when she asked for advice. . . . *Now that I think of it,* Acila realized, *the only time there's not at least one servant or guard within earshot, if not in sight, is when I'm alone in my room at night—and then Wolf is with me. The closest thing I get to privacy is when I come here to sit in the garden and look out at the river, and I'd bet that if I screamed, there would be a guard out here before the echoes died out. And the household duties I'm nominally responsible for seem to increase each week. I wonder if the Queen is doing this deliberately, to make sure that I'm busy, watched, and staying out of trouble. That could make changing places with Briam even harder.*

Briam was obviously going to be no help; Acila only hoped he wouldn't be too much of a hindrance when he found out the truth. So who could she get to help her save him?

The Queen had a full schedule: leading public prayers morning and evening, sitting in judgment, reading correspondence from all over her realm, planning for the upcoming Mid-Summer Festival (if she had started any planning for the Sacrifice, she wasn't involving Acila in it), and doing whatever it was she did alone in her private chapel for two hours every afternoon. And while she certainly seemed fond enough of Briam, she wasn't likely to try to save him.

Forcing herself to look at the matter from the Queen's point of view, Acila conceded that there was no reason for her even to think of trying to save Briam. He didn't have lands or responsibilities elsewhere, he had no family save Acila, he didn't have any particular plans for the future . . . in fact, he was virtually perfect as a Year-King. He was young, healthy, and good-looking (suitable for fathering a child), not given to worrying about the future. Briam resembled nothing so much as a farm animal being fattened for the slaughter, which was probably, Acila realized with a shudder, just how the Queen viewed him. She treated him kindly, and as for his coming demise, well, all men die sometime, and there are worse deaths.

The same objections applied to the Shield-Bearer. Although she had known Briam before he became Year-King, it had been too briefly for her to have any feeling for him as a person, a special and unique individual. Living in this culture, she probably didn't get too attached to men anyway; she probably regarded the death of the annual sacrifice the way some men regarded losing several wives in childbirth.

Druscilla, however, had seen Briam as a person, and probably would help if she could. But as long as she was four day's travel away, the help she could give would be limited. If there were only some way to get her back to court! *I have to at least talk to her again,* Acila thought. *She's the only one who knows how Lord Ranulf survived.*

Putting that thought into words, however, made her realize its obvious fallacy. If the Year-King who survived was, in fact, Lord Ranulf, which seemed almost certain, there was one person who knew even better than Druscilla how he had survived. *I can see it now,* Acila thought to herself. *I fly back home, land on the battlements—assuming I don't get shot as I come in—change back to human form, find some clothes—hopefully before anyone sees me wandering around naked—go to Lord Ranulf and say "my brother's been chosen as Year-King and I want to save him—tell me how you survived being sacrificed!"*

Maybe he would help, maybe . . . but he might just as easily say that this is Briam's fate, or that if Briam can't save himself, he should die, or worse—he might come here and tell the Queen what I'm planning, and if she even suspects, I don't have a chance! And if she had a son by him, he may still love her.

Aren't you forgetting something? He wants to marry you.

He wants my father's estates—

He has those—

. . . and he wants me to bear him children.

I wonder where his son is. He wasn't with Lord Ranulf when he invaded, and he doesn't seem to be here. . . .

I wonder about that, too. I'll ask Druscilla when I get a chance.

Yes, you'd better make a chance to talk to her. You could fly there some night—it's a long way by road, but you could fly there and back before dawn if you pushed it.

True, but then Druscilla would know for certain what I am—and I don't think she's ready for that. Haven't you noticed the things she's been careful not to ask me?

Yes, I have. But you had better think of something soon—I don't think you can come up with a workable plan at the last minute. You're going to need help, and time to prepare.

Acila went to dinner still mulling over plans. After asking her for the third time to pass the salt, Wesia was moved to comment on it. "You're rather moody these days, Acila. Are you with child?"

Acila regarded her in astonishment, but Briam jumped to his feet, eating knife in hand, and advanced on the swordswoman. "How dare you? My sister is a proper maiden, not some sluttish servant wench!"

Wesia disarmed him without even rising from her chair. "Sit down, boy."

"My lord," the Queen said softly, as Briam picked up his knife from the floor and sank back into his seat, still glaring, "the Shield-Bearer meant no offense. Why would it be so dreadful if Acila were with child?"

"She can't have a child without a husband!" Briam protested, as if stating some natural law.

"Why not?" Wesia looked amused.

"I am not with child," Acila announced firmly, "and I have no immediate plans in that direction." Time for a quick change of subject. "Did you say that you brought in a deer today, Briam?"

Briam nodded, and the Queen said quickly, "Wonderful! Venison for dinner tomorrow, Acila?" Acila assented, relieved that the Queen had picked up her lead!

"In that case," the Shield-Bearer said, "I'll wait until the next morning before I take the border patrol out. I do love venison."

"You're going away?" Acila asked, secretly delighted. Wesia often seemed to be everywhere at once, and she was a hard person to deceive. "For how long?"

"Depends on how things are in the border country. A few weeks, probably." She smiled across the table at the Queen. "I'll be back for the Mid-Summer Festival. With all the people coming for that, we'll need most of the guards here. You can send if you need me sooner— I'll leave a few guards here to look after things and run messages."

The Queen nodded. "I'm sure we'll be all right here. Acila is being a great help with the preparations for the Festival. It's easy to forget she hasn't lived here all her life." She smiled at Acila, and Acila smiled back. It really was nice to have one's efforts noticed and appreciated.

But Acila saw the troubled look Wesia gave the Queen, and she thought she could almost hear her think, "but she hasn't, and you'd best remember it."

CHAPTER 14

A few days after the Shield-Bearer left, the Queen was taken ill. She came down to breakfast after the morning prayers on the balcony, took one look at the food on the table, pressed a hand to her mouth, and fled the room.

Acila and Briam exchanged concerned looks, then Acila said, "You sit at the head of the table and start eating, so everyone can eat breakfast; I'll go see what's wrong."

"All right," Briam said. "I'm no help when people are sick, anyway."

Acila was not surprised to find the Queen in her bedroom, throwing up into the wash basin. She twisted the Queen's hair, which had come loose, out of the way, and held it clear until the spasm subsided, then dampened a cloth to wipe her face. The Queen thanked her in a faint voice, then collapsed on her bed, startling Wolf, who had followed Acila upstairs and then taken refuge under the bed.

"Don't worry, child," she said. "I'll be fine after I lie still for a while." Her right hand slid protectively to her abdomen.

"I may not be with child," Acila said, "but it certainly looks as though you are."

"Yes," the Queen said with satisfaction, "the Goddess has seen fit to send me a daughter."

"Can you really tell?" Acila asked, "or is it just that you want a daughter?"

"Both," the Queen replied, breathing slowly and

carefully. "I want a daughter, and I know that I carry one. I knew before, when the baby was a son; as soon as I knew I was bearing, I knew it was a boy."

"I didn't know you had a child," Acila lied. "Where is he now?"

"He's with his father," the Queen replied. "He comes to visit sometimes, although," she chuckled, "I think the boy's fonder of the Shield-Bearer than he is of me. Last time he was here, he followed her about like a puppy—or a wolf."

Acila laughed, looking down at the tips of the wolf's paws, which were all that stuck out from under the bed. "Did he crawl under the nearest piece of furniture at every opportunity, too?"

"No, he's not a bit shy." The Queen reached out, snagged an extra pillow, and propped herself up a bit more. "I'll do now, Acila, you go and eat your own breakfast. No need for both of us to starve."

"But you have to eat *something*," Acila protested, "especially if you're with child. If I have the kitchen send you some weak ale and dry bread, can you keep that down?"

"I can try. I'll stay in bed until it's time to start the morning petition hearings, that will give me a chance to digest at least some of it. I can read the correspondence later; I should feel better in the afternoon."

"Fine," Acila said, "I'll send you a tray." She paused, "Are you likely to get better soon, or are you one of the women who's sick for the entire term?"

"It's hard to say." The Queen frowned. "I don't get with child easily; the last time was nine years ago. I had a bad time of it then, but the circumstances were different." She shrugged. "Things will go as the Goddess wills."

"True enough," Acila replied, and went off to the kitchens. *But there's nothing that says we can't ask the Goddess for the outcome we desire.* Then it hit her. *I'm going to be an aunt! What fun! I love babies, and now I'll have one of my own kindred to play with.*

If the Queen lets you anywhere near it once she finds out what you're plotting.

She may not find out. Besides, she obviously knows that Lord Ranulf survives, and it doesn't seem to upset her. She's even letting him raise her son.

And you might wind up helping raise her daughter—she may not survive this birth.

No! Acila felt shocked and horrified at the thought. *She can't die; she's much too alive for that. Besides, she survived last time.*

Nine years ago—and she admits she was very sick then.

We'll just have to take extra care of her, then. I don't want her to die. The realization startled Acila. *I don't want to lose her. Now I understand why Briam can't even consider leaving her. Do you suppose I feel like this because Briam's my twin?*

Probably. So take good care of her—if you don't, Wesia will undoubtedly kill you—and concentrate on how you're going to get Briam out of here before he can be sacrificed, even if he refuses to go.

I think Druscilla will help there. I really do need to talk to her. Acila entered the Hall. Everyone had finished eating by now, Briam had gone off somewhere, and the servants were taking down the tables and starting to set up for the morning's hearing. Acila grabbed a hunk of bread and an apple and went off to the garden to eat, with Wolf still at her heels.

Briam spent the day out, presumably hunting again, and the Queen dragged herself to the morning hearings, then ate dinner, although she appeared to regard her food with trepidation, and disappeared into her chapel. She emerged in time for evening prayers, but when she sat at the supper table, she was so tired she seemed ready to collapse into her plate. Acila, watching her with concern, noted that she took only two bites of her food, then simply shoved it about on her plate.

Briam appeared to be lost in his own thoughts. Acila

wondered if the Queen had told him about the baby, but she wasn't close enough to touch him and use telepathy, and she didn't want to say anything out loud in front of the servants. It was the Queen's place to announce her condition or not, as she pleased, although she obviously wasn't going to be able to keep it secret for long.

The Queen called for the harper to play after supper. Briam, who had been learning from the harper to play a lap harp, picked his up and joined in. He was surprisingly good.

Every so often, Acila thought, *he does something that makes me realize I've underestimated him. Of course, this alternates with incidents that indicate I've badly overestimated him.*

Out of the corner of her eye she saw movement; the Queen was taking advantage of the fact that everyone was listening to the music and slipping quietly away to her room. Acila wondered if she should go after her, but decided that she probably wanted to be left alone. Certainly if she wanted company she had only to ask for it. Privacy was a rare commodity in the palace anyway, and the Queen was still sharing her room with Briam. *In a couple of months she'll probably be happy to be rid of him,* Acila thought irreverently, *if only so she can sleep undisturbed!*

Briam and the harper finished the ballad they were singing and started a popular—and loud—drinking song. Acila got up and quietly went to her room.

She found that she was still feeling uneasy about the Queen—maybe she should check on her.

If there were anything really wrong, surely Briam would know; he is *bound to her,* her other self pointed out. *You'd only feel what Briam did. You probably just had too much wine at supper.*

Acila still felt restless. Making a sudden decision, she shut the wolf in his den, with a command to stay there. Then she took off all her clothes—at least they were enough simpler than Druscilla's that she could undress unaided, even if she needed a maid to lace her up when she dressed. Since no one would expect to see her dressed before morning, she could now shift into any shape she pleased—but what shape should she use? She needed something fairly inconspicuous—like a mouse, perhaps, but that was too dangerous with the number of cats about. A cat? It had been over two months since she had been a wolf in heat; she should be able to become a cat without having to worry about bearing kittens.

She doused all the lights except the night-candle, shifted into a smallish cat, and adjusted the color of her coat for maximum invisibility. She wished that she had the gift the Queen possessed; she could be either the focus of everyone's attention or go totally unnoticed, apparently at will. But Acila would just have to depend on matching the color of the shadows and staying in them. At least she didn't have toenails to click on the floor, the way she had in wolf-shape.

She made it down the hall, past the Shield-Bearer's room, and into the Queen's room without attracting any particular attention, and found the Queen collapsed on her bed, still fully dressed, staring into space.

It was funny, but Acila seemed to be able to feel how the Queen felt; it was rather like the day Briam became Year-King, but that had felt good and this didn't. Not at all.

The Queen lay immobile, feeling nauseated, tired, and very scared. Acila couldn't hear her thoughts, the way she could Briam's, but she could feel sickness and terror. *Is she thinking that she might die with this child's birth? Or, worse, before it?*

In any event, I'm not going to stand here and endure this, and I don't want her to have to either. I hate feeling people suffer. She paced across the room and jumped up onto the bed. The Queen blinked, and turned her head slightly to look at her. Acila walked up to the Queen's hand and butted her head under it, demanding to be petted. The Queen smiled faintly and began to stroke Acila's fur. To Acila's great relief, the hopeless terror in the atmosphere dissipated. She purred happily and curled up at the Queen's side.

When Briam arrived an hour later, he found the Queen sound asleep with Acila still curled up at her side. He looked at them for a moment, shrugged, pulled the bell to summon the Queen's maid. Acila retreated to the windowsill to observe the girl's undressing the Queen and putting her to bed, then slipped quietly back to her own room while Briam was undressing. She was still satisfied with this expedition; Briam hadn't given her a second glance, and if he didn't recognize her it was unlikely that anyone else would. So now she had a shape in which she could prowl about with impunity. And the Queen seemed willing to tolerate her company in this form—which could prove very helpful indeed.

She changed back to human form, unlocked the den, and spent several minutes petting the wolf and telling him how wonderful he was not to make a fuss while she was gone, then crawled into bed. If she was going to be herself *and* a cat, she was going to need all the rest she could get.

The Queen managed to complete prayers the next morning, but her skin had a definite grayish tinge as she tottered past the table and went straight back to her room. Acila grabbed the nearest maid and told her to take the Queen a tray, then went to take her place next to Briam. There was nothing to be gained by starting the whole palace gossiping. Briam frowned at Acila as she sat down. "What's wrong with the Queen?"

So she hasn't told him. Maybe it's not the custom. After all, if the Year-King dies on schedule, he won't be around long enough for her to start showing. Acila reckoned up the time and was horrified to realize that the sacrifice should be taking place in about six weeks—*and the Mid-Summer Festival is in ten days!*

We'll never be ready on time, not with the Queen this sick!

"Acila?" Briam's voice interrupted her thoughts. "What's wrong?"

"I just realized we've only got ten days until the Mid-Summer Festival."

"No, not that," he said impatiently. "What's wrong with the Queen."

"I don't really know," Acila temporized. *If she doesn't want to tell him, it's not for me to do so—even if I am his sister.* "But I can tell you one thing, if she doesn't turn up for the morning hearings, I'm going to call the healers to look at her."

"Good," Briam said, applying himself to his porridge. "I'm going out with some of the townsmen; we're setting up an archery competition to run during the festival."

"Have fun," Acila said lightly, glad to have him out of the way. *It's sad, though,* she thought; *I can remember a time when I would have teased to go with him and join in. How did we grow so far apart?*

Briam finished his breakfast and left; Acila finished hers and supervised the clearing of the tables and the setting up of the hall for the morning hearings. When the Queen hadn't appeared a quarter-hour before they were due to start, Acila went to her room. Her breakfast tray lay untouched beside her bed, and she appeared to be asleep.

"Lady?" Acila bent over and spoke softly. The Queen's eyes opened at once.

"Acila."

At least she recognizes me—but she doesn't look well at all.

"I think you'd better send for a healer, child," the Queen said softly.

"Absolutely." *Never mind discretion, there's a limit to what you can hide.* Acila went quickly into the corridor, leaned over the railing to see who was about in the atrium, and called to the nearest servant to send the healer to the Queen's room at once.

When she returned to the Queen, her eyes were closed again, but she opened them again when Acila reached her side.

"The healer's coming, Lady." Acila reached out and patted the Queen's hand.

"Good." The Queen gripped Acila's hand. "It's time for the morning hearings, isn't it?"

"Yes, and the Hall is set up, but it really doesn't look like you're going to make it down there."

"Not in any condition to sit in judgment," the Queen agreed grimly. "They'll have to be postponed."

"Won't that upset people?" Acila asked.

"Not once the healer has announced my condition," the Queen replied, smiling faintly. "I had to cancel them for a bit before Rias was born, and it's amazing how much people can get settled among themselves when they know that they'll have to wait months for a judgment."

The healer arrived just as the Queen struggled to sit up. "No, you don't, Lady! Just lie still!"

"I'm not dying," the Queen said calmly. "I am with child."

The healer, an elderly woman who did not seem to be at all in awe of the Queen, sniffed. "Tell me something I don't know."

The Queen managed a weak chuckle as she lay flat. "I want you to make a public announcement of my condition; I'm canceling the daily hearings until I feel better."

"I'm glad you're showing that much sense," the healer said, already running her hands over the Queen's body. "You'd better delegate the morning and evening rituals as well."

"You know I can't," the Queen protested. "They must be done by someone of the blood, and I'm the only one here to do them."

"What about Lady Druscilla?" the healer asked.

"She's in the country." The Queen's tone was obviously intended to close that subject. "Acila, I don't want to keep you here all day; I'm sure you have work to do."

Acila curtsied and retreated in nervous silence. She then went straight to the Guard room and asked them to send an escort to bring Druscilla back to the city immediately. If anyone later questioned her decision, she could always claim that she had thought that was what the healer had ordered.

CHAPTER 15

One of the first household tasks Acila had to accomplish that day was to find another room for Briam. The healer ordered him moved out of the Queen's bed so that she could rest without having to worry about him. The healer also pointed out that Briam had already done quite enough for the Queen, but Acila wasn't about to tell Briam that.

There were four rooms at the back of the second floor, overlooking the garden: the large northwest corner room next to the Shield-Bearer's which was Druscilla's; two guest chambers; and another, smaller, room on the southwest corner, which the maids told Acila was used by Rias when he visited. Acila had Briam's things moved to one of the guest chambers. When Druscilla returned, Acila planned to move into the room between them.

The healer had also ordered the Queen to stay in bed all the time she wasn't leading rituals, and it was obvious to Acila that the rituals were quite taxing to the Queen in her current condition.

On the fifth day when she went to give her daily report to the Queen, Acila found her drinking some sort of greenish potion while the healer stood over her, scowling and watching to make sure she finished.

"See if you can talk some sense into her, Lady Acila." The healer treated her with respect, which rather surprised Acila. It was one thing to have the servants think one was wise and capable, but quite another to have people one respected respect one in turn.

"She must stop pushing herself like this—assuming that she wants to have this baby!"

"And I've told you, Healer," the Queen interrupted, "that only someone of the blood can lead the rituals."

"Is the Shield-Bearer of the blood, Lady?" Acila asked. She had wondered about this ever since she had met them; they seemed closer than most sisters.

The Queen looked startled. "No, she's not. She and I have been close friends since we were girls, but she's not kin to me."

"So the only people who could lead rituals would be you, Druscilla, and your children?"

"Our daughters," the Queen corrected absently, "but Druscilla has none, and mine is yet unborn." She put her hands protectively over her womb and bit her lip, obviously more worried about the child than she would admit.

"And as if the daily rituals weren't enough, she's proposing to spend an entire day on display for the Mid-Summer celebration," the healer said in disgust. "My Queen, you'll miscarry for certain if you do that!"

"Do you expect me to cancel the celebration after all the preparations have been made?" the Queen demanded indignantly. She turned to Acila, "Everything is ready, is it not, Acila?"

"Yes, Lady," Acila said miserably, "but I don't see how you can do it, either."

"The Goddess will support me through it," the Queen said grimly. "I can always do what must be done, especially when there's no one else to do it."

"But isn't that why you sent for me?" a soft voice asked from the doorway.

Three heads whipped around and three sets of eyes stared at Druscilla. The healer was the first to recover. "I am most glad to see you, Lady Druscilla. Maybe now the Queen will be able to get the rest she needs."

Druscilla turned a concerned gaze on the Queen. "I shall certainly do what I can to help—within reason—"

As long as it doesn't include sacrificing the Year-King, Acila mentally translated.

"—but what is wrong with you, Lady?"

"Nothing is wrong with me, Druscilla," the Queen said firmly. "I carry the heiress for the City."

Druscilla sagged back against the wall, staring in disbelief.

Acila winced. Wasn't tact considered part of a lady's training here? Then she took a good look at Druscilla, and noticed that she was covered with dust and looked ready to fall over. *The poor girl's probably so tired she doesn't know what she's doing.*

"Lady Druscilla," she said, "why don't you go get some sleep? You look as though you didn't stop on the road at all."

"Good idea," the healer seconded. "Take her away, Lady Acila, and put her to bed, but be sure to get her up in time for her to lead the evening ritual."

Acila nodded and dragged Druscilla from the room before she could make any more unfortunate comments.

"My things are still in your room, Druscilla, but I'll move them this evening, after you've had some sleep. I didn't expect you for at least another three days; you made incredibly good time on the road."

Druscilla winced. "Don't remind me; I'm trying to forget it. The two Guards made it to my estate in a bit less than two days—they arrived at dawn. Then they raided my kitchens, ordered me to throw some undershifts into a saddlebag, shoved me onto the extra relay horse they'd brought, and off we went. I lost track of the time; it feels as though I've been riding with the Wild Hunt throughout all eternity, and oh, I ache all over."

Acila reckoned on her fingers. "It's been almost exactly four days since I sent for you, so you rode only two days—but I can believe it seemed like an eternity."

"*You* sent for me?" Druscilla said in surprise. "I thought the Queen did, or at least the Shield-Bearer."

"She's out patrolling the borders," Acila replied. "I considered sending for her, but I think she'll be back as soon as she can anyway, and we needed someone who could take the Queen's place in the rituals. Besides, I wanted to talk to you."

"Yes," Druscilla said, stifling a yawn. "I think you and I have a lot to talk about." Then, as they entered her room, "Goddesses Above and Below, what is that?"

It was easy enough to guess what she meant; Acila had added only one thing to the room's furnishings. "It's a den for the wolf."

"You mean I have to *sleep* with that beast?"

"No, of course not. He's off with Briam someplace, and I'll have the den moved out this evening, along with my clothes. You'd better get some sleep before you get dragged out to do the evening ritual. By the way, do you know the ritual?"

"Yes, of course." Druscilla dragged the covers back and slipped into the bed. "I've done the daily rituals for the past year—until the Queen sent me away. And the Mid-Summer ritual is easy; it's mostly just standing around letting the people see us."

"Us?"

"The Lady and the Year-King." Druscilla closed her eyes. "Draw the bed curtains, and close the door as you leave, please."

Acila did as she was bid, and then went to order the servants to make up a bed for her in the room between Druscilla's and the one Briam was now occupying.

Then she returned to the Queen's room. The healer had left, and the Queen was resting, but she was awake and turned her head as Acila walked in.

"There you are, Acila," she smiled. "Did you get Druscilla settled?"

"Yes," Acila replied. "She's in her room, sleeping, and I'll make sure she's up and dressed for the evening ritual."

"Excellent," the Queen said. "Thank you, Acila."

The tension which had been keeping her going of late suddenly seemed to melt out of her body, and she looked more relaxed than she had since she became ill. She closed her eyes and to all appearances fell asleep instantly.

Acila tiptoed silently out of the room.

Druscilla got up, performed the evening ritual, and told Acila not to bother moving her things just yet. "I'll sleep in the guest chamber next to my room; you can keep my room—and the wolf," she looked at the wolf, sprawled at Acila's feet, and shuddered, "for the time being. I'm too tired tonight to want to move anything."

Acila regarded her with sympathy. "That's fine with me. The bed in the guest chamber is already made up; I had it prepared this afternoon while you slept. At the moment both of our wardrobes are in your room, but since we're next door to each other, your maid can just come to get what you need."

"Very well." Druscilla looked as if she didn't care at all about her clothes. In fact, she still looked near to asleep on her feet.

"I can have a tray brought to you if you'd rather not sit up for supper," Acila offered.

"Thank you," Druscilla said gratefully. "I'm still very tired. I would be happy to go straight back to bed."

"Go ahead, then," Acila said. "I'll give your regards to Briam when he comes in for supper."

Druscilla had turned to go, but at that she looked back over her shoulder at Acila. "Do that," she said, "and tomorrow you and I have to have a *long* talk."

"Indeed," Acila agreed. "Rest well."

The next morning, after the ritual and a quick breakfast with Briam, who was happy to see Druscilla again, the two girls retired to the back garden, accompanied by the wolf. Druscilla was not happy about that, but she confined herself to a sigh and a lot of sideways glances to make sure she always knew where the beast was.

The wolf paced about the garden courtyard with the soft clicking of claws, then lay down, sprawled across Acila's feet. Druscilla shrank away, shuddering. "I know it's silly of me," she admitted, "but every time I see that wolf, I seem to see Lord Ranulf's shadow hovering over him."

"Count your blessings," Acila said briskly. "I met Lord Ranulf when he crawled over the windowsill into my bedroom in the middle of the night. He was a six-foot spider at the time."

"Yuck!" Druscilla said with true feeling. "What did you do?"

"Grabbed the nearest torch." Acila grinned. "He never got beyond the windowsill."

Druscilla laughed, then sobered abruptly. "I didn't realize you knew Lord Ranulf."

"Unless there are two men by that name wandering around with blue circles on their foreheads, he's the man who captured our estate."

"It sounds like the same man," Druscilla said uncertainly.

"And he mentioned a son named Rias," Acila added, "so I really think he must be the same one. But he's not here now, and we have other problems. Will they let you leave the city the morning of the Sacrifice?"

"Let me?" Druscilla laughed bitterly. "They'll make me! They don't want me here at all. Furthermore, they intend to make certain that you come with me."

"Good," Acila said briskly. "That may be helpful. Now you said that the Year-King jumps into the river at the waterfall, right?"

"Yes," Druscilla nodded. "Off that terrace above the falls—the one at the north side of the city."

Acila made a mental note to examine the place for herself. "Has anyone other than Lord Ranulf ever survived the sacrifice?"

Druscilla shook her head. "Not that I know of."

"How did Lord Ranulf survive?" This was the one question Acila really had to have answered.

"He survived because he's a horrible, unnatural, in-human monster," Druscilla stated flatly.

Acila's "Druscilla, that's not much help" blended with a childish treble from the top of the wall behind her.

"Don't you *dare* talk about my father like that!" The outraged voice changed into a snarl as a half grown wolf cub jumped from the wall straight onto Druscilla's lap.

To call the next few moments chaotic, Acila thought later, would have been a gross understatement. Wolf dove under the bench Acila was sitting on and disappeared from sight, Acila jumped up to pull the cub from Druscilla, and Druscilla, in her frantic attempt to put as much distance between the wolf cub and herself as possible, fell into the pool in the middle of the garden.

Acila grappled with the cub until she had him pinned down as she had done with the pack leader months ago in the woods. She risked a quick glance at Druscilla, who, soaking wet and with her clothes weighing her down and clinging to her so that she could scarcely move, was now climbing awkwardly out of the pool on its far side.

"Go get some dry clothes, Druscilla," she advised. "I'll deal with Rias. I assume this is Rias?" It seemed a safe assumption.

"I can't claim to recognize every hair on his body," Druscilla snapped, "but I'd hate to think there were any *more* of them wandering about! And *he* is not supposed to be here during the summer anyway. He's only allowed to visit during the winter." She dripped her way out of the courtyard.

Acila turned her full attention back to the wolf cub. He wasn't trying to get loose or bite her hands, but his angry brown eyes looked straight into hers and held her gaze. *A real wolf would look away.*

This isn't a real wolf. Can you stare down an angry child?

Acila looked calmly into his eyes for several moments. Except for the occasional involuntary blink, neither of them moved. Rias still looked furious. Acila wondered what he was so upset about. This seemed to be an overly strong reaction to Druscilla's admittedly extremely rude comments about his father. *And what is he doing here? Surely he's supposed to be somewhere else with somebody watching him. Someone is probably worried about him.*

She released one paw and started to scratch his chest. A palm-sized patch of fur moved under her fingers, and Rias suddenly starting fighting to free himself. Acila grabbed his paw again and held on, watching the area that had moved. As he thrashed about under her she noted that the patch of fur appeared to be strapped to him with thin cords which would normally be hidden by his fur. One of them snapped in the struggle, and Acila released a paw long enough to grab the patch of fur, discovering as she did so that it was a thin pouch, camouflaged with glued-on fur. *The fur must have been easy enough to come by—a wolf sheds enough in a week to cover another wolf.*

She released Rias and sat back to examine it. It opened on the non-fur side and held several sheets of closely written parchment. "This is really ingenious, Rias. Did you make this?"

Rias growled and snapped at her hands. She turned and glared at him. "No," she said firmly. "Stop that." Rias continued to growl. "I'm warning you, Rias. I know you're an intelligent human. *Act like one!*"

Rias snapped at her again, and Acila decided enough was enough. As he lunged toward her she swung her free arm under his rib cage and tossed his body into an arc that ended in the pool The edges were high enough that he wouldn't be able to get out of there without changing back to human shape.

While he was still splashing around, she glanced quickly at the parchment he had found important enough to carry around with him in wolf shape. She recognized it from the first sentence. It was the formula she had used to change herself into a sword, obviously copied from the scroll in the temple library at home. She checked quickly. Yes, the entire formula was there: both the recipe for the potion and the spell to activate it.

The splashing from the pool had stopped now. Acila looked up to see a small boy with a towel wrapped around his waist approaching her. "Give it back." He extended a hand.

Acila handed him the parchment, studying him carefully. He was small for his age, and pitifully thin. His hair was dark and needed cutting, and his eyes looked hurt and cynical.

"Well?" he said after a moment's silence. "Aren't you going to start asking a lot of questions?"

"Just one," Acila said. "Where did you get that?" She indicated the parchment.

"I found the library my father was looking for," he said with pride. "*He* couldn't find it, and then he went haring off after *her.*" There was a wealth of disgust on the last word.

"It must have been a well-hidden library—or a very small one."

"It's big," Rias said simply. "But the entrance is hidden under an altar, you have to press the right cloud carvings to open it."

The cloud carvings on the Sky Father's altar. So this is our new priest. Acila felt stunned.

You were younger than he is when the Maiden chose you.

But I already lived there. He's never been there before in his life. I wonder what Marfa and Galin think of this.

Aloud she asked, "Does anyone else know you found the library?"

"No," Rias shook his head. "Nobody cares what I do these days," he added resentfully. And then the words just poured out—as if nobody had listened to the poor child in months. "My father left me behind when he rode out on campaign last fall, even though I begged to go. I'm old enough to run messages at least, and Father doesn't take stupid chances in his campaigns. I would have been safer with him than left behind to risk death from boredom. He captured an old temple way up in the mountains, and he only lost *one* man doing it! They say that the lady there was a powerful sorceress, and she turned herself into a magic sword so that her twin brother could use her to kill a man in single combat and win his freedom. Then she changed back, bathed in her victim's blood—and my father asked her to marry him!"

"What did your father say about these stories?" Acila asked curiously.

"He said she was a shapechanger, just as he was, and yes, he did intend to marry her." Rias scowled. "She refused to marry him; she rode away into the forests with her brother and no one has seen them since, but as soon as things were running smoothly on the estate Father left the Steward in charge and set off to find her."

"He did?" Acila asked uneasily. *Then where is he now? He probably couldn't find me while I was living with the wolves, but now that I'm back in human form and living here. . . .*

"Yes," Rias snapped. "He did. I barely even got to see him before he left. I'm just a disappointment to him 'cause I can't change properly. That why he wants to marry *her*, so that he can have children who are *real* shapechangers. He can turn himself into any animal that exists and quite a few that don't, and *she* can apparently turn herself into anything at all, alive or not, but the only thing I can be, other than human, is a wolf. It's not fair! They'll all turn into birds and fly off, and leave me alone. And Father won't care. After all, once he has children who are really like him, he won't need me, will he?"

Acila found herself totally at a loss for an answer to that question. She knew only too well what it was to feel like a freak whose father didn't approve of her.

"As for my mother," Rias continued bitterly, "I'm allowed to visit her only for a couple of months in the winter—and you saw what Druscilla thinks of me."

"She *was* awfully rude," Acila agreed.

"Spring, summer, and autumn I spend with my father—or wherever he leaves me. And Eagle's Rest is an incredibly boring place to be left. The Steward's in charge, but he and everybody else there are moping around missing *her*. Nobody seems to miss the brother. He must be a total idiot, but they all want *her* back. So I poked around until I found the library—and this," he waved the hand holding the parchment. "It looks as if it might be very useful. Maybe it will let me change to other things. Right now, I'm not a real shape-changer—I'm just a werewolf."

"But the moon isn't full," Acila protested, "so you can't be a true were-anything. Do you mean that wolf shape is the only nonhuman shape you've mastered?"

Rias nodded. "But this will let me change to *anything*."

Acila decided that this was not the moment to explain the disadvantages involved in that particular formula.

"Why come here with it? Why not stay at Eagle's Rest and experiment there?"

"I need Druscilla's help with the potion."

Acila stared at him. "You expect *Druscilla* to help you with a shapechanging potion?" she asked incredulously.

Rias nodded.

"But Druscilla hates shapechangers!"

Rias grinned. "Not as much as she hates wolves. Besides, I've got ways to persuade her."

CHAPTER 16

Druscilla walked into the garden just then, dressed in a loose robe and carrying a bundle of cloth and a tray full of food. Setting the tray on a bench, she tossed the bundle at Rias.

"I went by your room and got you some clothes," she said. "Get dressed and eat something; I suppose you're starved, as usual."

Rias's thanks were muffled as he pulled a tunic over his head. Then he sat down on the bench with the tray and tore into the food with single-minded concentration.

Druscilla picked up the towel he had dropped and tossed it into the basket for the servants to wash. Then she sat down on the bench beside Rias, nearly sitting on the parchment as she did so. "What's this?" she asked, picking it up and starting to read it.

Acila, seated on the opposite bench, watched Druscilla's face as she read through the parchment. Druscilla did not seem as horrified by it as Acila had expected. *Maybe Rias is right. Maybe it is wolves she doesn't like, not shapechangers.*

"Interesting," Druscilla murmured. "What are you doing with this, Rias?"

"I want to try it out," Rias mumbled around the meat he was chewing. "Will you make up the potion for me, please?"

Druscilla eyed him suspiciously. "Why should I?"

Rias swallowed his food and smiled up at her. "Because if you don't," he said, "I'll tell the Queen that you told me about the Year-King and the Sacrifice."

Druscilla's jaw dropped. She looked at him in horror and then turned to Acila. "Acila, you didn't!"

"Tell him?" Acila asked. "Of course not! I'm not supposed to know either, remember? I'll bet his father told him."

"Years ago," Rais said, then did a double-take. "*Acila?* You're *her,* aren't you?" he asked accusingly.

" 'She,' not 'her,' " Acila correctly automatically. "Yes, I am, but I haven't seen your father since the day of the duel."

Rias frowned. "But that was almost a year ago," he said. "Where *is* he?"

Acila shrugged.

Rias looked her up and down, as if trying to form an opinion. "And if you're here, where is your brother? I thought you went with him to look after him."

Druscilla raised her eyebrows at that. "Lord Briam is out with his Companions."

Rias, who had just taken another bite of food, choked on it. When he had his breath back, he started laughing. "Your brother is the Year-King? You're not doing very well at taking care of him, are you?" He doubled over with laughter, obviously finding this hilariously funny.

Both girls were easily able to refrain from joining in the laughter. As they sat waiting for Rais to get control of himself again, it occurred to Acila that the boy might be a valuable source of information.

"Just how much did your father tell you?" she asked, when Rias's laughter had diminished to the snickering stage. "Do *you* know how he survived?"

"Turned into a fish and let the undertow take him down river," Rias said calmly. "Not that it's going to help you much. How long can your brother breathe underwater?"

Druscilla bit her lip. "It would have to be a long

time," she said. "People line up along the river the length of the city and throw flowers in to mark the Year-King's grave."

"That's just great," Acila sighed. "Well, we've still got several weeks to think of something." She reached over and took a piece of fruit from the tray. Worrying always made her hungry.

"About my potion," Rias began.

"I'll think about it." Druscilla frowned at him. "Don't push your luck; you'll have enough trouble explaining to the Queen what you're doing here at this time of year."

"And you should at least send a message to Galin," Acila added. "I know he'll be worried about you."

Rias grinned cheekily at her. "Why don't *you* go tell him?"

Acila smiled blandly back. "I'm busy with the preparations for the Mid-Summer Festival," she said. She turned to Druscilla. "The Shield-Bearer left a few of the Guards here to run messages—do you suppose we could send one of them?"

Druscilla shrugged. "I don't see why not. You'll need to give directions on how to get there. How far is it, anyway?"

"I'm not sure, exactly," Acila admitted. "I took a rather round-about way getting here."

"So you did," Druscilla agreed. "Rias, how long did it take you?"

Rias shrugged one shoulder and kept chewing.

"He probably doesn't know," Acila said. "A lot of the way is through the forests. Since I doubt he took that route as a naked human, he must have been a wolf, and I don't think wolves have much of a time sense."

"I've never seen Wolf miss meal time," Druscilla pointed out.

"That's different from counting days," Acila argued.

Rias swallowed another mouthful. "It was moon dark the night I left," he said, stuffing another piece of meat in his mouth.

The girls looked at each other and counted on their fingers. "Five days as the wolf runs," Acila said finally.

"Apparently without stopping to eat on the way," Druscilla added. "Rias, remember that it will be dinner time in less than two hours."

"Don't worry," said Rias around his food. "I'll have room for dinner."

Druscilla shook her head. "I'll leave you to finish your 'snack,' " she said. "I've got to go put some more clothes on."

Rias grunted absently as she left and continued to eat. Acila shifted to his bench and picked up the parchment. Reading through the formula again, after having used it, she noticed just how vague it was about the results you could achieve with it.

"Rias," she said gently, "I'm not at all sure that this spell will help you. What you really want is to be able to fly, right?"

Rias nodded, still chewing.

"But you do want to be awake and have your mind still working, don't you?"

Rias gave her an "are you crazy?" look and nodded.

"Well, the one time I used this spell," she definitely had his complete attention now, "to turn myself into a sword—you heard about that, didn't you?"

He nodded again.

"From the beginning of the change until I found myself on the field at the end of the duel, I wasn't aware of anything. One minute I was turning into a sword, and the next minute I was changing back. There was absolutely nothing in between. And, of course, the change back is not something you can control. Somebody else has to dip you in either sea water or blood—and the river here is fresh water, so that leaves blood. Needing a supply of someone else's blood to change form is awkward, to say the least."

Rias frowned, looking thoughtful. "Druscilla doesn't know you're a changer, does she?" he asked.

Acila shook her head. "Briam knows, and you and your father know—and probably everyone at home knows by now."

Rias shook his head. "Father told them it was a magic spell."

"The sword part was," Acila agreed, "and it's not something *I* ever want to do again!"

"But nobody here knows," Rias said, coming to a decision. "If you teach me how to fly, I won't tell anybody."

"Is blackmail your normal method of operation?" Acila asked.

Rias nodded and grinned. "Knowledge is power—at least that's what Father always said when I complained about being so small; he just told me to study harder."

"I'm not sure this is exactly what he had in mind," Acila said, "but I'll do my best to teach you to fly anyway. Because you want to learn, *not* because you threaten to tell people my secret." She stood up, still holding the parchment. "I have to get back to work. Take the tray back to the kitchen when you're finished with it, please, and I'll see you at dinner."

Rias nodded, stuffing a large chunk of bread into his mouth.

Acila went to find the housekeeper and order his room made up for him.

Briam and his Companions all appeared at dinner. The Queen had a tray in her room, and while Acila suspected that she had been told that Rias had arrived, at least nobody was asking awkward questions at the table. Briam acknowledged the introduction absent-mindedly and continued his discussion of the forthcoming archery contest with his Companions, and the Companions tried, with a fair degree of success, to pretend that it was normal to have Rias around at this time of year.

Acila dragged Briam aside for a brief talk at the end of the meal.

"Lord Ranulf left Rias at Eagle's Rest, and Rias ran away from there. We have to send him back."

"Why? Is Lord Ranulf after him?" Briam bent to scratch Wolf, who was standing between the twins, behind the ears. As Druscilla had pointed out that morning, Wolf never missed a meal. "And even if he is, why worry? He's not going to blame *you* for his son's running away."

"That's not the point," Acila protested. "He has to go back because the Sky Father has chosen him to be His new priest."

Wolf cocked his head and looked up at Acila. He appeared considerably more interested in what she was saying than Briam was.

"So what? You're the Maiden's priestess, and you're here."

Acila ground her teeth. *Sometimes Briam is so exasperating.* "Are you saying that you can dispense with my presence here and that *I* should take him home?"

"No, of course I'm not!" Briam protested. "Stop twisting what I'm saying; you're my sister and you're supposed to be with me. I just meant that if the Gods don't care whether you're there, they shouldn't care whether he is either."

"I'm sending a letter to Galin about this," Acila informed him. "He must be worried at the very least; Lord Ranulf left Rias in his charge. Do you have any messages for Galin or Marfa or anyone else there?"

Briam shook his head. "No, not really. You can tell them where we are and how we're doing, and I'm sure that you'll say everything that is proper."

He turned and wandered over to join his Companions who were talking to Druscilla and Rias. Acila followed him, and Wolf followed her.

"Let's go hunting tomorrow," Briam said. "We haven't been out of the city in days." He turned to Rias. "Do you want to come with us?" Several of the Companions looked quietly appalled.

I imagine they don't care for the prospect of having

to watch out for both Briam and *Rias while hunting,*
Acila thought.

Rias looked questioningly at Wolf. "Does the wolf
go with us?" he asked after a moment.

Briam shrugged. "Usually he does. Sometimes,
though, you can't pry him away from Acila. He'll do
what he wants."

Rias grinned, the look of a child with a secret.
"Thank you, I would like to come with you. I've never
been on a King's hunt."

"That's settled, then," Briam said. "We'll leave right
after breakfast tomorrow."

Rias appeared at breakfast the next morning looking
pale and haunted. Acila hoped that she didn't look as
bad as he did, although she certainly felt as bad as he
looked.

"Bad dreams?" she asked quietly, slipping into place
next to him. Wolf quietly lay down under the bench
they sat on.

Rias cast her a startled look. "You really are a sorceress, aren't you?"

"Not exactly," Acila said. "I'm the priestess of the
Lady of Fire, and She's not too happy with my absence
from Her altar. What you probably didn't realize is that
the Sky Father has chosen you to be His priest."

"Is that why I dreamed I was being blown all over
the sky?" Rias looked crestfallen. "I thought maybe it
meant I was going to learn how to fly."

"It might mean that, too," Acila said consolingly.
"But which way were you being blown?"

"Back to Eagle's Rest," Rias admitted. "I could see
the walls, and Galin and Marfa were standing there—
except it wasn't exactly them—and Marfa was calling
me . . . it was a really strange dream." His voice trailed
off uncertainly.

"Marfa is the priestess of the Earth Mother and
Galin serves the Lord of Water." Acila spelled it out
matter-of-factly. Rias would just have to get used to

this. "You probably saw the Gods overshadowing them, which is why they looked different." *I know that's what I saw.* "I think they're just upset that both of us are away."

"But I've been away for days," Rias protested, "and I haven't had any dreams like that until last night."

"Until yesterday," Acila pointed out softly, "you were a wolf. That does make a difference in your dreams."

Rias shrugged. "You should know about that," he said, also keeping his voice low. "But what makes you think the Sky Father has chosen me as his priest?"

"You found the library," Acila explained. "Only the priests can get into the library; it won't even open if someone else is in the room. I tried to show it to Briam once and it didn't work."

"And the Sky Father is the priest you didn't have when I came?"

"The old priest died last winter—no, the winter before last," Acila said, "but the reason I know that it is the Sky Father that chose you is your description of how you got into the library."

She saw the realization in his face. "The clouds on the Sky altar," he said. "You get in differently, don't you? You'd have to use something on the Fire altar."

"Exactly," Acila said. *Good, he's already beginning to figure this out. It shouldn't be too hard to train him to do the ritual. I wish I could take him myself.* A sudden wave of homesickness washed over her.

Rias looked closely at her. "You miss the place." It was not exactly a question.

Acila nodded. "You may complain that it's boring, but I *like* boring."

Rias looked past Acila and Druscilla at Briam, who was laughing with his Companions. "Compared to the mess you're in now, I guess you would." He looked down at his plate. "Can I still go hunting with them?" he asked. "Or is something awful going to happen to me if I don't go straight back?"

Acila shrugged. "Except for the dream, nothing much has happened to me—unless you count Briam's being Chosen," she whispered. "You'll undoubtedly have strange dreams until you do go back, but you can probably handle that for a few days. I still think you should go back as soon as you can, though."

Rias looked sideways at her. "So should you, shouldn't you?" he asked. "You're having the dreams, too."

"Yes," Acila nodded. "And I do plan to go back as soon as I can—as soon as Briam is safe. Some nights the Maiden seems to understand that; after all, she has a brother, too."

"Are you going to marry my father, then?"

Good question. "I don't know." Acila took a bite of her breakfast and chewed it carefully to give herself time to think. "I don't know if your father really *wants* to marry me."

"Of course he does!"

"No, you don't understand. He doesn't even *know* me. I don't want to marry someone because he's interested in my heritage, or certain 'talents' I might have. When I marry, it'll be because my husband wants *me* because he loves me as a person. And since your father hasn't really had a chance to know me—" the words poured out of her in a rush, "I've been a *thing*—to my father and a lot of other people—all my life, and I don't want to be married as a *thing*. I want to be a person!"

Rias was staring at her, and even Druscilla, who was not a morning person, seemed to have noticed her last outburst. Acila blushed. "I guess that sounds pretty crazy," she sighed.

Rias shook his head. "No," he said slowly, "I think I know what you mean."

"So do I," Druscilla said quietly from Acila's other side. "I was the Queen's heiress, and then she decided that I wasn't good enough, so she's going to get another heiress. It's like I'm a building stone or something that can be replaced, as long as the replacement part is sufficiently similar."

Acila nodded. "And I don't want to be married as a 'suitable' bride."

Briam and his Companions began to get up from the table. "Rias," Briam called, "are you coming or do you plan to dawdle over breakfast all morning?"

Rias jumped up. "I'm coming," he said quickly. "I can always get something to eat while we're hunting."

Acila grabbed his arm and held on long enough to whisper in his ear. "Don't snack on raw mice; it upsets the people with you, and the bones are hard to digest in human form."

Rias looked startled, and then laughed. "I'll remember," he promised.

Acila released him. "Have fun, and be careful."

The hunting party left, accompanied by Wolf, and Druscilla turned a teasing look on Acila. "Are you sure you don't want to be the boy's stepmother?" she asked "You sound like his mother already."

Actually, Acila thought, *I can think of worse fates.* "He's a nice enough boy," she replied lightly. "Besides, I'm his aunt by marriage."

Druscilla blinked. "That's right. You are—at least for the moment."

CHAPTER 17

"Lady," Acila asked when she went in to visit the Queen the afternoon before the Mid-Summer Festival, "has anyone coached Briam for his part in tomorrow's ritual?"

The Queen looked at her in concern. "I thought you had."

Acila shook her head. "I don't know the ritual; I just arranged for the decorations and the dais to be set up, and the steward told me what needed to be done for that. And the cooks were here last year, so they knew what was expected for food. But, as far as I know, all that Briam has been preparing for is the archery contest. If his Companions have been coaching him for the ritual, he hasn't told me."

"Find Briam and send him to me after supper, then, and I'll tell him what he needs to do," the Queen said. "And I'll see Druscilla after the evening ritual; she's seen the Mid-Summer ritual, but she's never done it before." She sighed. "It's probably just as well that she's here, but I do hope that she'll continue to behave herself—"

Her voice trailed off, and Acila was reminded that she wasn't supposed to know the nature of Druscilla's previous misbehavior.

"She seems to be doing well enough, Lady," Acila said reassuringly.

"Yes, she can be amazingly capable when she wants to be," the Queen admitted. "I only hope that she will decide she wants to do the ritual well. At least she's

not likely to faint or become ill in the middle of it."
She sighed sadly.

"It's not easy to stand back and watch someone else
doing your work, is it?" Acila sympathized. "I felt awful when I had to leave my home and people in someone else's hands." She blinked back sudden tears; this
was not a subject she usually permitted herself to think
about. "I only hope he'll be good to my people."

The Queen raised her eyebrows. "Knowing you,"
she said, "I'm surprised you didn't disguise yourself as
the housekeeper and stay to look after things yourself."

"I might have if I could have gotten away with it,"
Acila admitted. "But Lord Ranulf knew I existed, and
one of his men would have pointed me out. He planned
to kill Briam, marry me, and use me to bear him children for his new estate. At least when Briam and I
fled, he couldn't pretend that he hadn't invaded and
conquered our home. And I had to take care of Briam;
there was no one else to do that." Then she looked at
the Queen's white face and realized what she had said.
*Oh, no, I should never have mentioned Lord Ranulf's
name!*

But the Queen was apparently thinking of something
else. "You're very protective of your brother, aren't
you?"

Acila forced herself to smile and shrug. "I suppose
most of it is just habit by now. After all, he is a grown
man and can probably take care of himself."

"He certainly seems capable enough to me."

For what you need him for, he is, Acila thought.

The Queen sighed. "I only hope that Druscilla be-
haves as well as he does."

"You don't trust her, do you?" Acila said slowly.

"Not entirely." The Queen frowned. "Last spring she
ran off into the forests to avoid taking part in a ritual—
and she is *not* suited to life in the wild."

"I should think not!" Acila forced a laugh. "And unless she swapped clothing with her maid, I can't see

how she could get beyond the city gates, let alone into the woods."

"It was certainly very odd behavior for her," the Queen agreed, "and it disturbs me that she would do something so incomprehensible; it makes it impossible to predict what she might do next."

"I see what you mean," Acila said slowly.

"Well, we'll just have to hope for the best," the Queen said. "I admit that it is a relief not to have to do the rituals, and I was dreading the festival tomorrow. I didn't think I could ever feel as sick as I did when I was pregnant with Rias, but I'd almost swear that it's even worse this time." She shook her head. "But it's probably just that my memory has mercifully faded over the last ten years. Be sure to send Briam to me immediately after supper."

Briam was delighted by the summons. "I shall be glad to go to her; I haven't seen her in days. How is she, Acila?"

Acila shrugged. "About the same."

Briam frowned in concentration. "There's something you aren't telling me," he complained. "Why is she sick, and why am I not allowed to sleep with her anymore?"

"So she's thrown you out, has she?" Druscilla had come up behind them on the dais. Acila and Rias hastily moved over so that Druscilla could take the center position at the high table, while the servant quickly set down the platter and withdrew beyond the range of normal conversation.

Druscilla sat down and continued, "I guess she feels that you've served your purpose, and she has no more need of you—for a while anyway," she added bitterly.

"What do you mean?" Briam asked, politely, if automatically, serving Druscilla from the platter in front of him.

"You know the truth, Acila," Druscilla said accusingly. "Why didn't *you* tell him?"

"Because it's the Queen's place to tell him, not mine," Acila retorted, forcing a smile on her face. "And, please Druscilla, lower your voice and try to look pleasant; people are starting to stare at us."

"You're as bad as she is!" Druscilla snapped in a furious whisper. "Act like a lady, don't upset things, don't disturb the Sacrifice—"

"What sacrifice?" Briam asked. Acila quickly looked around to see if anyone had overheard them. No one had, but what she saw at the far end of the Hall made her feel faint. The Shield-Bearer was back. At the moment her attention appeared to be focused on Rias, but if she heard any of this conversation, that would change in a hurry.

"Druscilla, for the love of the Lady," Acila pleaded. "The Shield-Bearer's heading this way. If she suspects we're plotting anything, she'll watch us constantly. Act innocent, if you possibly can—and if you can manage stupid, so much the better."

Sudden comprehension flashed across Druscilla's face. "Understood," she murmured, blanking her expression and turning her attention to her plate.

Briam, however, didn't understand anything. "Would one of you please tell me what's wrong with my wife?"

Druscilla stared at him; obviously she had never heard anyone refer to the Queen as "my wife." "She's with child, Briam."

"What?" Rias yelped.

"Really?" Briam's face lit up. "That's wonderful! Did you hear that, Acila? I'm going to be a father!"

The Shield-Bearer came to stand behind Rias just in time to hear Briam's announcement. Her face turned white, and Acila hastily shoved a cup of wine into her hand. Wesia downed it and the color came back into her face, but when she set the goblet down, her jaw was set and she looked at Briam as if she wanted to kill him herself. Now.

* * *

Wesia curtly refused to join them for supper and strode off toward the Queen's rooms. Acila hastily excused herself, ordered the wolf to stay under the table at Briam's feet, fled to Druscilla's room, shed her clothes as fast as she could get out of them, and changed into her cat shape.

When she slipped into the Queen's room less than ten minutes after the Shield-Bearer had left the atrium, she was relieved to see that the Queen was asleep. Wesia sat beside her bed, watching her as if she were afraid to take her eyes off her. Acila curled up on the windowsill and began grooming herself, being careful to present the picture of a cat with no concern beyond the condition of her coat.

It was a good half-hour before the Queen started to stir, and Wesia hadn't moved the entire time. But when the Queen's eyelids flickered, Wesia leaned forward and put a hand on her shoulder.

"Wesia?" The Queen turned to smile at her. "Good, you're back. How are things on the borders?"

"Well enough," Wesia said briskly. "But how are things with you? I leave you for only a couple of weeks, and look at you! How could you get into this state?"

The Queen reached up to pat Wesia's hand. "I find it difficult to believe that you have attained your present age and rank without at least theoretical knowledge of the process—even if you have never borne a child yourself." She looked around and added, "Where's Briam?"

"What do you want with him?" the swordswoman snarled. "I should think he's done quite enough already. Don't tell me you're still sleeping with him!"

"No," the Queen chuckled, "and that's exactly what the healer said when she ordered me to move him elsewhere. I think he's sleeping over the back garden near Acila."

"And Druscilla?"

The Queen frowned. "Acila was sleeping in Druscilla's

room, but she said she would move and put Druscilla back there. . . ."

Her voice trailed off, and the two women regarded each other in silence. "Yes," the Queen admitted, "we may have a problem there."

"Maybe, and maybe not," Wesia said. "They were bickering at the high table when I came in. What is Druscilla doing back here anyway? And *why* is Rias here?"

The Queen thought for a moment. "Now that you ask, I don't know. My mind isn't functioning all that clearly these days, and when Druscilla came in one day and said that the guards had come and dragged her back here at top speed, I thought you had sent for her—but you weren't here and didn't know I was ill. I do need her, of course, because I can't possibly stand through the presentation tomorrow, but I don't remember sending for her, and when she arrived, frankly, I was feeling too sick to care how or why she was here.

"As for what Rias is doing here, I have absolutely no idea. Acila told me that he had run away from the place where Lord Ranulf left him, and she asked leave to send a message to the steward there, so I imagine that someone will come to collect him in a few days. Druscilla hasn't been complaining about him, so he must have stopped teasing her the way he did last winter. The housekeeper reported to me when he arrived; she put him in his usual room. Yesterday he went hunting with the Year-King and his Companions, and they all came back safely, so he appears not to be causing trouble."

"And if someone doesn't come to collect him before summer's end?" Wesia asked.

"Then you can provide an escort to take him back to wherever his father left him." The Queen smiled up at Wesia. "I have every confidence in your ability to handle Rias."

"And Druscilla?" The Shield-Bearer's eyebrows rose skeptically.

The Queen shrugged. "She's here now, and she's needed here. Acila has been working very hard managing the household, but that's a full-time job, and she can't do the morning and evening rituals in any case. So Druscilla can take over my religious duties, she and Alicia can share the rest of the work between them. Right now, I can barely handle the correspondence. Any complicated problems can be referred to me—or to you, if I get any sicker. But I shouldn't; I usually do well enough as long as I stay in bed."

Wesia scowled. "I still don't like it, but there's not much we can do about it now. Done is done, and, in any case, Druscilla won't do at all as your heiress." She leaned over to stroke the Queen's hair. "You have a care to yourself; remember that we need both you and your daughter to come out of this healthy. It is a daughter, isn't it?"

"Of course," the Queen replied, shifting to prop herself up higher on the pillows. "I wouldn't go through this for another boy—I know the dangers involved. But, Wesia," she added, "there is one thing I need from you: watch Druscilla and Briam."

"I'm glad you're not being silly enough to trust them. What about Acila?"

The Queen chuckled. "That poor child is run off her feet; she doesn't have time to get into mischief. Besides, she comes to me faithfully every day and reports on what she's doing."

"Are you sure she's telling you the truth?"

"I'm not a fool," the Queen replied evenly, "and carrying a child is not rotting my brain. Why do you think I assigned Acila so much work if not to keep her busy and under nearly constant observation? As long as her accounts agree with those of the steward, the healer, and my maids, I shall be inclined to believe her—except about her brother and Druscilla. After all, she does love her brother, and she seems to be fond enough of Druscilla." She thought for a moment. "You know, in many ways, Acila and Druscilla are amazingly similar."

"Yes," the swordswoman agreed. "They certainly have at least a few things in common. Acila even runs the household almost exactly the way Druscilla did, and they weren't together long enough at Druscilla's estate for her to have learned it there." She frowned. "And it must have been Acila who sent for Druscilla. If you didn't and I didn't, who else could have? They could be a formidable combination if they decided to work together—"

She broke off abruptly, went into the hall, and shouted down for a servant to send for the Lady Druscilla. "We had better talk to that girl," she said, returning, "and make very sure that she doesn't tell Acila anything we don't want Acila to know."

"Sweet Queen of Heaven," the Queen gasped. "I had forgotten about that! Everyone else here has orders to watch what they say to Acila—but surely Druscilla wouldn't? It would only hurt the girl unnecessarily. There's nothing anyone can do about it now."

Druscilla arrived in a flurry of petticoats and embroidered overskirts.

"Are you feeling more rested, Druscilla?" the Queen asked as Druscilla rose from her curtsy.

"Yes, thank you, my lady," Druscilla replied formally. "You do still wish me to lead the evening ritual tonight?"

"Please," the Queen said. "I find that I tire very easily these days. And come see me afterward and we'll go over what you have to do for the presentation tomorrow. You'll have to give the awards to the craft masters and accept the first-fruits. We'd best have you try on the robes, too—then the sewing women will have all night to alter them if need be."

Druscilla bowed her head in assent, the picture of maidenly obedience. Acila hoped she wasn't overdoing it.

Wesia seemed to suspect this sudden meekness.

"What were you and the twins quarreling about at the table, Druscilla?"

Druscilla shot her a startled glance. "Nothing in particular," she said quickly. "I was hungry, tired, and still very sore from several days of near-constant riding. You should have seen the pace the Guards set when they dragged me back here! I'm afraid I was being snappish."

"Who sent the Guards for you?" Wesia asked.

Druscilla looked innocently up into her eyes. "I thought that you had, until I got here and found you were away. I suppose it was the healer, since she wanted me to take over the rituals."

"I trust," her aunt said quietly, "that you did not choose supper at the high table as a suitable place to inform Acila and Briam of his approaching fate."

"No, of course not!" Druscilla stared at her in honest astonishment. "I wouldn't dream of telling Briam; he'd be miserable!"

To the surprise of everyone present, she burst into sudden tears. "He loves you and thinks you're wonderful; how can I tell him you're planning to kill him?" She looked up at the Queen and added in anguish, "And how can you kill him? He's shared your bed and fathered your child—a child he'll never even see! How can you slaughter him like some dumb animal?"

"You must admit," the Shield-Bearer said, "that he's not overly endowed with intelligence."

"So he isn't as brilliant as you two are," Druscilla said fiercely, "well, very few people are! That still doesn't mean he deserves to be killed; he's a human being! You let Ranulf live," she added accusingly, "and he wasn't even truly human!"

"Lord Ranulf went through the ritual like every other Year-King," the Queen pointed out. "It was the Goddess' choice to spare him, not any doing of mine."

"Why would the Goddess spare a monster like him and let every other man die? It doesn't make sense!" Druscilla wailed. "You should have seen him when he came out of the river—all twisted up and melted together in a horrible mess of scales and fur and gills and flippers with his face right in the middle!" She pressed a shaking hand to her mouth and fought to control the gagging the memory was inspiring. Then she shook her head and shuddered. "And then he turned into a wolf and ran into the woods—he probably still spends his nights howling in the forests!"

That certainly explains why Druscilla feels the way she does about wolves, Acila thought.

"The sacrifice was properly performed," the Queen said firmly. "What happened to him afterward is no concern of mine."

"You let him take your son," Druscilla said accusingly.

"The boy is better off with his father."

"Yes, he certainly is," Druscilla said bitterly. "Better there than here, watching a series of stepfathers go to the annual slaughter!"

"I believe we are all agreed on that," the Shield-Bearer said, rejoining the conversation. "So you will say nothing of this to Briam and Acila—or to Rias."

"The twins will find out soon enough," Druscilla said, "and Acila, at least, may survive the experience—or do you do intend to kill her, too?"

Now that's a good question, Acila thought, waiting with interest for the reply.

"Of course not!" The Queen was shocked at the idea.

"Then what do you intend to do with her?" Druscilla asked. "Surely you don't expect her to stand calmly and watch her brother be sacrificed, then come back to the palace and make sure that dinner is properly seasoned and the maids have done their quota of spinning and weaving?"

"Lady Druscilla does have a point," the Shield-Bearer said reluctantly. "Year-Kings don't generally come with family—at least the wandering ones don't. And when someone from the town is the chosen one, his family all know what it means from the outset and accept it, knowing it means that the crops will grow and the harvest be good."

"We'll have to get her out of the city," the Queen said decisively. "If she's gone when he dies, we can tell her later that he met with some sort of tragic accident—that he fell in the river while fishing or something."

"It should do for the moment," the Shield-Bearer said, "but she isn't stupid; she'll figure out the truth next year."

"That still gives us a year to think of something," the Queen said, "and I have enough troubles right now, thank you. Where shall we send her?"

"She can bear Druscilla company on her trip back to her estate," the Shield-Bearer replied promptly. "It would be most cruel to ask either of them to stay and attend the Sacrifice."

"You don't care a bit about my feelings—or Acila's," Druscilla retorted. "You just don't want us to disrupt the ritual!"

"Quite right," the Queen said briskly. "Once in a year is enough. Now that we've settled that," she added, "please go find Briam and bring him here; I need to tell him what's expected of him for the presentation tomorrow."

Druscilla made an ironic curtsy, then turned and ran from the room.

The Queen watched Druscilla go and shook her head. "It's rather a patchwork solution," she sighed; "I only hope it will hold together."

"I'll watch them closely," Wesia promised grimly, scowling in the direction Druscilla had gone. Then she turned quickly to the Queen. "Druscilla hasn't enough training to break your bond with the Year-King, has she?"

The Queen shook her head. "I very much doubt it. You can see for yourself that she doesn't truly understand it. Remember her saying that first morning 'you can't have him; he's mine'—as if I'd deliberately chosen him!" She laughed. "The poor child doesn't even see that it's the Goddess who does the choosing; the Queen is only the vessel through which the calling flows."

"I wonder," Wesia said slowly, "if even the Goddess chooses. Perhaps She simply sings, and whoever truly hears Her answers."

"Perhaps," the Queen agreed. "But chosen is chosen, however it's done.

CHAPTER 18

Briam arrived, smiled dotingly at the Queen, and bent to kiss her cheek—very carefully, under Wesia's baleful eyes. Acila slipped quietly out of the room then; she didn't need to know Briam's part in tomorrow's ritual, and she did have plenty of household tasks awaiting her.

She headed back to Druscilla's room to retrieve her clothes. Wolf was already there, curled up in his den.

She was half-dressed when she realized that she couldn't lace up the back of her dress by herself and she had no reasonable explanation for being undressed this early in the evening. While she was struggling to accomplish the near-impossible feat of lacing the back of her bodice, Druscilla came in.

"What's wrong, Acila?" she asked in concern. "Are you feeling faint?"

Bless you, Acila thought fervently, you've thought of a reasonable explanation. *I think I'm about to become subject to sudden spells of faintness*

"A bit," she said, putting a slight quaver into her voice, "my gown suddenly seemed to be laced too tightly—but mostly I feel shaky. How long do we have before the sacrifice?"

"Do you still plan to save him?" ·Druscilla said sarcastically. "I thought you were in favor of going along with whatever the Queen wants."

"Druscilla," Acila said firmly, "I ran away from home and lived in the woods to save him, and I'm not going to let him get killed now."

"Then what are you going to do?"

Acila thought for a moment. Given Druscilla's recent remarks about Lord Ranulf's lack of humanity, she didn't particularly want to tell her the whole plan.

"Can you get him out of town the morning of the Sacrifice?" she asked. "Even if he doesn't want to go?"

Druscilla spread her hands wide and shrugged. "Well, yes and no. I can make up a sleeping potion—I know one that acts in less than a minute, and I can give him that, stuff him in one of my clothing chests, and head downriver toward my estate, but the Shield-Bearer would catch up with me before I'd gone two miles!" She paused and blushed. "I made a bit of a fuss when he was chosen, so I'm the first one they'd look for if he vanished."

"But if they didn't miss him?"

"How could they not miss him?"

"I can take his place," Acila said quietly. "They don't throw him into the river naked, do they?"

"No," Druscilla said slowly, "he wears a large, loose, elaborate robe, and a crown that covers most of his head, but the Queen dresses him! You couldn't possibly fool her—could you?"

"I think I can," Acila said. "She's pretty sick these days, so she's not taking that much interest in what's going on around her."

"That may be true of the Queen," Druscilla agreed, "but she's not the only one you have to fool."

"I can manage," Acila assured her, not wanting to go into too much detail. "After all, Briam and I are twins, and while we don't look much alike normally, I can occasionally fool people into thinking I'm Briam."

"With your dark hair?" Druscilla was skeptical, and Acila really couldn't blame her.

"It's a sort of glamour," she explained. *You could call it that, after all.*

"Well, if you say so," Druscilla said doubtfully. "I think the Queen identifies him more by how he feels than how he looks anyway—have you ever noticed how she always seems to know who comes into the room before she looks at them?"

"Now that you mention it," Acila said, remembering several times when the Queen had named her before opening her eyes, "yes. I've seen the Shield-Bearer do it, too." *Fortunately they don't seem to be able to do it when I'm in changed form.*

Druscilla grimaced. "They make quite a team. They've been closer than sisters for as long as I can remember—I've always been hopelessly outnumbered. And I'd swear they read each other's minds."

"They may," Acila said, "but they talk a great deal, too. Listening to them can be very informative."

Druscilla grinned. "I knew you were my kind of person. Have you taken up a career as an eavesdropper?"

"Well," Acila reminded her, "I *was* under your bed that first morning when they sent you to find your maids and start packing. If I'd entertained any thoughts that you were mistaken about their plans for Briam, I'd have known better after that."

Druscilla nodded grimly. "But can we really convince them that Briam is you? I don't think we can count on him to cooperate at all."

Acila frowned thoughtfully. "I'll have to get sick. If they're that anxious to get rid of me, they'll bundle me into a litter and send me with you anyway. So you come up with something to knock Briam out; we'll bundle him into one of my bedgowns and a nightcap, wrap him in a few blankets—as long as you leave before dawn, it should work. I'll make sure we've run a bit low on torches around then."

Druscilla nodded. "It does help sometimes, being the one to supervise the household. And if they think you're sick, they won't watch you that closely."

"I hope not," Acila said, "but I'm not going to depend on it. And you had best be very, very careful, because the Shield-Bearer is going to watch you like the proverbial hawk. I'm surprised she's not here now."

Druscilla looked sharply at her, then abruptly went and looked out down the hall. "No sign of her. She's probably guarding the Queen from Briam—not that there's any necessity for that. Her devotion to the Queen is her only weakness."

"Certainly the only one I've seen any sign of," Acila agreed, "but the Queen ordered her to watch you and Briam, so that won't help us much." She smoothed her bodice in place. "Lace me up, please; I have enough work to keep me blamelessly occupied until well after midnight. And you had best find something innocent to do. Why don't you start embroidering some baby clothes?"

Druscilla laughed. "I shall! Then the Shield-Bearer can watch me all she wishes, and I hope she dies of boredom!" Her hands made quick work of fastening Acila's bodice. "I'll go to the sewing room with you and you can help me choose fabric and thread." They left the room arm in arm, with the wolf trailing behind them.

Within the hour Druscilla had made a good start on what promised to be a very elaborate embroidered baby smock. She sat working on it as they sat around the Queen's bed, while the Queen went over their duties for the festival one more time. Acila had difficulty believing that Wesia needed any reminders about her part; she would have wagered that the swordswoman didn't need even to be awake to direct traffic and keep order among the crowds of people who came in from the surrounding countryside to see the Year-King. Druscilla and Briam had to proceed from the palace to a dias at each gate, sit there for a time, be admired and bless the people, then proceed to the next gate and repeat the performance, ending back at the palace again, where Druscilla would receive the first-fruits from the farmers and present awards to the craftsmen.

Acila's job was to keep the food coming from the palace kitchens to the tables set up in the square outside the palace. She was nervously hoping that there would be enough food. She knew she was worrying needlessly; with the amount of food in the kitchens now she could have fed her household, her father's treacherous mercenaries, and Lord Ranulf's entire army, but still she couldn't seem to help worrying. She felt restless, sitting quietly under Wesia's watching eyes, and wished she had followed her own advice to Druscilla and started some embroidery of her own. Tomorrow—no, the day after—she resolved she would start something; it was such a useful way to hide one's face, especially if one had long loose hair.

The apparently placid quiet lasted until Acila, Briam, and Druscilla went to their own rooms. Druscilla went to hers instead of the room she had been sleeping in, but she barely entered the room before she backed out again, screaming. Briam ran to catch her as she fainted gracefully into his arms. Acila cast a bewildered glance at the tableau as she stepped into Druscilla's room. From his den, still in the corner, Wolf looked innocently up at her. Acila sighed wearily and leaned against the door frame.

"What is going on here?" the Shield Bearer demanded from behind them. Rias popped out of his room at the end of the corridor to see what was causing all the racket. Wesia glared at him, but he just looked innocently at her and stood his ground.

"Nothing, Shield-Bearer," Acila said wearily. "Just Druscilla and her fear of wolves." *And, personally, I think she's overdoing the stupid and helpless routine. Even if this is intended to distract Wesia, what if the servants tell her that we changed rooms days ago? That's bound to make her even more suspicious.* Rias snickered softly, but everyone ignored him.

The swordswoman looked over Acila's shoulder into the room. "Just terrifying," she said dryly. She stepped back and plucked Druscilla from Briam's arms, just as Druscilla's eyelashes began to flutter. "Go to bed, Lord

Briam," she ordered. "Your sister and I will take care of Lady Druscilla."

Briam hesitated, and Wesia's eyes narrowed suspiciously. Acila moved from the doorway and brushed against his hand. *Just go,* she thought at him. *I'll look after her, and you'll only make the Shield-Bearer angry if you insist on remaining.*

Briam bowed stiffly and retreated to his own room. Acila opened the door to the room where Druscilla had been sleeping. "Put her to bed in here for tonight," she said, being careful to voice it as a suggestion. "We can move our clothes around as needed tomorrow. I forgot when I ordered my things moved out of her room to tell them to move the wolf's den." This isn't going to work, she realized, Wesia knows that Druscilla has been here more than one day—she's bound to ask what's going on.

But Wesia didn't; she strode into the guest room and dumped Druscilla unceremoniously on the bed. "The den wouldn't fit in here anyway; her room's the largest on this hall. She'll have to chose between sleeping in here or sharing her room with the wolf."

"I'll sleep here," Druscilla said faintly. "You can have my room, Acila, with my blessing."

"Very well," the swordswoman said. "That's settled, then. I'll get my bedroll and sleep in the hallway; that way you won't have to worry about the wolf prowling in the night and disturbing you. I'll send your maids to you." She stalked out of the room.

Acila grinned after her, feeling limp with relief. "I'll bet you're not worried about the wolf's sneaking into your bed one-half as much as she's worried about your sneaking into Briam's!"

Druscilla's eyes opened wide. "Why would she expect me to do that?"

"I thought they were training you as the Queen's heiress," Acila said softly. "What do you think binds Briam to the Queen?" Then, warned by the sound of footsteps in the hall she continued in a slightly louder voice. "I'm glad that you're feeling recovered, Lady Druscilla. I bid you good night." She stepped into the hall, nodded to Druscilla's maid in passing, and went to Druscilla's room where a maid was turning back the bed.

Wesia arrived while Acila's maid was still brushing her hair, a luxury she had never properly appreciated before spending several months as a wolf. By the time Acila was ready for bed, Wesia had set up her bedroll next to the hall torch outside Druscilla's door and was sitting on top of her blanket, apparently meditating. The maids stepped softly as they passed her, and Acila closed her door quietly and slid the bolt into place as silently as possible.

Acila looked longingly at the bed. It would be wonderful simply to slip between the sheets, close the curtains, and let the world and all its problems go away for a while. But she had been abruptly reminded of how little time they had left, and how large the holes in her plan were. If she was going to take Briam's place on a dive into the river, it behooved her to investigate what she was going to dive into. She blew out the night-candle, shed her bedgown, perched on the windowsill, and turned into an eagle.

The wolf came and sniffed at her in apparent concern, and Acila prayed that he wouldn't start howling when she left. If he did, she'd have to return immediately and explain the noise to the Shield-Bearer, something she was not at all anxious to do. But when she pushed off the windowsill and flapped her wings to catch the wind, he simply rested his jaw on the windowsill and watched her silently as she rose high above the palace, out of the glow of the torches in the courtyard.

She swooped out over the waterfall, being careful to stay far enough away to avoid the worst of the spray. Even with an eagle's eyes, it was too dark to see the rocks below it clearly, so she flew downstream to where the water was calmer, dove into the water as if she were about to catch a fish, and began to change again.

She needed to breathe, so she developed gills as she changed her feathers to scales and elongated her body to adapt to currents in water instead of air. Her beak merged into her throat, which was now part of her chest, but she kept the eagle's eyes, adapted slightly to see under water; she didn't particularly want to lose the ability to see ahead of her. She knew that she must look strange indeed, but, after all, she wasn't likely to encounter anyone she knew.

Her wings, or arms, were now small steering fins, and her legs had become a forked tail fin. She spent several minutes maneuvering about under water, getting a feel for how this shape responded to both her attempts to move it and the water currents, before heading upstream toward the waterfall. She wished that she had seen the sacrifice ritual before, but she would just have to do the best she could with what she knew. She also wished that she had been getting more physical exercise—swimming against the current was hard work, especially as she got closer to the waterfall.

She got to the area just under the fall and was relieved to discover that the rocks were not as bad as she had feared. Apparently the sacrifice drowned in the undercurrent, rather than being smashed on underwater rocks. If she wore padded clothing under the ritual robe, which would also help her look like Briam, who was certainly bulkier than she was, that would help keep her from being hurt by the rocks. The fall was high enough so that it would take her a few seconds to reach the water, and during those few seconds nobody would see her too clearly. After all, anyone watching would be above her, and once she disappeared into the water, nobody could prove they'd seen anything unusual. The spray would probably help, too. So she could use those few seconds to start the change into water-breathing form and to shrink enough so that her entire body would be protected by the robe when she hit the water.

No, it might be better to change to something very small and heavy, so that she would sink to the bottom as quickly as possible. She thickened her scales and pulled herself in toward her heart, quickly reaching the point where she was too small and heavy to keep swimming. She sank like a stone, skittering over the rocks in the river bed on her way down. She landed on the bottom, feeling mildly abraded about the edges and very much aware that she couldn't stay in the form for long—she couldn't breathe!

She stretched out again into something midway between a fish and an eel—after all, she would have to get out of the clothing once she reached bottom—and wiggled her way through the rocks. Once she was clear of the worst of them, it was easy; she floated downstream, relaxing in the current . . . peacefully resting, drifting. . . .

She shook herself and headed for the surface. This was no time to fall asleep! She swam to the bank of the river, developed arms, and pulled herself out, starting to turn human as she did so.

At this point she discovered that the transition from water-breather to air-breather was not as easy as changing the other way. When she changed to a fish, she had simply released the air from her lungs and taken in water, but the water was in no hurry to leave her lungs now. She couldn't breathe; she was drowning!

She slipped back into the water, developed gills again, and took stock. She now had a human face and hair, gills on neck and shoulders, a human torso, and the body of a fish from the waist down—that part of her had stayed in the water and she had never gotten around to changing it. This arrangement reminded her of something she had seen in one of the scrolls in her library—a creature half-woman and half-fish, which was reputed to sing and lure sailors to their deaths. It sounded silly to her; certainly the idea of eating a sailor was just as repulsive to her in this form as it had been in human form.

Well, she couldn't stay here forever; she had to supervise the food for the festival tomorrow.

And won't you be wide awake and alert! her other self pointed out sarcastically.

Do you have any helpful suggestions? she shot back.

Try going out feet first, upside down. Maybe then by the time you get your head out, you will have been able to drain the water out of you. And if that doesn't work, figure out what Lord Ranulf would do—after all, he survived it.

True, but Druscilla's description wasn't very helpful; apparently it made no sense at all to her until he turned into a wolf—come to think of it, it might be easier to cough up the water in that form!

A minute later a wolf stood by the river, apparently choking to death. It was miserable, but it worked. When the coughing stopped and Acila's vision cleared, she looked up at the stars. *Oh no, I've been gone for hours! I hope nobody missed me.*

She changed to eagle form, flew back to her room, changed back to human, and collapsed in an exhausted heap on the floor. This was not much help; even with the furs on it, the floor was cold, and she was upsetting the wolf. He whined and shoved at her until she finally managed to drag herself as far as the bed and crawl into it. Her bedgown still lay beside the pillow, but she didn't care; she didn't have the strength to put it on.

You'll be freezing by morning, the voice in her head told her, but she didn't care. She fell asleep so quickly that she scarcely felt the jolting of the bed as the wolf scrambled up and curled up on top of the blanket, practically on top of her, in a position guaranteed to keep her warm, as well as in one place, until he deigned to move.

CHAPTER 19

S omeone was banging on her door. "Acila!" Briam sounded worried. "Open the door! Are you all right?"

Acila opened her eyes. The sun was just starting to rise, and she wished with all her heart that she didn't have to follow its example. But Briam seemed about ready to break down the door she had bolted last night, so she had to get up and reassure him before he wakened everyone in the palace.

"I'm coming, Briam, just a minute!" She jumped out of bed and almost fell over as everything turned black before her eyes. She grabbed the bedpost to steady herself until normal sight returned, then carefully picked up her bedgown and put it on before opening the door.

Briam looked at her and said, "You look awful! Have you been changing again?"

"Hush, for the love of the Lady! Do you want Druscilla and the Shield-Bearer to hear you?"

"They're with the Queen," Briam said sullenly. "I'm not an idiot, you know."

"No, love, I know you're not," Acila said hastily. "I'm just worried, that's all."

"What have you got to worry about?" Briam asked. "I'm the one who has to spend all day being on display. I only hope I remember the right words to the blessings. Oh, well, no doubt it will be easier next year."

"I certainly hope so," Acila said, reaching for her

clothes. *I wonder where we'll be next year.* "As long as you're here, Briam, would you please lace me up?"

Once she was dressed, they went downstairs together, followed by the wolf. The atrium was full of servants, most of them awake and excited about the festival, but a few laggards were being shaken awake and moved from their sleeping places so that the tables could be set up for breakfast. Except for the cooks and servers, Acila knew, the servants were to have a day's holiday, so there was not much grumbling at the early hour of breakfast.

Druscilla came down the stairs from the Queen's rooms, firmly escorted by Wesia, and joined the twins at the high table. The wolf settled down under Acila's feet with a sigh of what she would have sworn was relief. She didn't blame him; she would have been happy to hide under the table herself. She felt cold, shaky, and very unsure of herself, and she hoped she would get through the day without any major blunders. *At least I don't have to take part in the ritual,* she thought, *and the kitchen staff has set out food in the plaza before, so they'll doubtless tell me if I make any mistakes there.*

Besides, her inner voice pointed out, *you'll feel better after you eat something. If you're going to be doing more changing, you'd better start keeping dried fruit in your room.*

Then I had best get some dried fruit, because I do plan to do more changing. I want to be absolutely sure I know what I'm doing before I go into that river, and some practice at impersonating Briam might not hurt either. She applied herself diligently to her food.

Acila went to the kitchens immediately after breakfast and found no more than the expected amount of chaos there. The steward was waiting for her with a question, though.

"The first-fruits are here, Lady Acila," he said holding up a small basket of pears. "But who gets the first one, the Queen or Lady Druscilla?"

Acila could understand his quandary; the first fruits were given to the Queen as part of the ceremony when she and the Year-King returned to the palace.

"Has the Queen's tray gone up yet?" she asked.

"No, Lady Acila," the head cook replied. "We're making it up now."

"Very well," Acila said, "give it to me when it's ready, and I'll take it up." She reached out and took a pear from the top of the basket. "Give the basket to the Lady Druscilla at the proper place in the ritual," she directed the steward, "and the Queen can have the first one on her breakfast tray."

The man bowed. "Very good," he said, then went off to his office, basket in hand.

Acila took the tray to the Queen's room and found the room full of people. The wolf took one look, dove through the crowd, and vanished under the bed. In addition to the Queen, the room contained Briam, Druscilla, her maid, the Queen's maid, Wesia, and four of the Queen's guards, in full dress uniform.

"Shield-Bearer," the Queen was saying as Acila entered, "I am pleased to approve your choice of escort." Apparently this was some sort of formality, for the four guards bowed to the Queen, to Druscilla, and to Briam, before taking up a position in the hall just outside the door. Acila stepped aside to let them pass, then approached the bed.

"I'll be about my duties, then," Wesia said, bending to kiss the Queen's hand. "Rest well." She turned and saw Acila. "I'm glad to see that someone remembered her breakfast."

"No fear of anyone's forgetting," Acila replied; "they were making up the tray when I went in."

Wesia gave a brief nod of acknowledgment, then looked at the pear. "First-fruits?" she asked softly. Acila nodded, and Wesia smiled approvingly at her. "Good girl," she said, bestowing a quick pat on Acila's arm as she left. *Goodness,* Acila thought in relief, *if I'm getting approval from that quarter, I'm doing well indeed.* She placed the tray on the table next to the bed and watched as the Queen supervised the adornment of Briam and Druscilla.

Druscilla's face had been painted so that her eyes looked enormous; in fact, her maid had covered her eyebrows with powder and redrawn them half an inch higher on her forehead. The Queen's maid was now doing the same thing to Briam, ignoring his protests.

"Calm down," Druscilla advised him, pausing long enough to let her maid redraw her lips slightly larger with a brush dipped in some sort of red paste. When her mouth was free she continued, "I know it looks strange close up, but when we're up on the dais we'll look normal to the people below us—remember we're doing this for their benefit, not ours."

"Very true," the Queen said from her bed, "and I'm glad that you realize it."

Druscilla turned to look at her. "I'm not an idiot," she said. Acila smiled quietly; the words and tone were those Briam had used earlier.

"I never thought you were," the Queen said mildly. "You'd better finish dressing; you'll have to be leaving soon. Acila," she added turning her head, "would you get the orb, please?"

Acila fetched the box that held the orb and brought it to the Queen, while the Queen's maid finished painting Briam's face and helped him into a loose-fitting overtunic of dark blue velvet, richly embroidered with small gemstones set around the neck. Then both maids helped Druscilla into three petticoats, a pale blue undergown, and an overgown that matched Briam's tunic, but was even more elaborately embroidered, and laced it tightly to show every curve of her figure. Acila felt stifled just looking at it, but Druscilla barely seemed to notice its weight. Her maid coiled the young woman's hair up high on her head, then helped her to kneel beside the Queen's bed.

The Queen opened a drawer at the bottom of the box that held the orb and took out a crown which appeared to be a representation of the city in stone. *So that's why the box is so heavy,* Acila thought. She watched Druscilla's neck muscles tense as the weight of the crown came down on her head, and felt very glad that all she had to do was supervise the kitchens. *I certainly wouldn't want to stand about all day wearing that!* The Queen opened the top of the box and put the orb in Druscilla's hands, and both maids assisted Druscilla to her feet. She looked beautiful, but quite unreal, like a puppet or a doll. She shifted the orb to her right hand, held out her left hand to Briam, and drew him to stand beside her, facing the Queen.

The Queen lifted her hand and traced a sign in the air in front of them. "May the Lady bless and keep you both," she said. Briam bowed, and Druscilla curtsied slightly, keeping her back perfectly straight and being very careful not to dislodge the crown, then they went out into the hall where the guards fell in around them. The maids gathered up the paints and stray garments, curtsied to the Queen, and withdrew.

The Queen sighed and lay back against her pillows. "That's done," she said softly. "Now it's up to them. They should do well, though; Druscilla's very good at ritual when she wants to be, and Briam looks imposing—almost godlike."

"Yes," Acila agreed, "he's quite good-looking, and that dark blue color suits him. He has a nice voice, too, as long as he's been coached in what to say." She picked up the pear from the tray and extended it to the Queen. "The first fruit of your harvest, my Queen," she said formally.

"I thank you, my daughter," the Queen replied, taking it from her. She bit into it and smiled. "Delicious. Here, have a bite." She patted the bed next to her and extended the pear.

Acila curled up in the spot indicated, took a bite of the pear, and handed it back. "Yes, it is delicious," she said as soon as she had swallowed it.

The Queen reached for her tray. "Sit and talk to me

while I eat," she requested. "I'm doing well enough in body as long as I rest, but I do get bored. What's happening in the palace these days?"

"Lately everyone's been working hard preparing for today's festival," Acila said, "so things have been running fairly smoothly; everyone's too busy to get into mischief."

"And the screams I heard last night?" the Queen asked. "That wasn't part of the smooth running of the palace when *I* was up and about.

"Oh, that." Acila chuckled. "That was just Druscilla. You knew that I had been sleeping in her room?" The Queen nodded. "Well, when Briam asked me to have the wolf sleep with me, I had the carpenter build a den for it—it's just a big box, but it's a place where the wolf can curl up and feel secure."

"An excellent idea," the Queen approved. "I take it this den is located in Druscilla's room?"

"Yes, and when I gave orders to move my clothes, I forgot to have it moved as well, so Druscilla walked into her room last night and there was the wolf looking at her—"

"Hence the screaming." The queen nodded. "What did she do next?"

Acila giggled. "Fainted gracefully into Briam's arms, and he just stood there with a 'what do I do now' look, and then the Shield-Bearer walked up and plucked her out of Briam's arms as if she were a rag doll! So we wound up changing rooms back again, and the Shield-Bearer slept in the corridor so that the wolf wouldn't prowl into Druscilla's room in the middle of the night—though that seems pretty unlikely to me."

"To me also," the Queen agreed, "but if the Shield-Bearer is willing to sleep on the floor, I have no objections. And Druscilla is unusually timid around wolves."

"She certainly is," Acila said emphatically, "and it's silly. Wolf has never bitten anything larger than a flea—well, not since he came here and didn't have to hunt for food. But he sleeps with me, and I'll bolt my door at night, so Druscilla has nothing to worry about. I'd be astonished to find he could open a bolted door."

"I'm sure Druscilla will find that reassuring," the Queen said. "I've noticed that she's very fond of you; in fact, she has asked me if you can visit her when she returns to her estate next month. Would you like to do that?"

"Yes, my Lady, very much, if you can spare us," Acila replied. "But I'm happy to stay here and help as long as you need me."

The Queen reached out and patted Acila's hand. "I appreciate that greatly, and you have been most helpful. But after this month I can spare you both for a while; after summer's end there are no petition hearings and no daily rituals for a month, and by then virtually all of the harvest is in, so it's a good time for you to go away and get some rest."

"Then I shall be happy to accompany the Lady Druscilla," Acila said, "and I thank her for the invitation. What day does she intend to set out?"

"I'm not sure," the Queen said; "you will have to ask her."

Very well, Acila thought, *I'll ask her what day you told her to get me out of here—as if I couldn't make a very good guess.*

There was a sound of running footsteps in the hall, and one of the kitchen maids appeared in the doorway and sank into a deep curtsy. "Your pardon, my Queen," she murmured. "Lady Acila, you are wanted in the kitchens, if you please."

The Queen chuckled. "It's a good thing you sat with me, Acila," she pointed out, "it's probably the only chance you'll get to sit down today." She extended the empty tray to the maid. "Here, you can take this with you; I'm done with it." The girl took the tray, curtsied again, and scurried out.

"Acila," the Queen continued, "hand me that pile of correspondence before you go, please. Maybe I can get some work done before I fall asleep again." Acila did as she was asked, then proceeded to the kitchen, preparing herself to cope with the next disaster life was handing her.

Fortunately, the disasters of the day were all minor enough for Acila to handle easily, though she was tired enough by the end of the day to fall straight into bed. *Never mind shapechanging practice; I've still got time, and there's no point in doing it when I'm this tired—I'd only do something stupid and get hurt.* She did bolt her door, though. *Better to do it every night and have it known as a habit than to do it only when I'm going out and have people get suspicious.*

The next day, the Shield-Bearer announced that now that Rias had seen the Mid-Summer Festival, it was time for him to return to his father. Rias didn't even point out that his father was missing; he meekly agreed that it was time he went home and thanked the Shield-Bearer for providing him with an escort. *His night-mares must be even worse than mine,* Acila thought. He took polite leave of her under Wesia's watchful eyes, but whispered in her ear as he hugged her. "Remember your promise. You have to come home and teach me to fly."

Acila hugged him back. "I'll remember. Behave yourself, and give my love to Galin and Marfa."

She missed Rias when he was gone, but she was just as happy to have one less complication in her life at the moment. For the next few weeks she slipped out at least two nights a week to practice swimming under the waterfall, until she knew the rocks and currents there as well as she knew the furniture in her bedroom. She noticed after the first week that her gowns laced more loosely, so she started eating more at meals, gradually enough so as not to invite comment; she

didn't want anyone commenting on either her sudden
weight loss or her increased appetite.

Wesia stuck to Druscilla every waking moment and
slept in the corridor at night, so private conversation
with Druscilla was impossible. At dinner one day Acila
told her that the Queen had consented to their proposed
visit to Druscilla's estate and asked which day
Druscilla wished to leave. Druscilla, of course,
promptly named the morning of the Sacrifice, and
Wesia looked grim for a moment, then announced that
she would supply them with an escort. Druscilla and
Acila both thanked her politely.

There is no help for it, Acila thought, *I shall have to
get "sick" so I can travel by litter—a closed litter. Sick
headaches and fainting spells should do it.* So she
started "fainting" occasionally in the evenings, then
once or twice in the morning, and admitting to terrible
headaches which were eased only by her lying down in
a darkened room.

The Queen sent the healer to examine her, and the
healer, predictably enough, said that Acila was over-
worked and overtired. *True enough,* Acila thought
grimly, *anyone would be, working all day and swimming under a waterfall at night!* The Queen ordered
Druscilla to take over some of the household duties, to
which Druscilla agreed gladly.

Druscilla also insisted on going to the stillroom and
brewing a tonic for Acila. Acila drank it obediently,
thankful that it didn't taste too bad and didn't seem to
do her any harm. She trusted that Druscilla was making good use of her time in the stillroom, but she didn't
have a chance to ask.

The day before they were to leave, Wesia brought
the healer with her when she and Druscilla came to see
Acila. "Will the Lady Acila be well enough to travel
tomorrow?" she asked the healer.

The woman passed her hands over Acila's body,
checking the energy currents. "I wouldn't try to put her

on a horse for a four-day trip," she replied, "but I see no reason she can't ride in a litter."

"And she's certainly not getting well here," Druscilla pointed out. "She'll do much better to come with me where she can get some rest and not have to worry about anything."

"Absolutely," the Shield-Bearer agreed.

I wonder what she would have done if the healer said I wasn't well enough to travel, Acila thought. Aloud she said, "I think I can manage well enough in a litter, but can it have thick curtains? I find that daylight hurts my eyes these days."

"Certainly," the Shield-Bearer said. "I'll arrange everything; you just stay in bed today and rest."

"All right," Acila smiled wanly. "Thank you." Acila dozed fitfully all day and had nightmares all night, so that by morning she had no need to pretend she felt ill. Then Druscilla came in with her "tonic" and gave Acila a warning look as she handed her the goblet. Acila held it carefully and asked, "Where's Briam? Isn't he coming to say good-bye to us?"

"I think he's still asleep," Druscilla said, "but I'll get him." She dragged Wesia out of the room with her, and Acila, listening carefully, could hear her say. "Please, Shield-Bearer, would you see to having my chests loaded? Let them say good-bye to each other alone."

There was a moment of silence, and then the Shield-Bearer said, "Very well." Acila sighed with relief, changing places under Wesia's eyes would have been nearly impossible.

Druscilla returned a few minutes later, dragging a sleepy Briam with her. Acila was glad to see he was wearing only his nightshirt with a blanket wrapped over it; that would make changing places with him much easier—his nightshirt was almost a twin of hers.

Druscilla looks nervous, just the way I feel, Acila thought. "Druscilla," she asked, "did my clothes chest get put in with yours?"

"I'll go make sure," Druscilla said, picking up her cue, and left the room.

Acila patted the bed beside her, and Briam sat down. "How are you feeling, Acila?" he asked sleepily. "It's a shame you're sick; did you know that you're missing another festival today?"

"Yes," Acila replied, "but considering the breathless excitement of the last one," she grinned at him, "I think I can survive missing this one." Her voice quivered slightly as she realized what she was saying, and she forced her smile back into place. "Druscilla will take good care of me. She makes really nice potions, too; they're not bad-tasting at all." She extended the goblet to him. "Here, try this."

She was relieved to see that Briam had not totally lost the habit of obeying her; he drained it off in one gulp. "Not bad," he said, yawning. "I'm sorry," he apologized, "it's too early in the morning—" he slumped across her lap.

Acila scrambled out from under him, pulled the blankets aside, and tucked him into her bed. Then she pulled off her nightcap, tied it over his head, and arranged him and her blankets so his face wouldn't show. The wolf left his den, padded across the room to sniff at him, and started whining.

"Be quiet!" Acila snapped, just as Druscilla came back. "Den!" she added, and the wolf slunk reluctantly back into his box.

"Did it work?" Druscilla came to bend over the bed.

"Yes, it's all right," Acila said, hastily wrapping Briam's blanket loosely around her so that it covered her head, and stretching her body a bit to make herself as tall as Briam. "You'll have to give him more on the road, though, unless you're planning to tie him up."

"I'll manage," Druscilla said. "Don't get yourself killed, though." She gave Acila a quick hug. "I want you to live to see our children."

"So do I," Acila said. Sensing a presence in the door, she said, in her best approximation of Briam's voice, "Take good care of my sister. I'm going back to bed; tell them to call me when they need me." She left the room, making sure that the blanket hid her face as she nodded to the guard in the doorway, went along the corridor to Briam's room, and closed the door.

She listened, holding her breath, as Druscilla ordered "Acila" carried to the litter. No one suspected anything; from the conversation it was apparent that the guards thought "Acila" was asleep. The only fuss occurred when the wolf tried to follow them, and that ended with one of the guards shutting the wolf in the room, bolting the door from the inside, and climbing out the window. Acila felt guilty about the wolf, but there was not much she could do about him now; he would certainly be very much in the way during the Sacrifice. She would simply have to fly back afterward and let him out.

She finished changing her face and build so that she looked like Briam, then sat on the windowsill and gazed out at the garden and the river, mentally reviewing her knowledge of the rocks and currents under the waterfall. Acila prayed that Druscilla would be able to manage Briam, though as long as she kept him away until after the sacrifice, that should be enough.

What time is the Sacrifice, anyway? There are still too many details of this I don't know. She dressed in Briam's clothes and headed down to the atrium in search of breakfast. *After all, Briam knows even less than I do, so someone is bound to tell me what I'm supposed to be doing.*

The servants seemed subdued as they placed a large breakfast in front of her. Acila forced herself to eat with the appearance of unconcern and to smile at Wesia when she arrived, wearing her dress uniform, midway through the meal. "Did my sister and the Lady Druscilla get safely on their way?" she inquired politely. "It certainly is quiet here without them."

"Yes," Wesia replied, helping herself to rapidly cooling porridge and shoveling it in with no apparent knowledge of what she was eating. "I went with them as far as the South Gate, and they have an escort of six of my best guards. They'll be fine."

"Good," Acila set her spoon down. "What's the schedule for today's ritual? Is it like the last one? Nobody's told me much about it."

"It's not all that different from the last one," Wesia replied. "Your clothing is different for this, but basically you just walk in procession and do what you're told."

"Sounds easy enough," Acila said casually. Wesia swallowed the last bite of her porridge and rose. "Come to the Queen's room, and we'll get you dressed."

Acila followed the swordswoman obediently up the stairs, but was surprised to find the Queen up and dressed, although she was definitely pale. "Should you be out of bed, my Lady? Are you feeling well enough?"

The Queen smiled faintly. "I'll do," she said. "It's not a long ritual."

"Good," Acila said cheerfully. "Standing around all day in fancy robes is tiring."

The Queen gave her an odd look. *Does she suspect something?* Acila wondered. But the Queen only gestured to a set of robes laid out on her bed. "Take off everything but your undertunic, and put those on."

Acila untied her belt, pulled her tunic over her head, took off her shoes and hose, and stood obediently while the Queen and the Shield-Bearer dressed her in a long loose robe and put a crown on her head. The crown was light; Acila suspected that it would come off in the water and float downstream to where it could be fished out later. It seemed strange to her that her mind was focusing on trifles like that as she stood with two people who were planning to kill her. *In fact, it's really very difficult to believe that they intend to kill me. They're so calm and matter-of-fact about all this.*

The Queen picked up a goblet from the table beside

her bed, took a sip of it and passed it to Acila. "Drink this, my Lord," she said quietly.

Acila found herself draining the goblet without even thinking about it. Wesia took the empty goblet from her hand, and Acila realized that she seemed small and far away. In fact, everything seemed far away, except the Queen, and Alicia felt strangely calm. Nothing seemed important to her now, not even her realization, in one small corner of her mind, that Druscilla wasn't the only person in the palace who could drug a cup of wine.

CHAPTER 20

Flanked by the Queen and the Shield-Bearer, Acila left the palace and joined the silent procession of the Year-King's Companions and the Queen's Guard to the north terrace above the waterfall. There was a dais set up next to the wall so that the floor of the dais was level with the top of the wall. *No doubt,* Acila thought with the same odd detachment, *so that I can simply step off the wall into the river.*

But something stood between her and her fate; Wolf stood at the top of the steps leading up to the dais, growling softly through bared teeth. A small group of the Queen's guards stood in a semicircle facing him, regarding him warily. Seeing the Shield-Bearer, one of them hurried over to consult her.

"What is he doing here?" Wesia demanded before the unfortunate guard could open her mouth. "I gave orders that he was to be locked in his den."

"Shield-Bearer, we did!" the woman protested. "I locked him in the den myself, and then I bolted the door to Lady Druscilla's room, and climbed out the window—in case he got out of the den!"

"So you're claiming that he got out of his den, either unbolted the door or climbed out the window, and made his way here—all without anyone's noticing him?" Wesia did not sound as if she found this easy to believe. The guard shrugged unhappily.

"Well, never mind that now," the Shield-Bearer continued, sounding irritated, "just get him out of here!"

"Yes, Shield-Bearer," the woman said hastily. "Do you mean us to kill him?"

"No," the Queen said quietly. "Acila will have enough grief from her brother's death. Do not harm the wolf."

Wesia cast an appalled look at the Queen, and then at Acila, who stood there quietly, not reacting to anything. *Is she not supposed to mention my death in front of me?* Acila wondered. *It's certainly too late for me to do anything to prevent it now.* She idly considered asking, but it was too much trouble to move her mouth.

"Get some fishing nets and trap it," Wesia ordered the guard. The woman nodded and ran off, and Wesia turned to the Queen in concern. "Are you feeling well?" she asked. "Was the drug made too strong?"

"I don't think so," the Queen replied after a moment's thought. "I seem to be feeling as well as can be expected under the circumstances. Why?"

Wesia jerked her head toward Acila. "He seems to have gotten a bit too heavy a dose."

The Queen frowned. "He shouldn't have, I calculated it very carefully for his body weight."

Briam's body weight, not mine. That must be why I feel so strange.

The Queen took Acila's face in her hands and looked her straight in the eyes. "My Lord? Can you understand me?"

Acila blinked and focused her attention on the Queen. "Yes," she managed to reply after a moment. Then her mind drifted off again, and everything was far away once more.

Dimly she could hear the Queen saying, "Well, at least he won't suffer," but she didn't feel that the words bore any relation to her.

"We had better get the ceremony started soon, though," Wesia said. "We don't want him collapsing before the end of it."

"Neither him nor me," the Queen agreed. "But they have the wolf netted now, so we can begin."

The three of them, with Acila still in the middle, walked through the assembled townspeople and guards, ascended the dais, and faced the crowd. Acila could see the wolf, tangled in the nets the guards had thrown about him, struggling frantically to escape, but the only thought this aroused in her was *now I won't have to go back to let him out of Lady Druscilla's room.*

In her dreamlike state, it did not seem odd to her when he stopped struggling, blurred, and appeared to be turning into a snake.

The Queen started speaking then, and all of Acila's attention focused on her.

"For answering our call, we thank thee. For thy service to us and ours, we thank thee. Thou hast done well."

A young girl came up the stairs of the dais and handed Acila a large sheaf of wheat. It took a good deal of Acila's remaining concentration not to drop it. "Receive the fruits thy life provides," the girl said, bowing low to Acila before returning to her place in the crowd.

Acila stood there, clutching the wheat, as the Queen continued to speak. "Now thy time is come," she intoned, "Now do we release thee. We loose our claim upon thee and yield thee to Water, the Blood of Earth, Mother of us all, from whence we come and to which we return. Let that which binds thee to us be severed."

From the corner of her eye Acila saw the Shield-Bearer unsheathe an ornate and very sharp sword, obviously intended only for ritual use. The Shield-Bearer raised the blade high and then whipped it downward in an arc between Acila and the Queen. It didn't touch either of them—it didn't even pass close to either of them—but even through the drug Acila could feel its action as it severed the psychic bond which had tied her and Briam to the Queen since the day they had met. Not only could Acila not feel her link with the Queen, she couldn't feel the twin link with Briam, her link to the Lady of Fire, or the link with Wolf that she hadn't realized existed until now. Suddenly, she was alone, alone as she had never been in her entire life. She was empty, used up. *Is this how it feels to be dead?*

The Queen seemed to feel it, too; she looked pale and cold. Acila wanted to move toward her, to hold her and comfort her, but Acila knew now that she was dead, and the Shield-Bearer's sword blocked her way back to the land of the living.

"Bow to the Queen, and take three steps backward," Wesia's voice said in her ear.

Acila, numb from the drug and the shock of the severed bonds, obeyed. The third step carried her over the edge of the wall and then she was falling straight down, through the air beside the waterfall, splashed by the spray. Just before she hit the river she thought she heard a sound over the noise of the water, the scream of an angry eagle. Then she reached the river, the water closed over her head, and she heard nothing more.

She was being tossed about by the water and bouncing from rock to rock, she couldn't breathe, she was choking on water. *This isn't right,* a small part of her mind thought, *I should be able to breathe.* Then the responses she had trained into her body during her nights of practice took over. With no further conscious thought her body changed, and now she could breathe again. With a few flips of her tail she freed herself from the mass of wet cloth around her and let the current carry her downstream.

Yes, this was right, she had returned to the water as she had been commanded, now she was where she belonged. Her work was done; now she could rest. She settled contentedly into the nearly mindless life of a fish and lost all track of time.

A shadow blocked the light, and sharp talons fastened about her and tried to lift her out of the water. With what remained of her human mind she knew that some fish-eating bird held her. *No doubt it will give up once it finds I'm too heavy to lift out of the water.* Then, with a flash of returning humor, she thought, *Poor thing, how confusing for it—nothing my size is supposed to weigh this much!* She thickened her scales in case it tried to bite her, but it didn't. Instead, it dragged her steadily toward the river's bank, out of the crushing current, and held her there.

A pair of human hands reached down and replaced the talons, then hauled her out of the water onto someone's lap. Acila changed almost automatically from fish to wolf, rolling free of her captor as she did so, but then she had to devote the next several minutes to coughing up the water she had been breathing. When she could see straight again, she turned her head to look at what had pulled her out.

It was certainly strange-looking. The talons, still dangling in the water, were attached to human legs. The rest of the figure was human male, except for the head, which was animal. Acila had no difficulty recognizing that head; it had followed her about for months. It was Wolf, looking at her as he always had, with his tongue hanging out of the right side of his mouth behind his lower fangs, and therefore Wolf must be . . .

"Druscilla was right!" Acila said in astonishment as she shifted back to human form. The midday sun was warm, and skin would dry faster than fur. "It *was* you all along! And I thought it was just that whenever she saw a wolf she thought of you."

The talons changed to human feet, and the face shifted to Lord Ranulf's normal features.

"She probably does," he said, laughing, "But yes, it was me. I wanted to be sure that you stayed out of trouble—or at least alive."

"Then why didn't you stop Briam from being Year-King?"

Lord Ranulf sighed. "I couldn't," he said simply. "You know that I was once Year-King."

Acila nodded, "Ten years ago, right? Rias is your

son and the Queen's, and he's a changer, too—does this mean it's an inherited trait?"

Lord Ranulf nodded. "I strongly suspect so. It will be interesting to see what the Queen's daughter by Briam is like."

Uh-oh, Acila thought. "But if he marries Druscilla . . ."

He grinned broadly. "What an enchanting thought! Seriously, though, I'm sure that Druscilla will love her children no matter what they are like. People tend to underestimate Druscilla."

"Yes," Acila agreed, "it's one of her greatest weapons. But you were telling me why you didn't stop Briam from being chosen."

Lord Ranulf looked straight into her eyes. "Do you remember how you felt about the Queen at the Choosing?"

Acila remembered. "She was the center of the world, and everything moved toward her."

"Exactly. When she does the Calling, anyone who truly hears it is drawn to her. Fortunately, not too many people can hear on that level, but if you can hear it you're vulnerable. Last spring was the first time I'd been there for that Calling since the day I was Called, so that was when I learned that the spell still works on me. I would recommend that you and I and Briam all avoid that ceremony from now on."

"I certainly intend to," Acila said, "and I imagine that Druscilla will make sure that Briam never goes near the place again—after all, he *is* supposed to be dead." That brought her mind back to her current position. "And I'm supposed to be alive and at Druscilla's, so I had better get there fast, before someone comes looking for me. Besides, I need to make certain that Briam is all right."

Lord Ranulf shook his head. "I'm sure that Briam is just fine," he snapped. "Really, how much more of your life do you intend to waste looking after your brother?"

"But he needs someone to take care of him!" Acila protested. "He's not very practical."

"Acila," Lord Ranulf was clearly trying to be patient and reasonable, "I have just spent the better part of a year living with you and Briam. Briam is a reasonably intelligent young man; he's just not as brilliant as you are. You only think he's not bright because you keep comparing him to yourself. Don't you realize that most of the people in the world are not as capable or as intelligent as you are?"

"Well, of course the servants aren't," Acila began, "but isn't that why they are servants? And the Queen and the Shield-Bearer and Druscilla are all quite intelligent."

"And you've lived such a sheltered life that you've not met many other people," Lord Ranulf said grimly, "but tell me this: was your father as intelligent as you are?"

"Of course he was!" Acila replied automatically, then, as several unfortunate incidents rose in her memory, added, "it's just that he wasn't home enough to understand how some things worked out in daily life."

"You mean that he meddled in things he didn't understand when he came home." Lord Ranulf had no difficulty translating that. "And what did you think of Stefan?"

Acila made a face. "I hated him. I had to push him down the stairs once—it was the only way I could get him to stop grabbing at me every chance he got. And I swear to you," she added indignantly, "that I did nothing whatsoever to encourage him. Ever!"

"But your father trusted him and wouldn't listen to you."

The silence stretched out until Acila admitted, "Well, yes, I guess you're right." Then she added accusingly, "But *you* were willing to work with Stefan!"

"He came to me with your father's body," Lord Ranulf said, "and a story of a defenseless castle with only two children to hold it. He expected to be richly rewarded for his treachery; it was widely known that I wanted your father's plundering stopped, and Stefan doubtless thought my character like his own. I doubt he understood that viewpoints other than his existed. I didn't trust Stefan and I don't regret his death; he clearly earned it. I can't pretend to be particularly sorry for your father's death, either, except that I believed at the time that it left you without a protector."

He paused and smiled at her. "Now that I know you, I realize that you are much better off without him. I am even willing to admit that you can take care of yourself—most of the time. I do confess, however, to some curiosity as to how long you intended to remain a fish."

Good question, Acila thought. "How long *was* I a fish?"

"Six days," Lord Ranulf replied. "And I've spent the last three of them trying to catch every fish in this river, looking for the one which weighed too much." Acila blushed, but said nothing. "I care for you very much, Acila," he continued. "I don't believe I have ever been as frightened as I was when I realized that you actually *were* changing places with Briam. And when I finally got out of those damnable nets you were already falling, and even in bird form I couldn't have stopped you—" he shuddered.

"It wasn't really all that dangerous," Acila said. "I'd been practicing swimming in that part of the river for weeks."

"When you slipped out at night and came back exhausted. Funny how you never collected all those bruises in practice," Lord Ranulf remarked dryly.

Acila took a good look at her arms and legs. She really did have quite a crop of bruises. "It was the drug," she said. "That was the one thing I hadn't planned for, which was silly of me—after all, they'd have to have some way to get the Year-King to go into the river without making a fuss."

"And I never mentioned the drug to Rias, so he

couldn't warn you about it." Responding to Alica's surprised look, he reminded her, "I was under the bench in the garden the day he came, remember?"

Acila cast her mind back. "That's right, you were with us, and you disappeared while I was pulling him off Druscilla."

"I stayed out of sight until you left him alone, then told him to keep his mouth shut about my current form and location."

"He is pretty good at keeping his mouth shut when he wishes to," Acila agreed.

"True, when it suits his interests," Lord Ranulf agreed. "But we're straying from the point of this discussion once again—I'm trying to ask you to marry me!"

"You asked me to marry you last year," Acila pointed out.

"Yes, I did. I thought then that you were a defenseless maiden, who should not be driven from the only home she had known by her father's greed and folly.

"And now," he continued, "I know that you are far from defenseless and could probably make a home for yourself almost anywhere, but I still want to marry you, and I shall count myself a very fortunate man if you will agree to marry me."

Acila stared down at her hands, totally at a loss for words. It was very strange to have a choice; she had always thought that if she married at all, her father would choose a husband for her and she would do as her father told her.

Oddly enough, Lord Ranulf seemed to understand something of her dilemma. "All I ask now is that you think about it," he said gently. "I'm going home to Eagle's Rest. Briam and Druscilla arrived safely at her estate, and the guards that went with them headed back to the city, apparently without suspecting anything; I watched them long enough to be sure of that. Then, when you hadn't turned up at Druscilla's after a couple of days, I went looking for you."

Acila felt her eyes fill with tears. "Thank you," she said.

Lord Ranulf took one of her hands and kissed it, then released it and rose to his feet. "There's a chest of your clothing at Druscilla's, a gown and some under-gowns in the extra clothing chest in Druscilla's room at the palace, and, of course, all the clothes you left at home are still in your room there. You'll have clothing wherever you decide to go. I hope, however, that I'll see you at home soon." His eyes held hers as he changed to bird shape, then he spread his wings and flew away.

Acila stared after him for a long moment, then changed to eagle form herself and went aloft to find out where she was in relation to Druscilla's estate.

CHAPTER 21

Acila found that she had drifted downriver much further than she had planned; none of the area around her was recognizable. But she certainly didn't consider herself lost; she had no doubt at all as to the direction she had come from. She began to fly up river, staying high enough to have a good view of the countryside.

In the fields below her she could see laborers gathering in the harvest. It was obviously a good harvest, and if her fall into the river, along with assorted bruises and sore muscles, had anything to do with that, Acila was glad of it. *And who's to say that it didn't help the harvest? There's certainly no way to prove it either way, and I do know that magic exists and works.*

She flew slowly since her muscles were protesting her attempts to use them. It was infinitely easier to be a fish floating downriver than a bird using its wings to stay aloft—or even a human walking around. But no doubt she would recover her strength in a few days. *Some food would help, too,* she thought, suddenly aware that she hadn't eaten anything to speak of in days. *But I don't dare eat now; I'll have to change back soon, and I don't want a repeat of what happened the time I ate in wolf form and then changed back. Well, maybe just one mouse. . . .*

She ate three of them before her stomach stopped aching, and she was convinced that they were the most delicious things she'd ever eaten in her life. Darkness had fallen before she was done, so she found a suitable tree in which to spend the night. *This way I'll have time to digest the food, and besides, I don't think Druscilla and Briam want me bursting in on them in the middle of the night.*

She woke at first light, feeling less hungry than the day before, but much stiffer. She would have sworn that every feather in her wings had petrified. *Well, waiting won't make it any easier,* she thought, forcing her wings to beat and carry her aloft again. After a few minutes it hurt less, but she was still conscious that she wouldn't be able to go on for much longer in this form.

Fortunately, she was beginning to recognize landmarks, and soon she reached the point where the road to Druscilla's estate branched away from the river. There was a rider on that road, and even from Acila's height she could see the uniform of one of the Queen's guards.

Coming to tell me that Briam's dead? Acila forced an extra burst of speed from her tired wings so that she would reach the estate first. *Now where did Druscilla put my clothes?*

The servants were up and beginning their daily chores, and Acila could hardly land in the middle of the courtyard and turn into a naked human so she went in the window of Druscilla's room. She hit the floor with claws outstretched, changing as she landed. As she rose to her feet, the bed curtains were pulled aside from within and Briam looked at her crossly.

"Acila, why can't you use the door—and knock first—like normal people?"

"What?" Druscilla's sleepy face appeared over Briam's shoulder. "Acila. When did you get here?"

"Just now, and there's a Queen's guard not five minutes behind me—where did you put my clothes?"

Druscilla rolled out the far side of the bed and went to open a chest in the corner. She threw several garments at Acila, then opened the next chest and began to dress herself as well. "Why is she coming?" she asked, her voice muffled by her undertunic.

"I would imagine," Acila said, pulling on her skirt, "that the Queen sent her to notify me—" Her eyes slid sideways to Briam.

Druscilla considered briefly. "You're probably right. Just one guard?" Acila nodded. "Then that's probably it. If anything had happened to the Queen, they would have sent a full escort to drag me back. And I just got rid of the *last* royal escort!"

Briam got up and reached for his tunic. "I'll come down with you," he announced.

"No, my love, please," Druscilla pleaded. "Please stay out of sight."

"But, why?" Briam asked. "You said the Queen was done with me—why would she care that I've married you?"

"Probably because until her baby is born, Druscilla is still her heiress," Acila put in hastily. "I'll go down now—before the servants say I'm not here. I'll send someone if she asks for you, Druscilla, all right?"

"Yes, fine," Druscilla said, advancing on Briam with the obvious intention of keeping him in the room by any means necessary.

Acila arrived in the Hall just in time to hear Druscilla's steward say, "I'm afraid that the Lady Druscilla has not arisen yet. Would you like some ale until breakfast is ready?"

"Thank you," the woman said. "It was a cold ride this morning." Acila recognized the guard now; it was the one who had asked if she should kill the wolf.

"Good morning," she said, approaching the swordswoman. "Lady Acila," the guard bowed, looking uneasy. Acila wondered idly if this assignment were punishment for letting the wolf escape—*as if anyone could have stopped him.*

A servant came up with a mug of ale, gave it to the guard, and looked inquiringly at Alicia. "No ale for me, thank you," Acila said. "I'll wait for breakfast." He bowed his head and departed, still looking puzzled, but Acila was fairly sure the guard had thought nothing of it; her attention was now concentrated on the ale.

"We'd best get out of the way while they set up the tables," Acila said, smoothly drawing the woman to the end of the Hall by the stairs and positioning her so that her back was to them. "How is the Queen?"

"Well enough," the guard replied. "She still spends much of her time resting, but they say the baby grows well. And of course there's not too much for the Queen to do this time of year—" she stopped abruptly and took another gulp of ale.

"And my brother?" Acila asked lightly. "How is he?" The swordswoman looked around wildly. *No doubt,* Acila thought, *she's looking for a place to put my fainting body.*

"I am truly sorry to have to tell you, Lady Acila, of your brother's death."

"My brother, dead?" Acila gasped, swaying artistically, as the guard put an arm around her to steady her. "Dead? How?"

"Drowned, my lady; he fell in the river. A tragic accident." The woman propped her against the wall and looked around for help. "Let me call your maid."

"No." Acila resolutely dragged herself upright. "No, I'm all right, and I don't want a fuss made." She made a show of pulling herself together. "How is the Queen taking it? Does she want me to return to the city?"

The guard looked relieved, now the worst was over and she could fall back on her instructions. "The Queen is grieved, of course, but she has the consolation of her child. She bids me say to you that you need not return on her account, but that you have a home in her palace as long as you wish. In any event, she hopes that you will return at winter's end for the birth of the child."

"I shall, gladly," Acila said.

"If you choose to stay here, you can ride back with Lady Druscilla then," the woman said kindly. "She'll be summoned for the birth, and the Queen will send an escort."

"Of course," Acila said. "I thank you for coming to tell me. Do you wish to see the Lady Druscilla?"

"No, Lady Acila, my errand was to you. If you have no need of me, I'll start back to the city now."

"You may leave when you like," Acila said, "but I'm sure the steward will be glad to feed you before you leave, and if you need additional provisions, have him see to it. If you will excuse me—"

"Certainly," the guard bowed. "My deepest sympathies, Lady Acila."

"Thank you," Acila said quietly, then turned and headed up the stairs.

At the top of the stairs she almost tripped over Briam, who was crouched behind the railing. Druscilla knelt behind him, with one hand held firmly over his mouth. Together the two women dragged him into Druscilla's room and bolted the door.

"What does she mean 'your brother drowned'?" Briam demanded furiously as soon as Druscilla released him. "I'll show her how dead I am!" He started toward the door.

It took the combined efforts of both girls to wrestle him into a chair, and they could never have done it if he had been willing to hurt them to stop them. "Please, my lord!" Druscilla said.

"Briam, for the Lady's sake, stop and think for a moment!" Acila said in exasperation. "Doesn't it occur to you that she might have a good reason for thinking you're dead?"

Briam looked suspiciously from Acila to Druscilla and back. "All right, what is it you two haven't been telling me? Doesn't it ever cross your minds that I might get tired of being treated like a stupid child?"

"I'm sorry, my love," Druscilla said contritely.

Of course, Acila thought wryly, *that does not constitute a promise of amendment.* "How much did you tell him?" she asked Druscilla.

"She said that I was the Year-King," Briam replied, "and that the Queen's marriages only last a few months, and then she releases the King and is considered a widow until the next Spring Festival. And even I can feel it—the bond with the Queen isn't there anymore; it went away the day of the Festival." He frowned, "You know something, Acila? I can't even feel you the way I used to; I still can a little bit, but not all the time like when we were children. Druscilla's the one I can feel most strongly now." He reached out and took Druscilla's hand.

"I know," Acila said sadly, "the twin bond has been fading out for months. I think it was bound to happen when we left home and started meeting other people." *I feel almost as close to Lord Ranulf as I do to you,* she thought, *and when I marry him, no doubt I'll bond with him the way you have with Druscilla.* "And you should be bonded to your wife," she went on. "I just realized; I haven't congratulated you yet." She hugged them both. "Be happy."

"Thank you." Druscilla hugged her back and smiled.

"I thank you, too," Briam said, "but you still haven't explained why the Queen's guard thinks I'm dead—or for that matter, where you've been and how you got all those bruises." He looked critically at her. "You look awful—what did you do, get caught in another rock slide?"

"They think you're dead because they sacrifice the Year-King by throwing him into the river at the foot of the waterfall, and I got the bruises on the rocks under the waterfall," Acila said bluntly.

"You took my place." Briam stared at her. "Why?"

"Because it would have killed you, silly," Acila snapped, "and I didn't go to the trouble of saving you when our estate was invaded so I could watch you get killed within the year!"

"But why didn't you just tell me to run away?"

"I tried to, months ago—don't you remember? You

wouldn't even think of it. Don't you remember how you felt about the Queen *before* she released you?"

Briam nodded slowly, and Druscilla shuddered.

"Which reminds me," Acila said. "Don't ever go back there for the Spring Festival. Having been Chosen once doesn't give you an immunity; you'll always hear when the Lady calls."

"But surely his bond to me—" Druscilla began.

"Maybe," Acila said. "I'm not sure. Lord Ranulf told me he can still hear it, but as far as I know he's not bonded elsewhere. Anyway, I still wouldn't risk it."

"I won't," Briam said. "I'm content where I am." He smiled at Druscilla in a way that made Acila suddenly feel very useless and out of place. "But where did you see Lord Ranulf?"

"He fished me out of the river," Acila said. "Literally."

"You mean you were a fish?" Briam chuckled.

"It seemed reasonable at the time, I had to breathe somehow."

"You *are* a shapechanger, aren't you?" Druscilla said in a small voice. "Like Lord Ranulf. I thought you might be."

"But you were very careful never to find out for sure," Acila finished the sentence. "I noticed that, so I didn't tell you. But, yes, I am—and Briam is not." She saw Druscilla relax slightly on the last words and decided not to share Lord Ranulf's theories about shapechanger children. *Time enough to worry about that if it happens.*

"What are you going to do now?" Druscilla asked. "You're welcome to stay here if you like."

"Thank you," Acila said, "and I'll gladly stay for a few days. I need to eat a few regular meals and get my muscles back into shape and the bruises healed—I really don't recommend long periods of life as a fish, not if you ever intend to be anything else again."

Druscilla smiled. "Maybe you should have been a mermaid instead."

"Perhaps I'll try that someday. But what I intend to do next," she looked at Briam, "is to go home and marry Lord Ranulf. I hope you don't object."

"Why should I?" Briam shrugged. "You're the one who'll be living with him."

"Why are you marrying him?" Druscilla asked. "To get your estate back? Because he's a shapechanger? What on earth will your children be like?"

"Probably a rare handful," Acila laughed. "For one thing, it's almost impossible to lock a shapechanger in his room; I always used to sneak out of mine when I was supposed to be sitting alone and considering my faults. But, yes, it will be nice to be home again. Lord Ranulf may have done well enough with the farms, but the spinning and weaving will need to be checked, and I hate to consider the state of the stillroom."

Druscilla nodded, obviously perfectly able to understand that line of reasoning.

"When Lord Ranulf first asked me to marry him," Acila continued, "he asked me where I'd ever find anyone else who would understand me so well. At the time I just thought he was trying to manipulate me into marrying him so he'd have a claim on the estate. But now he *has* the estate, and he still wants me, so it can't be that; he must truly want me for myself. And it's a good feeling to know that someone knows your darkest secret and still wants to marry you. It's such a relief not to have to *pretend* all the time. Oh, that reminds me, Druscilla, you were right, about Wolf; it was Lord Ranulf the whole time."

Briam's jaw dropped. "You mean all those months in the cave, all winter, hunting in the rain and snow, and living cooped up with us and the horses and all the rest of the wolves—that was Lord Ranulf?"

Acila nodded.

Druscilla looked warily at her. "You were one of the

wolves, weren't you? The one who wasn't afraid of people."

Acila smiled sheepishly and tried to lighten the tension. "It's not people who bother me in wolf form. It's loud noises, screaming, for example," Druscilla blushed, "and smells, such as perfume. It may smell nice to a human, but to a wolf it really stinks! And I had to be a wolf; I didn't manage to take enough of my clothes with me when we escaped to live through the winter in the woods. Remember when you found me in the city and all I was wearing was Briam's undertunic?"

Druscilla nodded, obviously rethinking many of the events of the last few months.

"Anyway," Acila pointed out, "if Lord Ranulf still says he wants to marry me, after living in a cave with me all winter and following me around the palace most of the summer, he at least knows what he's getting for a bride." She paused, then continued. "I think I'm going to enjoy living with him; I'm only now beginning to realize that. And I'll be so very glad to go home again; I've missed it so much."

"But you will still visit us, won't you, Acila?" Briam asked anxiously.

"Of course I will," Acila said happily. "Often. I know the way, and it's not far at all—as the eagle flies."

After spending several days at Druscilla's, enjoying regular meals and sleeping in a proper bed, Acila was ready to go home. For one thing, now that she was back in human form, she dreamed of the temple every night. Rias was there now, so there were three of them calling her in her dreams. And the Lady of Fire still threw lightning bolts at Acila's heels, but she seemed to understand that Acila intended to return to the temple as soon as she was strong enough, so the lightning was more reminder than attack.

As soon as she had her strength back, Acila rose before dawn in the morning, wrote a letter for Briam and Druscilla, and changed to eagle form. She took off quickly, going high enough to be unobserved, and then cast her mind back to the shapes she had seen Lord Ranulf use when he wanted speed above all other considerations, like a semi-normal appearance. She discovered that his mostly wing with very little body shape was much faster than she had anticipated, it was only mid-afternoon when she sighted Eagle's Rest.

She changed to her normal eagle shape for the descent; the people around Eagle's Rest were accustomed to seeing that form. In fact, she noticed that the sentries on the walls had spotted her and were announcing her approach. She banked around to her room, hoping that the shutters had been left open, and saw that there were two familiar-looking wolves sitting on her windowsill.

She studied their relative positions, remembering her promise to Rias. *I'll probably never get a better chance,* she thought, *and if he can't manage the change, Ranulf and I should be able to catch him in time.* She swooped in fast, at an angle designed to knock the wolf cub off the sill into the chasm. It worked as if she had rehearsed it for months.

Rias fell, howling and thrashing about, Ranulf launched himself from the sill after him, changing to bird shape, and Acila dropped after Rias, extending one wing out just enough to warn Ranulf off. After about a fifty-foot drop, Rias started to sprout wings from his shoulders, running the length of his back on both sides of his spine. Aside from the wings, he was still a wolf, but he did manage to get his wingspan large enough to hold his body, and catch the updraft. A few minutes later he managed to beat his wings enough to get himself back to the windowsill. He jumped from there to the floor, twisting his head in an effort to see what had happened to his body.

Acila landed on the windowsill, dropped to the floor,

and changed back to human. "Congratulations, Rias. You can fly."

Lord Ranulf landed on the sill behind them, still in bird form, with the most surprised look that Acila had ever seen on an avian face. The expression didn't change much as his form changed to human. "Acila, *why* did you do that? You could have killed him!"

Acila shook her head. "No, both of us were in range to catch him before he hit the ground; it's a very long way down. As for why—I was keeping my promise to teach him to fly."

"But I've been trying to teach him for years!"

"The same way you learned?" Acila asked. *I'll bet it wasn't.*

"No, of course not!" Lord Ranulf replied. "I learned by accident when I fell off a cliff as a child, but I'm certainly not going to shove my own son off a cliff!"

"I fell off a shed roof," Acila said, "but I was only three and it seemed an awfully long way down. I think you really *need* the feeling of absolute terror to start the change—at least the first time." She looked at Rias, who was still bemusedly regarding his wings, which were a beautiful silvery-gray color that blended in nicely with the wolf's body.

"Rias?" she waved a hand in front of his face. "Speak to me." She snapped her fingers to get his attention.

A shudder ran through the boy's body, then it blurred and reformed in human shape. "I did it!" Rias said in surprise. "I really flew, didn't I?"

"Yes, you certainly did," Acila agreed. "You need more practice, but we can work on that tomorrow." She smiled at him. "Why don't you go get dressed now; it's almost time for the evening ritual."

Rias leaned over and hugged her hard. "Thank you," he said, "for everything." He stood up and headed for the door. "Galin and Marfa are sure going to be surprised when you show up for the ritual. Shall we tell them it's magic?" He grinned at her and left without waiting for an answer, his bare feet padding down the stairs to the second floor.

Ranulf jumped lightly down from the windowsill, took the quilt from the bed, and wrapped it around Acila as he cradled her in his arms. "Welcome home, my dear," he said, dropping a light kiss on her forehead. "Dare I hope that this means you are willing to marry me?"

"Yes," Acila said, looking up at him shyly, "if you're really sure you want to marry *me*."

Ranulf's arms tightened about her. "I'm positive," he said, "even though I did just watch you push my firstborn child out the window." He shook his head. "It wouldn't have occurred to me as a teaching method, but I won't quarrel with success. And nobody can claim that you don't keep your promises."

Acila tilted her head up and kissed him lightly on the jaw. "Marfa will be claiming exactly that if I don't get down to the sanctuary for the evening ritual. Please let me go so that I can dress."

Ranulf released her reluctantly. "Very well, I yield to the claims of the Gods. But after the ritual, I want you back."

Acila laughed, happier than she'd ever been in her life. "I'll sit beside you at dinner—and probably steal half the food from your plate. I'm still starving!"

Ranulf laughed. "I'll order a large dinner." He changed to wolf form and left the room, doubtless to return to his own room and clothing.

Acila dressed and went downstairs to join the ritual. They were waiting for her; Rias had told the others of her return. Galin and Marfa both fell on her neck, thanking the Gods for her safe return.

Acila embraced them in turn, then moved to her place at the south side of the altar. "It's good to be back. Shall we begin?" Galin, Rias, and Marfa moved to their places at west, east, and north. Marfa picked up the basin at the center of the altar and moved it to the Earth Mother's side.

"In the beginning was Earth, mother of all life." Marfa took a bit of a mixture of rich brown earth, green leaves, and dry twigs from the small bowl on the Earth section of the altar and placed it into one of the shallow divisions of the basin. "From Her body all are born and to Her all return at the proper season. Honor the Mother, thank Her for Her blessings, and remember that our roots are in Her body." Marfa passed the basin to Rias.

"The partner of Earth is the Sky, Father and Observer of life." He picked up a small cone of incense from the bowl on his section of the altar, touched its tip to the flame from the lamp on the Fire section to light it, and placed it in the next division of the basin. "Under His gaze we live our lives, and under His inspiration we dream. Honor the Sky Father, and thank Him for the dreams, by which our souls are fed." He passed the basin to Acila.

"Fire is the daughter of Earth and Sky, Lightning, the firstborn of the children which link them." She took a twig from the earth part of the basin and lit it from the small lamp that burned perpetually on the Fire section of the altar. She wondered who had kept it filled with oil and burning while she was gone. But it still burned, and now she was home where she belonged; that was what was important. Placing the twig into the Fire division of the basin to burn, she continued, "All life is changed by contact with Her, yet Her essence never changes. In all the changes of our lives, remember that, though the form may change, the reality is eternal." *And, Lady know, my life has certainly been through changes.* As the form of the twig converted itself to a line of ash, Acila passed the basin to Galin.

"Water is the son of Earth and Sky, Rain, the secondborn of the children which links them." Galin picked up the vial of water and slowly poured some of it into the Water division. "Water flows through all that lives, yet Water never changes, however far He may travel. The reality is eternal." Galin placed the basin carefully back in the bare center of the altar, between the carved portions allotted to each of the Elements. He reached out to Acila and Marfa as they reached out to Rias, and the four of them stood silently holding hands until the last rays of the sun passed below the sanctuary windows.

When they left the sanctuary, Lord Ranulf waited just outside the door. "Is all well, my lady?" he asked, smiling as he took Acila's hand.

"Yes, my lord," Acila replied, smiling in return. She was back where she belonged; she could feel it through every nerve in her body. "Very well, indeed."

Hand in hand, they went in to dinner.